Introduction

Shallowton. Bewitching, mysterious, en
lake, deep in the village of Lurwood. Ste
surround it, visible for miles, sure to capture the stares of many. Catching a glimpse of the sharp, blue water and the lush, beauteous grassland caused individuals to fall in love with the otherworldly sight.

As fascinating as it may seem, not all of Shallowton held this happiness. Two years before, a ferocious storm struck Ruby's Rising Shopping Centre, ripping its roof off, while the graves of hundreds were wrecked, destroyed, gone - along with the town's fine, gleaming beauty. Everything disappeared in such a short period of time.

Avery Hayloft would switch the heartbreak for delight and creativity, bringing a brand-new design to this significant, remarkable place. Ruby's Rising Shopping Centre would no longer be known for misery, but become famous for showing individuals how they could deal with their trauma or their illnesses. It taught them a valuable lesson: their mental health determined neither their worth nor their ability to overcome suffering. Ava desired to add the spark back into their smiles, to prove they weren't alone. Battling with her own issues put Ava's long-time dream at risk ... but she didn't give up. Neither should you.

Chapter 1

Losing your dad could never be easy. Whilst you might strengthen past your heart shedding into millions of pieces, the bitter voice in your head doesn't go away. It lingers, almost like it knows when it might snap out and rasp at you, blaming you for his death.

It wasn't my fault. Wasn't my sister Keira's wrongdoing, either. It had been some wicked, malicious human. Not even a human - humans don't attempt that sort of behaviour. They don't push your mum to the edge, causing her to sit and weep until she's raw from crying.

Dad's murderer hadn't been located. It didn't matter that the word was out in every newspaper and on half the billboards in England, most countries in Europe and states in America. It had no effect, made no difference to the heart-breaking truth: my dad wouldn't ever receive justice, not if the police didn't do something soon. They focused on the case, and two lovely officers were round our house the next morning, but not long after, the case was closed. Only the public continued to search, especially individuals in Europe.

Now, it's just me, Ava Hayloft, my little sister, Keira, and Mum who live together. It's a comfortable house; however, all traces of hope got swept away with Dad's murder. I allowed Mum and Keira to release their emotions during the few days after it sunk in, to some degree, that Dad wouldn't ever see us grow up, wouldn't experience any more outings we'd had as a family that had always been upbeat and exciting.

As much as it hurt me too, I sucked in the tears and focused on viewing the positives. Not that there were any positives in someone so important to us dying, but all of the giggles we had shared. Dad's belongings were sprinkled around the house, along with photos of us with him. I had a whole collection of his sprays, clothes, even one of the teddies he'd owned as a child in my wardrobe. For as long as we lived, his face would never be forgotten, his smile never lost and his generosity and charm never far away from our hearts.

Shuffling into Dad's old office, I inspected the room. My eyes danced over the area that had been abandoned since his death. His office was fresh and open, his smell lingering even after years of him gone, adding a spark to the space somehow, similar to the strong scent minutes after a firework explodes. Not me, Mum or Keira had stepped foot in the room where Dad toiled at night when he'd finished the chores. Dad's job had been working from home which allowed him to enjoy time with me and Keira. He usually got his head down at ten o'clock when Keira and I were snuggled in bed. Mum would accompany him by the computer, where they'd hug each other.

Mum and Dad had agreed on a swift break from their marriage days before he died. Of course, they'd never get together again. That was unattainable. Impossible.

I was in search of Dad's significant binder in which he held personal notes for himself and his work. I was desperate to discover any jottings, maybe a description of who his enemies were. Dad's murderer hadn't been found after years, and Mum had given up hope. She spent her time accomplishing tasks but she never disclosed her work to me, and barely took a holiday.

I hadn't lost faith. I never would.

As I reached under Dad's wonky desk, I dragged my hand around on the floor, hoping it would hit the binder.

It did.

Positioning myself upright, I thumped the binder onto the desk as my sister, Keira, knocked on the door.

She'd expected no one to be in the room. The look of shock on her face told me that.

"Keira." I smiled. "Are you searching for this too?" I lifted the heavy binder up for her to see.

Keira shook her head. She didn't reply.

"Keira?" I repeated. "Are you OK?"

Keira stared intently in my direction, peering into my soul as if she'd never taken a glimpse of me before. She backed out of the room. I frowned, shrugging the feeling of confusion away.

I rested on the desk chair, relaxing my arm on the desk, flicking through to the diary entries Dad had written when he was anxious.
He'd recorded individuals he disliked, either because they'd tried forcing him to quit his job or made fun of him for having a child so young. A lot of people had loathed him for that minor reason. Dad had been sixteen when I was born.
I flicked the pages, getting quicker, yet making no progress.
I sighed, then gasped.
Dad's second to last note read:

<u>16.12</u>
Today has beaten yesterday, being the worst and hardest day I've had for a while. Mr. Chanell mistreated me, yet again. I'm tired of it, exhausted.

Mr. Chanell had been described by Dad to be kind-hearted and an inspiration to him.
He'd really abused Dad. But mentally, or verbally? I wouldn't know. He didn't jot this on the page.
Near to the bottom of the page, in awfully small letters, was Chanell's address.

If Mr. Chanell somehow proceeds to hurt me and goes too far, Sandra, this is where he lives. Give it to the police. I'll be fine. However, it's just in case. Of course, unless that occurs, you won't read this.

I swallowed, ripping out the page and shoving it into the bag I'd dragged into the study. I slid off the soft chair and sprinted downstairs.
"Keira?" I shouted, my voice shaky.
No reply.
Mum must have taken my sister to work with her. She usually did this, so I wasn't surprised.
I slipped on my trainers and slid Dad's old jacket over my shoulders, letting my brunette hair fall down my chest, resting at my waist.

I realised I was wasting time and grabbed the key from the silver hook, unlocked the front door, then hurried out and scrambled my way clumsily down the road.

I stood at the bus stop. It was rusty and stank of weed. I held my nose with my hand and was entirely grateful when my bus arrived. I jumped onto it, nearly missing the step, and thrusted my cash at the bus driver. He wasn't in a rush, printing out the ticket and handing me some change, taking as long as a sloth would.
I took a seat at the back, pulling out the Coke I had just bought from the small Tesco around the corner.
Setting it beside me, I straightened out my hair. It was knotty from crawling around under Dad's desk. I then peered out of the glass window, staring at the beautiful sights of Shallowton. As large as Shallowton was, the broken-down shopping centres were my favourite. It doesn't sound very appealing, does it? It *is* beautiful, partially thanks to the meaningful story behind it. Years before, it had consisted of a forest with tiny cottages of all colours. Pastel pinks and blues. Candy danced from the branches of scattered trees, mouth-watering, sticky and sickly treats just waiting to be demolished.
Many animals had roamed around, even fluffy bears. Friendly bears. My dad had let the story unfold in front of my excited little eyes as they'd filled with hunger to learn everything there was to know about Shallowton, then hope that he would seize the hint with both hands and tell me. However, the topic had turned into heart-breaking misery as he explained about the wicked individuals destroying all the trees, cutting them down and even killing some of the older people living beneath them in quaint cottages. The shopping centres had been built shortly after, a thoughtful memorial included in the centre - a place of worship to remember the victims who had unfortunately lost their lives. Two years later, a ferocious storm struck, swiftly carrying all the delicate flowers away from the cemetery graves. It was all wrecked. Ripped out. Gone. The two shopping centres had been demolished, only a few remainders surviving, including the outline of the centres in which only part of the roofs had been

wiped out. But the glorious wildlife, the cherished memories of the sweet victims, and half the fancy, fragrant shops? Disappeared.

Still, finding light in the place was one of the things I felt truly thankful for. No one else agreed. It was deserted. Numerous employees had lost their jobs, the economy crashing rapidly, therefore this spot of Shallowton had quickly become unattended.

Maybe part of the reason I loved to visit was because of the peace. I felt relieved when sitting on the cranky, uneven bench, breathing in the winter air, letting it drift up my nose. Almost as if Dad had told me about this place when I was little and left it for me when he died.

Of course, it was devastating that so many had been forced away from their loved ones so soon. A single haunting thought often shifted its way into my brain: I wouldn't know where those bodies were buried and therefore could tread on them with my trainers at any moment...

Oh gosh, no. It made me feel sick.

The bus halted and I stood up, grabbing my bag and the Coke. I regained my balance after travelling over such bumpy roads. Thanking the unhurried bus driver, I leaped off the bus, immediately breaking the slow pace and beginning to run. I knew exactly where Chanell's house was. Mum and Dad had taken me there for random dinners plenty of times whilst Keira stayed with the babysitter. Chanell was familiar with who I was, but probably wouldn't recall my existence. I didn't care. If he'd killed Dad, I only cared that he was punished. But would he tell a girl my age? Building on from this, if he was the murderer, he wouldn't give himself up, especially not to the victim's daughter.

I gathered some confidence as I placed myself outside of his three-floor apartment. It was a tall, oval building in a dirty grey colour. It made my eyes feel tired just glaring in that direction from far away, let alone closer up.

I yawned, moving forwards. People around weren't paying attention to me but if I walked up to the apartment and darted away again, they definitely would.

A small button sat beside the door. I assumed it was the bell. I pressed it weakly, stepping back as I did so. Hearing the sound of it ringing from inside made my heart bash against my chest, giving me chills.
I wasn't scared...
Until the door swung open.

Chapter 2

The man who opened the door was not Chanell. No way. He was too old, too rounded.
Not meant in a mean way, of course.
"Mr. Chanell," I said. "That's who I'm here to see."
The man stepped closer.
"Aren't you that man's daughter?" he enquired, looking down at me.
He meant my dad, obviously. I nodded, feeling a sharp, terrified feeling slipping through my body.
The man hesitated, clearly wondering why Darren's child was standing outside of his apartment. Obediently, he retreated inside.
He coughed. "Who did you say you were here to see?"
"Mr. Chanell."
"Third floor. Would you like to be escorted?" the man asked grumpily.
I shook my head, racing past him and up the stairs. I came to a halt outside of the door on the third floor. Well, there were plenty of doors, but Chanell's name was printed on the front.
I knocked.
The echo of the door being unbolted resonated across the hall. Mr. Chanell scratched his bald head as he let the door slam against the beige wall.
"Hi," he said sternly. "Do you deliver the mail? You look young, but good on you." He frowned as he realised I wasn't holding anything in my hands. "Who are you?"
He was acting so innocent.
"I know you're the culprit," I accused him, anger gripping my thoughts and pushing them aside, not allowing me to think of anything but this murderer in front of me.
Chanell scowled. "Culprit?" he muttered. "Who are you?" he asked again.
I parted my lips to answer but he held his hand in front of my face rudely. "More importantly, what are you doing? You're Darren's daughter, yeah?"

I rolled my eyes. "Yes, I am. I know you killed him."
He slowly withdrew his hand and stared at me, wide-eyed. "No, I didn't," he insisted.
I removed the paper from my rucksack, ramming it into his face. "From Dad's binder. Says you abused him," I said. "So, did you stab him that night too? Just to finish off the job? Murder a man and pretend you're a good person?"
"I... Yes, I abused your dad. But killing him? Bold of you to assume, lass. I might look rough, but I wouldn't murder anyone, especially not someone I worked with. I didn't particularly like him, no, but... I regret bullying him. I used to be repulsive and wicked... However, I received therapy and I know better now. I promise," he insisted.
I replaced the paper in my rucksack.
Could I desert my suspicions and walk away from there, pretending to be satisfied?
Truth is, satisfaction would be the last thing I felt... until Dad received justice.
Regardless, I carried no more than a dodgy diary entry, not conclusive in the slightest.
"Fine. Thanks." I surrendered, turning around and strutting to the top step.
"Avery?"
I swivelled.
"Don't worry. The culprit will be found."
He sounded tender, captivating. My churning stomach eased at his gentle assurance. I smiled and raced down the two flights of stairs, speeding out of the front door and into the fresh air once more.

Returning home, I propelled myself onto the couch, glaring at the family photo placed over the fireplace. It had been taken at a beach in Somerset. I was much younger, and blonde. My hair had darkened over the years, unlike Keira's - she was still blessed with gorgeous light curls. Keira was about six months old in the picture. Her round head was bald, her blue eyes electric. She was only wearing a nappy. Dad, in shorts and an ugly shirt, was holding Keira on his shoulders, a big, friendly grin on his face.

Beside Dad, Mum stood in a flowery, emerald dress. She was smiling too, staring at Keira with ocean eyes. I was crouching in the front, Mum's arm draped over my chest. My hair was frizzy from the shock of playing in the salty waves and I had a grey jumpsuit on. The frame was smashed from where Keira had had one of her temper tantrums, but Dad had gone to buy it the same day he died so we kept it, feeling it was selfish to not do so.
I viewed my tears in the reflection of the TV before I felt them. I gritted my teeth, shocked at my sudden outburst. Foolishly, I picked up a tissue and rubbed my face, feeling the tears sticking to my skin like they wouldn't let go. That's what I felt about Dad. No matter what anyone said, his memory would be with me forever.
I decided I couldn't sit still at all, so jumped up, yanked the bus ticket from my rucksack and rushed outside.

Shallowton stood boldly in front of me. The two broken shopping centres glanced at me, maybe expecting me to be a full-blown storm, ready to send the remainders flying.
I strolled, my hands flushing purple in the coldness of the late October afternoon. The first shopping centre wasn't very attractive, with just one shop left inside - the shop my dad used to work at years before. A mechanic store. He wasn't a mechanic but sold the items to people who were. A few pieces of equipment remained and the inside smelled strongly of metal and rubber mixed together.
I held my nose.
At the back of the shop, there was a door. I walked right up to it until I was less than a few inches away and reached my hand out.
"No!" a voice cried.
I screamed, spinning around, my eyes closed.
When I opened my eyes, I wondered vaguely why I'd been so dramatic.
It was only Mum.
"What..." I gasped, "...are you doing here?"
Mum lifted an eyebrow. "Let's reverse the question. What are *you* doing here?"

"This is my favourite place, remember?" I said. "Now, let's switch back to the original question. What's your reason for being here? No one is ever seen here anymore, except maybe a few farmers from the field next door."
Mum nodded. "OK. But this is my treasured spot too."
I laughed. "Liar. You never come here!"
"I do, Ava."
I shook my head, exasperated. "You're always at work," I pointed out.
"Not always. I have the evening off today," she bragged.
I stared at her for a moment, then went to transfer my stare to Keira. She wasn't there. "Where's Keira?" I snapped. "Did you leave her at work with the colleagues who are seemingly more reliable than you?"
Mum looked offended, but tried to come across as unbothered. "She's outside. I just wanted to look for something, but you were about to peek in that room. What, are you being nosy?" she sneered.
"Well, what's so unwelcoming in there?" I motioned to the door.
Mum ignored me. I sighed, trudging in front of her, out into the early night as the moon grinned down at me from the sky.

We all arrived at the house, groggy and tired. Getting a Chinese always cheered us up, but I couldn't get my mind off what could've been behind the door.
Was it Dad's body? No, he had a grave.
I didn't know, and probably never would.
After dinner, Keira and I searched for a jigsaw puzzle, unwinding before Keira's bedtime.
We were a quarter of the way to completing the puzzle when Mum rushed into the room, almost stepping on our masterpiece.
"Mum!" Keira moaned. "Watch your footing."
Mum grinned. "Sorry. I have some good news."
I tensed, not familiar with good news. "Tell us," I urged, stress rising in my stomach.
Mum smiled. "I booked a whole week off work. I'm taking us away overnight tomorrow!"

I bit my lip anxiously. “Are you sure? You’re able to be away from work for that long?”
“Yeah!” Mum confirmed. “They’re OK with it.”
Keira leaped up happily, kicking the puzzle and sending the pieces across the carpet. I tried to remain calm. Keira hugged Mum not so gently, squeezing her waist. Without warning, she twirled her round in a perfect circle and rolled onto the floor, giggling with wild laughter. Mum fell with a sturdy thump onto the carpet, just missing hitting Keira with her hand. She burst out laughing, loud and content.
I blinked, pretending to be a typical moody teenager. Well, nearly teenager.
Keira farted and I couldn’t hold the giggles in any longer. I crawled over, tickling my sister. “You’re disgusting,” I screeched. “That stinks.”
Keira chuckled harder.
“OK Keira, shower time,” Mum demanded, as if Keira wasn’t nearly into her double-digit years.
Keira obeyed, tickling me quickly in return.
I sauntered up the stairs too, trudging into my bedroom. I went to open the door and thought I perceived the noise of a razor. I instantly registered Keira being in the bathroom. Did my sister need to shave already? I paused for another moment, then continued to make my way to bed.

Chapter 3

Mornings were always hectic in our house, even if there were only three of us. Mum always yapped at me for leaving a trail of mess on the floor and Keira followed, picking it all up.
That morning, I woke up slower than usual, taking time to rub my eyes and glare around. I remembered the trip Mum had prearranged for us that day. In a daze, I rolled out of bed and shook my foot as the sharp shock of a cramp filled my toes. Groaning at the unpleasant sensation, I made my way to my wardrobe, searching through the contents to find my favourite dress. It wasn't summer, but I was usually oblivious to that. I thumped my hand on my forehead as I recalled shoving the dress into my suitcase. Rolling my eyes, I decided to just pick out another.
Shortly after getting dressed, I whisked out my mascara and carelessly brushed it across my eyelashes. They were already considerably lengthy, so it took less than a minute to feel comfortable with the finished look.
I vaguely caught the racket echoing from the bathroom, instantly labelling it as Keira. Irritatingly, I realised there was little possibility of me being lucky enough to use the bathroom and be sat in the car in approximately half an hour, especially knowing Keira would be at least twenty minutes.
Deciding smartly not to bother waiting, I strolled downstairs to greet Mum good morning.
As I straightened out my light blue dress, raising my hand to open the living room door, I heard Mum's voice, croaky and flat, highly unlike her everyday tone.
"Yes, I'm planning it out later. We will return tomorrow from our night away. I'll plot it all for then," she growled.
Ten seconds passed; I counted on my fingers.
"The money should have transferred to you last week. I told you that. You remain big-headed. As usual," Mum snapped, her tone becoming suddenly heated. "I explained to you what you had to do, which isn't anywhere near as difficult as what I need to do." Mum groaned as the conversation went on. "Ashley, I'm about to travel on a short holiday with my two daughters. Don't make me

tense because whilst one is gullible and uncertain, my eldest isn't dumb. She isn't foolish when it comes to hearing unusual information and can tell when the happiness in my eyes deflates. Don't be the cause and effect of that."

I could just hear Mum tapping her nails on her phone. She doesn't ever have acrylics; instead she is privileged with slim, immaculately long fingernails.

"Yes, I will indeed create an excuse to get her there. Ang knows, Ashley. I made..." Mum hesitated, the thought pending in her head. "Never mind, you shouldn't know that. I'll email over what you must do, it's simple. I have to go now." The beep of her ending the call hit my ears and I walked into the room.

"Good morning, Mum," I said, as if I didn't just experience a whole discussion about something extraordinary and mysterious.

Mum briefly glanced at me, smiling. "Hi, honey. Looking forward to our trip?"

I nodded, but couldn't think too much about the upcoming days. Mum had marked Keira as gullible and uncertain, and me as not dumb and not foolish. Moreover, to an individual named Ashley, who even Mum didn't seem to be too familiar with.

"I wasn't eavesdropping, but I walked in as you said goodbye on the phone. Who were you speaking to? Anyone I know?" I pried.

Mum shrugged her bony shoulders. "They were trying to bribe me to help them. Wanted to send me cash, but I was certain it was a scam," she answered.

I understood that she wouldn't explain any more, due to the fact that I'd told her it was only when she'd ended the conversation that I'd strolled in. Of course, I was aware of everything, but Mum would undoubtedly become distressed if I revealed that.

I retreated quietly and chose to put my effort into carrying the two suitcases out and into the car. We had a dark blue Range Rover. It was roomy and comfortable in the vehicle. I lugged the suitcases into the large boot and slammed it shut.

My thick brunette hair rapidly tangled in the unsteady breeze, causing it to flutter into my face.

Keira appeared in the wide window of her bedroom, grinning out at me. She unlatched the window, a heap of blonde curls gliding behind her as the wind blew into her room.
"Please say it's time!" She clasped her hands together in a hopeful manner. "Are we going?"
I opened my mouth as Mum marched out of the front door, her handbag hanging limply off the inside of her elbow.
She peered up at Keira, beaming. "It's time, Keira," she confirmed. "Let's have the best trip!"

A storm brewed overhead as we reached the motorway. The sky grew dark and gloomy. Glaring menacingly through the window, the clouds hugged one another, threatening us with a downpour. It arrived soon enough, the pelting rain falling fast and splashing onto the roof of our car.
"How far away are we?" I questioned. "Because if there's not much further to travel, this rain might be sticking around."
"Very helpful, Ava," Mum quipped sarcastically.
I let my body flop back against the seat, folding my arms as I looked through the window, feeling as moody as ever. Mum was miming the song that played on Heart Radio, tapping each finger in order on the steering wheel.
One seat across from me to the left, Keira was enjoying some self-amusement as she engaged herself in Minecraft on her iPad.
The rain slowly subsided and soft flakes began falling to the ground.
"SNOW!" Keira squealed with excitement. "It's SNOWING!"
Mum pulled the Range Rover to a standstill in the lay-by, turning the engine off. "It's October," she said flatly.
"Nearly November!" Keira reminded her.
Silence filled the car as we all stared with admiration at the snow. Apart from Mum.
"Mum, are you OK?" I asked, shifting over slightly so I was able to see her face. Well, half of it.
"You went to visit Chanell yesterday, didn't you?" she guessed. She sounded let down, as if I'd committed the worst crime possible.

"I thought he'd murdered Dad," I admitted, and the way she glared at me made me feel guilty, made my heart descend.
Mum covered her face, sliding her hands down her cheeks. "He didn't though, did he? You found that out the difficult way. He bullied your dad, but he didn't kill him. Yes, if he'd continued to abuse him, it could have resulted in death," she fumed. "You're so stupid. What you did was wrong."
My eyes widened. "You said earlier on I wasn't foolish."
She was panicking. I could tell. I could easily hear it in the way her breathing switched from standard to overpowering. I'd overheard information that she'd feared I would. However, she'd known I would, one day. I hadn't made sense of the details but if Mum understood that I'd discovered one thing, she'd tell me the rest.
Or she wouldn't. Not if it was beastly.
Which it was.
"You lied," Mum panted, as if she'd run out of the car and around the woods that surrounded the main road. "You heard the whole conversation I had with..."
I leaned forward. "Ashley," I whispered, positioning my hand over my mouth so Keira was unable to catch the name. "What did the rest of it consist of?"
I turned when Keira shook my shoulder.
"Can I go and play out in the snow? Maybe I'll eat some like I did last year. It sounds disgusting, but it's very tasty. Like... water, when it melts on your tongue!"
I shuddered at the thought of my sister eating snow. *Who does that?*
"We're on a main road." Mum folded her arms.
Nonetheless, Keira's sudden outburst of confidence was clearly tempting Mum to say yes, which was a mistake. "Go on, then. Just on the path along the trees, OK?"
As I thought. Giving in to my cute sister's request.
"Mum, maybe Keira shouldn't-"
Mum faced me, smiling. "I'm the parent, I know what's best."
Keira giggled, skipping out of the car and into the thick, powdery snowfall.

"Ava, Ashley and I were speaking about a surprise for your birthday. She got annoyed because she thought I hadn't paid for the gift, and thought I might have been ungrateful because she put it together," Mum shared, adjusting on her earlier conversation.
I raised an eyebrow, unsure.
"I told her Keira wouldn't notice there even was a surprise, unless I dropped a hint myself. Ashley was paranoid that Keira would spill it to you if I did. I explained you might be able to break it apart and guess nevertheless, if we weren't careful."
Someone else might not have fallen for it as effortlessly as me. Maybe they'd live with uncertainty or go searching deeper into it. After my false accusations about Chanell yesterday, I felt the need to believe her.
So that's what I did.
The snow was harder now, thicker too, settling on the bonnet of the car.
I asked Mum when we were going to resume driving. She responded by removing herself from the car and going to locate Keira.
Mum disappeared for five minutes before I became concerned. My body began shaking as I couldn't spot Mum or Keira. I came to the conclusion that I should trace my family. I didn't have the key to the car, Mum did, so I couldn't lock it. If I couldn't track them down, the main road was in my view, meaning I could wave my arms frantically to catch someone's attention.
Despite the snow, the ground was still bare apart from water from the downpour flooding the walkway into the forest.
The forest was deserted. With each step I took, my shoes sank into the dark brown sludge. I tumbled over many thick tree roots, ending up throwing my arms out for balance like I was an acrobat.
I grew apprehensive after a few moments and contemplated whether to keep moving forwards. Deciding after all to persist, I hauled my legs along, feeling sick with the panic that clutched at every muscle it could reach. I was gasping for air by the time I came to a standstill once more, my throat dreadfully sore and

moist, clammy sweat sticking to my back and my neck as if it wouldn't let go.
I stuck my foot out to take another step when a hand reached out, covering my mouth tightly so I was unable to release the scream that caught in my throat.
They spun me around, gripping my wrist, cutting my circulation off. I let out an aghast breath as they threw me to the ground. I hit the floor, my head half-buried in the dank mud. This time, I knelt over and let out a raspy squeal.
I gazed at the man standing tall and stern in front of my eyes. He was about sixty, unsmiling with round, brown eyes and dirty blond hair.
"Who are you?" I stuttered, scrambling to return to my feet.
He aggressively barged into me, sending me flying for a second time. I hit the soil, feeling its wet surface clinging onto my skin. I shielded my face as I glared up at the man.
A metal tip met my right arm. I didn't process that it was a weapon until later on.
"Get up, idiot," he demanded, as if I hadn't just attempted to do so. He chucked the weapon into his back pocket.
"Do I know you?" I questioned, rubbing sticky muck off my dress. I felt awkward as the realisation of the thin material sticking up over my thigh in front of this man fogged my brain, forbidding me to reflect on what had just occurred in front of my eyes. I instantly pulled the dress down.
The man seized my wrist again, tugging me, making me move. "No, you don't," he acknowledged. "But I know you. You accused Chanell, didn't you?"
I hesitated. Clearly he knew the truth, so why ask me?
"I SAID, DIDN'T YOU?!" the man roared, thrusting me in front of him. I felt ill, like I was on a roller coaster, being tilted and thrown around at full pelt.
"Yes. I did. It was only because Dad wrote about Chanell bullying him. I'm sorry."
The man resumed walking, leaving me to stagger behind.
"Don't run. Don't even think about it. You're in trouble," he snarled. "Your sister didn't act out, so I kid you not, if you do, I'll hurt you."

My lip trembled like I was five years old. Again, my brain didn't comprehend his remark until minutes after.
"Where am I being taken?" I cried, fear circulating my body, coursing through my veins, almost squashing them. I didn't understand what was happening. Chanell had been amiable and polite about the situation. I thought he'd think nothing more of it.
"Just for questioning. You know - what, how, why. The basics," he said. "If you answer truthfully, you go. If not, your sister dies."
Keira... He had Keira captive.
"You won't hurt Keira," I insisted. "Why'd you take *her*?"
The man took a right turn, a car becoming visible under the gloomy October sky. He clutched my arm as I tried to dodge him.
"Make this a bit simpler!" he shrieked. "Stop moving, girl. I didn't bring the knock-out drug. Doesn't mean I won't strike you unconscious."
I used his chest to brace my hand against whilst I tried to pull my wrist out of his tight grasp. This resulted in him taking both of my hands and carrying me over his left shoulder.
I lashed out by attempting to scream. This didn't work either as the man sat me down, his knee digging into my throat, then removed his sock and stuffed it into my mouth. Filthy. I almost vomited.
I recalled being on the verge of the main road. As my feet stuck up over his belly I raised my head, gathering my bearings. My heart dropped.
We weren't on the main road.
Therefore, I was stuck. Stuck with this reckless man, who could assassinate me or make me suffer brutally.
He shoved me face-first onto the edge of the damp grass. My mouth was still gagged with his foul-smelling sock. I could just imagine it on his sweaty foot. Realising he had no shoes on of any sort, I predicted this sock also held dirt and soil. Delightful.
"Are you capable of getting in the car yourself? Or should I lug you inside?" he asked, kicking me onto my back so he could examine my expression and hear my response. But didn't he remember I was heaving against his sickening sock? I pointed

my finger towards it. Sighing, he pressed firmly onto my chest and yanked it out.
"Ouch!" I responded. My lips had been parted for so long they were numb.
The man crossed his arms impatiently.
"Yes, I can get in the car myself," I grunted, my hand scraping against the mud as I leaped up.
I entered through the car door which was ajar and scrambled to neaten my dress, protecting my thighs; it had lifted again, and I cursed myself for not wearing jeans.
It was only when we were sat inside and he had started to drive that he replied to my earlier enquiry. "We saw your sister first. Knew you'd be with her." He glared at me. "Your whole damn family are on the billboards; we could tell it was her."
I grimaced. "We?" I echoed.
The man grinned. It was pure evil, making me shudder with unease - an unpleasant feeling that lunged at my lungs, shaking them up until I hardly dared to speak.
He didn't answer.
"Where's my mum?" I tried to change the subject away from Keira and this whole state I'd gotten myself caught up in.
"Your mum?" he screeched. He laughed. "I dunno. Haven't seen her."
I kept quiet as we passed Mum's car over in the lay-by. I missed her, remembering how I'd always cling to her when I was scared or panic-stricken at a younger age. I was twelve now, thirteen next month. I had never been as stunned - in a negative kind of way - or as freaked out as I was now. I couldn't remove the feeling of this man's hand snatching my wrist, making it throb with unbearable pain.
"How'd you locate us?" I demanded.
The man shifted his head slightly, a glint of guilt glowing in his eyes. Then he scowled, reaching into the glove box and revealing three pink, bizarre-looking devices.
It was my turn to frown. "What are *they*?"
We advanced over a sharp bump as the man dropped the devices onto my lap.
"Cameras." He returned his hand to the steering wheel.

I curiously swept them up, inspecting them in my palms. A little, nearly invisible silver circle was surrounded by a pink base. "These are weird cameras," I commented, unimpressed.
"Do you think I care? I didn't create them. But I trailed after your mum's car yesterday evening and slipped them in through the windows, attaching them to the coving in your rooms. Your bedroom, your mum's and the living room. A beautiful house you live in." He curled his lip in disgust.
"I guess you don't live in such an attractive house?"
"If your tone continues to be so mocking, I'll intentionally throw one of the cameras at your face. It will certainly shatter your nose and, if I'm lucky, shut you up," he threatened.
Sticking my tongue out in response to his weak threat, I focused on the plain, dull forest spreading out around us. As the satnav directed us around the bend, the man grunted lightly.
"Will I be killed if I remain silent?" I asked him abruptly, keeping my head up, acting unbothered.
I *was* bothered all right.
He unhooked a gun from his belt. I hadn't noticed it before; I'd been unaware of it earlier on, oblivious, and instantly raised my hands.
"I can kill you right here, right now if you would prefer." He lifted it up so that the tip aimed at my jaw. "Joking." He lowered it again. "But I told you, if you don't answer, your sister will have a gun to her head. You'll get a second chance and if you still don't say a word, explaining WHY you did it, I'll shoot."
"You'll shoot? You don't look like the kind of man who would fire a gun," I informed him sassily.
The man didn't hesitate to lift the gun higher. "Want to dwell on it?" He hoisted up a bushy eyebrow.
"No thanks." I gulped. And then, like an idiot, my nerves pushed me to say something I regretted afterwards. "Maybe later."
The man, who was focused intently on the road, temporarily scowled. A flash of shock covered his face, settling like a mask.
I leaned back, his expression allowing me to feel satisfied for the first time.

Chapter 4

To take my mind away from this man kidnapping my sister and taking me too, I tried to guess what my birthday surprise might be. I'd received birthday surprises before, mini parties with delicious foods of all kinds, including warm sausage rolls and colourful party rings and a big, towering cake. Not chocolate; Keira was allergic. Turning nine, I'd received a miniature sculpture of my dad. It was detailed, his body's features perfectly distinguishable. I couldn't possibly describe nor imagine it whilst being forcefully trapped in a vehicle with a giant beast of a killer. A *stalker*. He had stalked my family, followed us home and arranged cameras around our house.

Relaxing my mind - I'd lost count of how many times I'd done that before - I thought about how I had always wished for a pet, like a friendly dog or a fluffy bunny. Disappointingly, Mum was sensitive around any animal. Her skin flared up, her eyes watered and she developed rashes all over her body. She'd been rushed into hospital several times due to this and had been diagnosed with a condition I couldn't ever pronounce.

Eventually, I grew restless again and gave up on thinking about my birthday. Let's just say, if Keira died because of me, I wouldn't care for a birthday at all.

I promised myself that.

The man stopped the car and ushered me out, holding my wrist for a third time. He didn't fuss much over cramming his foul sock into my mouth again, just slid it in lightly. As he slammed the door, I felt the circulation cutting off my wrist and tried to create a small gap so my arm could breathe. Ahead of us, I could see what looked like an abandoned building, dirty stains covering the bricks and many broken pieces of metal scattering the ground around it.

"I'll release my grip a bit on one condition. You won't run?" the man barked, sneering at me.

I looked at him as if he had gone crazy, which technically he had. I spat the sock out. "My sister is in there!" I reasoned, outraged. "I'm not running away even if you wanted me to."

"I'll have to put the gun to your waist as we enter anyway," he warned.
My eyes widened in horror. "You won't pull the trigger, right?" I asked, struggling to breathe.
"Nope," he promised, still sneering. "My colleague likes set rules in place. You hurt our mate, we make you sorry. Until the questioning is over."
I whisked my hair off my face as the breeze faded to hot chills, and stepped inside the old, wasted-looking building. It seemed crusty from the outside and didn't look much fancier on the inside.
As he'd warned, the man pushed his gun against my ribs as we walked further inside and up a grey, spiral stairway. I jumped, trembling slightly, and eased my shoulders backwards, inhaling a deep breath. The man continued to drag me along, often pausing to dig the fingers of his free hand into my back and give me an extra boost.
"Please, your gun is hurting me." I struggled, feeling his finger once again mark my back, as sharp as a large needle.
He released it slightly, but not enough for the anxiety that filled my body to reduce. I was nearly knocked off my feet as he plunged me into a room. I glanced around the space: the fat hole in the middle of the ceiling, the disgraceful wee stains on the carpet, the several worn chairs scattered around the area.
Keira was perched on one of those chairs.
Wasting no time, a woman came into view, a sly look on her face. She had grey hair that clashed unappealingly with her dark eyes and her monobrow slid halfway down her tanned skin.
"Hi, Avery Hayloft. Glad to see you," she greeted, attempting to sound thrilled. It couldn't have been more fake if she tried.
"Couldn't think of anything better," I sassed sarcastically, gritting my teeth.
The woman muttered under her breath, warning me to 'watch how I speak to her.'
I'd pass on that.
The man slowly dropped the gun from my waist when the woman gestured for him to do so. I cringed with excruciating pain as he let go of my wrist.

"Sit, Ava. Dan, position the gun against the young girl's ribcage," the woman demanded without hesitation.
I placed myself on the chair opposite Keira. It was warm and I could sense all the germs it must hold. I cringed again, praying I could stand instead.
"What do you think you're doing?" the woman shrieked, and Dan's gun swivelled round.
"Standing is more ideal than sitting on the filth you call a chair."
Dan's eyes flamed and I obediently sat. I didn't want to die, especially not in front of my sister.
The woman kneeled in front of me, her dark, threatening eyes dimming further, as if insulting me internally. Dan put the gun at Keira's side, making her quiver. It was like I'd committed the biggest crime in Shallowton, not disappeared for an hour to speak to someone about my dad's murder.
"So, Avery," the woman spat, clicking her unhygienic fingers centimetres from my face. "Why did you visit Chanell?"
I put my hands behind my back, carelessly. "I've said. It was because I read in dad's diary that Chanell had abused him. I instantly assumed he might have killed him too."
"It wasn't too smart of you, was it, Avery?" she taunted as if I were two.
I held back a sigh and shook my head. "It wasn't. I thought I did the right thing."
"You didn't." She stood up, clicking her knuckles. "You thought you did, correct. However, Mr. Chanell has been trying to change his ways and is currently going to therapy to guide him to being less violent. He's been attending for at least three years. Your accusations yesterday made him highly upset."
Dan moved the gun a few inches from Keira.
"PUT THE GUN BACK!" the woman bellowed, her face turning purple. She faced me, her eyes angry.
I kept my gaze on Keira, the guilt gnawing at my insides, consuming me.
"Did you think you would get something positive out of blaming an innocent man?" she drawled.

I shrugged, beginning to feel less frightened and more frustrated. Keira should be experiencing resentment and anguish for our current situation, not me.
I didn't reply.
The woman glanced at Keira and Dan, disdain leading her lips to twitch. "I thought us threatening to kill your sister would get the information out of you." The woman sighed, her back to me but still speaking with an alarming tone. "Apparently not."
I waited for a minute for something to happen.
Something happened all right.
"Dan!" the woman growled, anger seeping from her lips, squeezing all feeling of self-assurance from my system and ripping the faith I held, crashing it down to the ground. "Put the gun to Avery again. Maybe if she realises we WILL murder her, she might SPEAK!"
I stood up, my legs feeling stronger, sturdier than moments before. "I'M NOT SPEAKING BECAUSE I DON'T HAVE AN ANSWER!" I yelled furiously.
Keira covered her ears, terrified.
The man seized me, thrusting me onto the chair and raising the gun to my forehead.
I folded my arms, indignation sucking at my patience. Keira hid her eyes, petrified. The confidence she had shown earlier evaporated as she became quickly traumatised by the action in the room.
"No, I didn't think I'd get anything out of it. I had to try," I replied at long last.
The woman motioned for Dan to take the gun away.
"Finally, Lisa," he said. "My arm is awfully tired, and this girl is pushing my temper."
I grinned to myself at my effortless attempt to irritate this man.
Lisa rolled her eyes, exasperated. "Grow a pair. Men are meant to be strong," she snarled.
A banging sound echoed around the small room, the noise vibrating every wall and stunning us all. Lisa and Dan held still, Dan still clutching the gun. That was when a man entered the already claustrophobic area, and everything happened from there...

The man squared up and jumped, kicking fiercely at Lisa and sending her flying across the room. She lay in agony, grumbling to herself and clutching her ribs. The man, whose face I couldn't see, turned to Dan, his bald head shining and glinting in the dim light. His eyebrows were clenched with contempt, his posture steady. He lunged towards Dan, hitting him with his hefty fist. The gun almost flung out of his palm, but not quite. He curled his fingers around it, guarding the weapon with his life.
"You idiot! You vile piece of-"
Dan shoved his other hand to the man's mouth. "There is a child in the room," he said bitterly.
The man set free a flat, meaningless laugh that I could only guess had been hidden since he'd knocked out Lisa. It, too, vibrated off the four grim walls. As the man's fist aimed to bash into Dan's chest, Dan stumbled up, avoiding him and regaining some balance and pointing the gun in my direction without realising. I peered at the woman still lying stretched out on the stained carpet and I was sure she'd landed on the patch of wee.
Gross.
I swivelled around to face Keira. She was next to invisible behind a chair in the very corner of the room. I could see her trembling hands and the tears that swamped her eyes.
She didn't look at me.
I moved my feet to depart from this wretched building, ready to run and no longer wanting to put up any sort of fight or argument. Not that I had voluntarily wanted to in the first place. I was too slow, stiffening as the man pounced once more at Dan, this time hitting his arm, making his hand shake and his fingers move.
I straight away thought about the gun in his grasp.
And that along with his moving fingers, the trigger had been pulled. Opposite to where I stood.
I dived sideways as the bullet fired my way. Keira screamed and Dan gasped. He clattered to the ground, moaning. The bullet hit the wall as my head banged into part of the floor where the carpet had peeled away. As I ordered my body to budge, I lost stability. My forehead pressed against the wood and, before I

passed out from concussion, I noticed that the man was the individual I had made a visit to yesterday. The man I'd blamed for murdering my father.
Chanell.

As a little girl, my biggest fear had been hospitals. I'm sure many shared the same anxiety. I wasn't alone.
I awoke in a hospital bed, my head throbbing. The cream sheets were soft and comfortable, clasping onto my skin and sending a warm sensation through my body.
I focused hazily on the person beside me.
Keira.
She handed me a mirror without a comment. I was afraid to take a peek but did anyway, once I'd built up enough courage. I had a bleeding scratch across my forehead that would most likely leave a scar forever.
"Battle scar," Keira assured me.
"Me? You faced the battle, Keira. You're amazing," I praised.
Keira looked blankly at me. "I was scared, Ava. So afraid." Her voice shook.
I took hold of her hand. "How did they capture you?"
A fragile tear escaped Keira's eye, misting over the light blue shade. "I was playing in the snow, remember? Out of the corner of my eye, I could see candy on the grass. My favourite kind. I followed the path into the forest. A woman jumped out at me, swearing as she shoved duct tape across my mouth. She held her fist against my head and pinned my arms behind my back. When lowering her fist, she covered my eyes with her sleeve. I was taken to that depressing building you were drawn to shortly afterwards." Her arms trembled as she wiped her eye with her thin jacket sleeve.
I brought her directly next to me so that I could wrap myself around her. I yelped with pain as I lifted my head. Keira automatically retreated, apprehensive.
"You were kidnapped?" I growled, feeling the frustration and deep burning anger seep through my arms and legs like a hot liquid. My sister was clearly terrified - she could barely open her mouth to speak, she was so disturbed - and that woman had

proceeded to traumatise her by thrusting a gun to her head, thinking it was amusing.
Revolting. I hoped she rotted.
"How did the man catch you?" Keira demanded, trying to let her face rest from the stress.
"I tried to find you and Mum. A little later, a hand gripped my wrist and knocked me to the ground - Dan. He manipulated me into the car. Said I'd have to answer questions or else you'd die. I doubted him and he intimidated me with that gun of his."
Keira began shivering, movements that she couldn't control. I could tell she wouldn't ever overcome what she had seen. She'd sat with a gun to her front, felt the forceful, cold metal pressed against her own skin, one harrowing thought piercing her ears, biting at every vein: *I will die if my sister doesn't obey.*
My own blood ran coldly through my body whilst recalling the latest events. I desperately wanted to overlook them, to continue with my week eager and optimistic, but even if I was able to disregard these last hours, Keira wouldn't. She was too young, too vulnerable.
I altered the topic. "Where's Mum? Prior to me searching for you, Mum was certain she'd inform you we were ongoing with our journey. I couldn't find her in the forest, and she wasn't in the building - so where is she?"
Keira knew where she was at. Her eyes told me everything.
"You're telling me she didn't actually go and look for her daughter, who for all she knew could have been kidnapped?" I seethed.
"*Did* get kidnapped. So did you," Keira insisted.
I leant on my elbow, my head still sore. "I didn't," I said.
"You did, Ava," she insisted.
Sitting up properly, I focused on my sister. Her face had paled, and her eyes darkened with worry. I cradled her tenderly. Her eyebrows lowered and pulled closer together. She emitted a small snorting noise. Whether it was of sadness for herself or scorn towards Lisa and Dan, I didn't know.
"Aside from the gun in his pocket, I could've escaped. I didn't have to follow him, be manipulated into the car. But he said you

were imprisoned inside so I had to. That was a choice. I wasn't abducted."
Keira seemed sceptical, but didn't comment.
Another thought rose to the very front of my brain. "That woman, Lisa, didn't have a weapon. Couldn't you have run for it?"
This snapped Keira to attention, her eyes widening as she digested what I'd asked. "Ava... did you see the size of her? Her muscles were practically two times the proportion of the rest of her body."
She was a burly woman, almost as intimidating as Dan.
"I'm glad we're safe. Hey, did they notify you about where Dan and Lisa were taken?" I wondered. I didn't even know how we'd got to this hospital or why Chanell knew anything about our whereabouts.
Keira tapped her chin thoughtfully. "No. Well, the nurse that checked you over mentioned that Chanell alerted her that both Dan and Lisa were still unconscious on the carpet of that building. Someone was going to fetch them, take them in for questioning of their own," she confided. "I was told to keep quiet, but you were there too so it's only necessary to alert you."
"And... how did we get here?"
"An ambulance, Ava. That man phoned one and said it was an emergency, which it was because you could've died. It's two days later but the police struggled to locate them, and the man was too paranoid that the concussion would result in death."
I shot up, too nervous to observe my injured head, pulling up my knees and swinging off the bed.
Keira urged me to retreat under the covers, but she'd well and truly disturbed me, pushing any hope of rest aside.
"They're here. They could be here, in this exact hospital. They could threaten us with the gun again!" I shrieked.
I could see I was making Keira uncomfortable and that she hadn't a clue how to calm me down. Nothing could calm me at that moment. I was disrupted and the unfamiliar type of fear I was experiencing in that spacious hospital room that smelled of heavenly, fresh lavender forcefully caused me to feel sick to my core.

A nurse of some sort rushed into the room as a dizzy spell wavered across my vision. I traced it with my finger and the nurse probably thought I'd gone mad.
I clutched anything my hand could hang onto, extending my head over a sink and throwing up, bile following shortly after.
I couldn't see, couldn't hear, couldn't smell.
I whirled round, pirouetted and finally embraced the darkness begging for my attention.
Fainted.

Chapter 5

I woke up with five doctors surrounding me. I shivered a few times; however, I was fortunate and incredibly grateful that the earlier fear had subsided.
"Hello, Ava. A little someone told us you prefer your nickname." The doctor closest to my bed smiled.
I stretched my arms, almost knocking off the oxygen mask that was perched over my mouth and nose.
The terror returned.
"It's OK my lovely, you're all right. Your concussion hadn't worn off fully and the added stress didn't help much. You began acting oddly and after vomiting, you collapsed."
I sensed the thick snot running from my nose, hearing a sodden splash on the oxygen mask. I felt horribly humiliated.
"Your sister explained that she'd told you Dan and Lisa hadn't been tracked. That the police knew they were in a building, but not how to get to the destination," the doctor said, stroking my hand. I clutched onto her fingers, desperate for comfort.
The four other doctors said nothing.
Eventually, the one on my other side spoke. She had beautiful red hair and perfect brown skin. Her beige lipstick hugged her lips as if it was made for her.
"Leanne, loosen the oxygen mask," she demanded, her strong accent matching her appearance flawlessly.
Leanne nodded, readjusting my oxygen mask.
"Is the child's mum anywhere to be seen?" the red-haired doctor queried.
"They believe she's lost in that forest. Her car was in the lay-by for forty-eight hours, abandoned," Leanne declared. She glanced in my direction.
I somewhat shrugged my shoulders.
Leanne coughed before speaking again. "I don't understand how the ambulance arrived to pick up Ava and Keira, but the police cannot locate the building," she said, confusion filling her blue eyes.
Red-haired lady fixed her posture. "Yes, but the police aren't paramedics. Chanell didn't mention anyone else, therefore they

didn't search until the little girl cried in distress about being imprisoned. Kept captive and held at gunpoint. Leanne, we can't even trace the same paramedics to question where the building is," she stressed.

Leanne dropped my hand and I instantly grasped the air, as if to beseech for her touch.

"Celia, calm. Your outburst won't get us any further and most definitely will not help Ava."

Celia bowed her head. I peered past the two of them. The other three doctors were men, frantically jotting sentences on cream sheets of paper.

My body rushed with a hot sweat and I shuddered. I gestured to Leanne, asking if I'd be OK.

"Yes, honey. You're all good. A concussion takes some time to recover from. Don't worry."

Somewhere along the way, I fell asleep. Not a sleep I'd ever have expected to encounter. A harsh, deep sleep that gripped at my heart, pushing and pulling it around wildly. I tossed in my sleep and yelped as I gazed into the distance, vaguely spotting Dan. As I spun, I realised I could see myself from an overhead angle. Me from a few days earlier. I could visualise the man trudging towards me, sneaking up behind me and yanking my wrist.

He booted me to the ground.

I lashed out, screeching as Dan kicked my body and glanced up, towards my present position. He stormed up, nearing me, and I stiffened.

I yelled out as I felt his foul breath. It smelled of onions and a disgusting flavour of peppermint. I gagged at his stench as his outline blocked my eyesight, his mouth watering with drool as he clasped his thick hands around my throat...

I awoke with Leanne right beside my hospital bed. She wore a frown of concern and bags underneath her eyes.

As her walkie-talkie buzzed, she lifted it to her ear. She hummed, waiting for the individual on the other end of the line to talk. "Yes, she's still in Room 10," Leanne replied after a minute. She inspected my face. "She's just woken up." She lowered the

walkie-talkie, her eyes fixed on me. "How are you feeling? I think you had a nightmare, didn't you?" she asked.
I grumbled.
Leanne touched my forehead, then returned to chatting on her walkie-talkie.
I kicked my feet, attempting to move. My legs had cramped, causing shooting torment through my bones. I struggled until I couldn't anymore and fell with a thump backwards, my head knocking the headboard.
Leanne sprung up, instantly tapping the back of my head to ensure I hadn't done any damage. "Please, Ava. You'll be able to go home really soon, but only if you stop giving yourself extra injuries," she said sternly.
I listened eagerly as she continued her conversation.
"Her mother has been tracked down? Perfect. When will-" Leanne cracked her knuckles as she waited for the second person to finish before she carried on. "At home... She was in her house this whole time? Surely she noticed her daughters weren't with her?"
Now I was suspicious. They were discussing my mum. I felt a pricking in my eyes as tears brimmed to the surface. Mum didn't care; she couldn't have, otherwise she'd have been looking for us. She'd have phoned the police or the hospital to ask where we were and if we were OK. But she didn't, and therefore may well lose my respect. She had two responsibilities. I understood she was significant at work as an apparent paramedic, but she wasn't much of a hero if she couldn't even protect her children.
I used my hands to fold my ears inwards, no longer wanting to hear a word. But when I did close my ears, I could recall the shrill tone of Lisa's voice and it sounded so close I almost screamed.
I couldn't breathe, couldn't find the strength in my body, until I overheard a simple comment coming from Leanne.
"If he wishes to visit Ava, I'll happily remove the oxygen mask. She seems to be breathing normally again."
I shook my head. I wasn't breathing properly, not at all.
But as she turned to me, her eyes were hopeful, and it reflected how sanguine I'd been just days before.

I reluctantly gave up fighting and let her remove the mask. She unwound a strand of hair from inside the breathing apparatus where it must have fallen over my face, ensuring she didn't hurt me in the process.
"Chanell would like to stop by and see you. Is that OK?" she asked.
"Is that who was on the other end of the walkie-talkie?" I tilted my head, flattening my hair.
Leanne opened a drawer and threw the mask inside. "No. It was Reception."
I shot her a puzzled look.
"The person on front desk," she elaborated.
"I know what a receptionist is," I mumbled. "But how did they receive the information about Mum being tracked down?"
Leanne ripped open a packet of tablets and tipped two into her palm. She poured a glass of water and passed them to me.
"Chanell cautioned us, in case your mum took part in Lisa and Dan kidnapping you and Keira, but everyone phoning in goes straight to Reception." She scratched her cheek.
I downed the tablets, flinching at their lack of flavour. "I wasn't kidnapped," I said firmly.
Leanne didn't respond and I knew she wouldn't believe me. She saw what Dan and Lisa had done as abduction, when in reality Keira was unwillingly captured, while I could have escaped. Despite the fact that Dan owned a gun, he wouldn't have shot me. He *would* have murdered Keira, however.
I handed the glass back. Leanne poured the remaining liquid into a nearby sink, chewing on her lip as she gazed in my direction. She shifted her weight from her left foot to her right foot.
"What's the matter? You're acting nervous. Should I be anxious too?" I froze, concern swamping my body, catching me off guard.
Leanne peered briefly over her shoulder towards the doorway. "Chanell should arrive in a moment. You're all right being left alone with him? He's lovely, but you're a kid," she said. She slurred her words so much I could hardly tell them apart from one another.
"Yes," I confirmed confidently. "I visited him the other day and I'm still alive."

Leanne laughed half-heartedly. A rap on the door sounded. It was already ajar but Leanne's shaking legs moved her to open it wider.
Mr. Chanell charged into the room, his bald head almost taking over half the original lighting. Not that it was as shiny as three days earlier, but still bright enough.
"Hi, Miss Ava," he greeted.
I waved, gently gesturing for Leanne to exit the room. "Hi, Mr. Chanell."
He perched on the edge of the bed, almost catching my toes under the cream sheets. "Call me Eric. How are you?"
I nodded, motioning to my head as I pulled it forward, wincing. Eric folded his arms.
"Does that answer your question? I'm doing better. Thank you for saving my sister and me."
"I knocked Dan's arm and he pulled the trigger. Towards *you*. If we're being practical, I could have killed you," he whispered regretfully.
I paused, cautious. "Do you know Dan and Lisa?"
He bowed his head. "They're my parents. I let them know a girl came to visit me, basically blaming me for her dad's murder. I didn't tell them who that girl was," he admitted, remorseful.
I scowled, spitting as I spoke. "Lisa and Dan are your parents? Geez, I apologise. No wonder you used to abuse my dad; you grew up in the same house as two unhinged criminals."
Eric's eyes widened dramatically from the shock of my remark. "Stop bringing that up, please. It's over and done with. Nothing can take me back to change my actions."
I strained to sit up, balancing my head upright. It didn't pain me anymore.
"Could Dan and Lisa - your parents - have killed my dad? They terrified me and my sister. All of us from the same family."
Eric shook his bald head. He glanced around, his eyes meeting every nook and cranny in the area except the headboard end of the bed. He assumed something I would disagree with.
I chewed my lip. He noticed and sighed.
"We think your mum was involved in murdering your dad. Not Dan nor Lisa. It might come across as impractical to you, but

your mum often had dinner with my mum and dad, departing from you and Darren on the nights she stopped by my house. The doctor, the police and I think she planned for you and your sister to be abducted so she could go ahead with some sort of plan," he said, scratching behind his ear.
I gazed at him in horror and disbelief. There was a stunned silence. Eric wrung his fingers together, awaiting my reply. Meanwhile, I stalled, sitting tight as I ran his allegations through my brain.
Usually, when you're a child, your mum informs you about all of the stalkers, murderers, thieves and criminals of any sort that could seem kind, but deceive you in a blink of an eye. I'd learned that the hard way. After I'd grieved for my dad and it had sunk into my system that he'd been killed, I'd understood that there were evil individuals out in the world. Beforehand, I hadn't had a clue. My mum hadn't notified me about these people, therefore if I was at gunpoint - like I had appeared to be the other day - I'd have stood no chance.
Is there a possibility I might have awoken under the same roof as a killer? Furthermore, the same roof as my *dad's* killer?
I broke out in a cold sweat, my hair clinging to my skin which ensued in it erupting into visible goosebumps.
"May you provide proof? Your accusations might fully be correct, but without evidence, I can't take your word for it. My mum is remarkable in many ways. For the last years, you've practically been a stranger to me and even before, I was too young to get to know you as a person." I pursed my lips.
He scanned my face, considering what his response should be, and shrugged. "Unfortunately, I do not possess any evidence at this moment," he admitted openly. "However, in the meantime, I can give you a number. If you discover anything appropriate, ring it. Contact the police too." Reaching into his pocket, he removed a beige contact card. A number stared at me in large, thick letters.
Eric retreated backwards, aiming to leave.
I lifted up a machine next to my bed. I hadn't seen it before, but nevertheless, I had one more question to bother Eric with. I

dropped it to the ground. It thumped onto the wooden floor, smashing in the process.
Eric rotated, faster than I'd ever noticed someone turn before. Not even Dan or Lisa had moved as strikingly. I gripped my tongue with my teeth to withhold an unexpected laugh at his rapid movement.
He had to have been a policeman himself at one time, always on guard. The way he manoeuvred told me this.
He raised an eyebrow, looking expectant.
"Would you be willing to meet up again? To look more in-depth into this situation? Who knows, perhaps it will be beneficial," I suggested, inspecting his expression. "You can ask your... *parents*... about why they bothered an innocent family..." I faltered, reminding myself how I'd accused him falsely too. Correct, he hadn't been guilt-free four years earlier, but for all I knew, he could have changed. I thought he had. "I'm sorry... I know I blamed you the other day..."
He nodded, smiling. "It's fine, Ava. You live to learn from mistakes, speaking as a first-hand expert in a topic like this. I'm unsure if I will be able to have words with my parents, though; once they're tracked down, they'll be sent to prison."
I said nothing. Recalling Lisa and Dan made my heart race. I couldn't think of them whilst still being so traumatised.
Eric placed his arm out and then yanked it back again, angling it as if to say goodbye.
I remained wary of him. As expected, I'd certainly become wary of everyone going forwards.
At least I'd receive justice for being held at gunpoint.
But my dad? His murderer might not ever be punished for taking his life.
Puffing up the pillow, I lay against the snug material. I missed my dad. A lot.
Just like that, I grieved myself to sleep.

Chapter 6

Keira returned the next morning as I was devouring breakfast: a beautifully buttered croissant with jam on the side for me to dip it into if I wished for the pastry to be sweeter.
Keira wore a fake smile as she neared me.
"What's up?" I enquired, wiping soft butter from around my mouth.
She plonked on the end of my bed. "Mum. Two nights camping at the police station and I'm being forced to go back there tonight." She sighed. "I don't want to. Especially not if you won't be there. Mum has been proven blameless but I'm cautious of her."
I licked my lips. "That's not fair," I agreed.
Keira rolled her eyes. "Yeah. I know. But I'm a child so I don't make the decision. As if I chose to be born when I was." She hesitated. "You'll be home soon, won't you?"
I'd often wondered bitterly why Mum hadn't visited me. She must have been aware of my concussion and my current recovery. "I hope so."
Leanne sauntered into my hospital room. It was time for my medication, I assumed. "Morning, honey. Good morning, Keira." She saluted and walked over to the tray of antibiotics.
"I didn't think it was antibiotics I took?" I asked, partially suspicious.
Leanne paused awkwardly, her hand midway to the tray. "Celia said it's safe to swap now, since you'll be given antibiotics to take home..."
Something was going on. I didn't open my mouth when she offered me my tablets.
"I need to ask, what's going on? You're acting strangely." I observed her carefully.
Leanne returned the box of tablets to the tray and swivelled to face me. "Celia informed me it's mandatory you go home today. She clearly stated this room is going to be occupied by someone new tomorrow," she confessed.
"But... what if I'm not recovered? I haven't left this bed for ages-"
"I know. That's why you've got to take these antibiotics and then I'm going to support you walking again. If you collapse, we'll

move you to another ward. If not, you're discharged," she explained, pouring me a glass of lukewarm water.
I downed the tablets, gulping.
I didn't necessarily fantasise about seeing Mum, but if I didn't recover, my little sister would be alone.
I accepted Leanne's plan.

It was difficult edging myself off the bed and standing upright. Honestly, I'd forgotten I even owned two feet of my own.
I wobbled briefly, Leanne supporting my left side, Celia my right.
"Go on, Ava. You weren't unconscious for long, it's more the recovery we're worried about," Celia said, gripping my arm as I toppled right.
I took a few steps and tripped.
"Darling, this won't work if you think about it too much. I know every time you sway, your mind is on Dan and Lisa. But they will be caught as soon as possible," Leanne assured me, hanging onto my left arm tightly.
I attempted to shift again. This time, after tripping, I managed to switch my thinking to something positive.
"Good girl," Celia praised as I positioned one foot in front of the other several times.
I tensed as the thought of the gun at my waist made me shiver.
"Keep going," Leanne pushed, detaching her hand from my arm.
I closed my eyes as I moved a step closer towards the door. I doubted myself, yelling inwardly that I'd be defeated by the flashbacks.
But as Celia released my arm, I walked forward. Five more steps. Ten.
Leanne and Celia clapped, Leanne jumping for joy.
Out in the narrow corridor, we repeated. As I got halfway down the hallway, I'd strolled for ten minutes by myself. Up and down, back and forth.
I grinned at my success. Behind the grin, deep down, I felt the fear of what Eric Chanell had drummed into my brain. This information didn't just exist, going through one ear and out the other. Instead, the voice inside my head grabbed it.

My mum could be a murderer. The voices would taunt me, leading me to feel sceptical and confused. A disadvantage for me. Because until I could properly tell apart good from bad, I had no clue what Mum really might be... or what she could have in store for my sister and me...

Dinner wasn't the same as the previous week. The atmosphere was hollow, almost fake. Mum knew we suspected her, thought of her as a killer. Not Keira and me - we couldn't be sure - but Eric, the police and the doctors. If that was correct, my sister and I wouldn't have been sent home.
Mum took a swig of apple juice, her fork pointing in the air. "I received a phone call today," she mentioned.
I gestured for her to explain.
"They called us in for a meeting. Heard the inconveniences of me getting tied up in this, and... want to ask what we are currently aware of and what we don't yet know."
I smiled unconvincingly. "Right. Where will this... *meeting*... be held?"
Keira's eyes dropped to her food, an anxious expression masking her face. I supposed she couldn't be definite that Mum wouldn't drive us to the lay-by again, sprinting off and allowing us to be captured.
"A&E," Mum replied.
I glanced at Keira. Her face turned the colour of beetroot.
This gathering, this 'meeting' thing, was unlikely to be serious if it was taking place in A&E.
I soon gave up eating the soft homemade pasta. My appetite departed, leaving my throat parched.
Keira and I decided to have a slumber party, with each other as company. We created a den out of bedsheets and disclaimed cushions from the attic. Mum entered and approved of our bed for that night.
Stepping in the shower was the hardest challenge. We hadn't practiced back in the hospital, mostly because after I'd gained confidence in walking, I was worn out.
Cuddling up under our den, I read to Keira. Both of us were home-schooled; after Dad's death, Mum had refused to send the

two of us into school. I hadn't cared because the school I'd attended had dismissed the fact that my dad had been killed and that I was bound to be upset. This could possibly have been the reason I'd suppressed my emotions.
On the other hand, Keira's only source of socialising came from waking up and travelling to nursery each day.
Keira lacked a lot of things an average nine-year-old might have. The ability to read was one of them.
We picked at a medium bag of toffee popcorn, four hands rooting inside, digging at the contents; two mouths consuming the sugary, rich texture.
Settling down was strenuous. My head felt as if it were suffocating, even though the material underneath it wasn't anything less than standard comfort.
I kissed Keira on her soft cheek, fondling her hair. Fifteen minutes later, I was asleep.

I estimated the time I woke up to be seven o'clock at least. But it was four o'clock. Raging voices came from outside. I unlatched Keira's bedroom window and stood, cold in my summer pyjamas.
I focused on Mum to begin with, her silhouette freaky in the dark. I strained my ears, begging them to pick up everything she was saying.
"You idiot! Why the heck are you standing on my driveway at this time?" she yelled, loud enough to wake the next five streets. If she assumed she was talking discreetly, she'd be wrong.
I was unable to see the second individual. He too was casting a shadow on the pavement under the dim streetlamp. He remained unknown.
"I'm here because you forgot to lock the gates before leaving. You're useless, Sandra. If this is how you're going to behave, I'll reveal myself in front..." His voice lowered as Keira stirred.
I shifted towards her, replacing myself by her side.
I'd recognised the voice.
I didn't recall where from.
I couldn't remember how come.

All I knew was that Mum had kept significant information confidential... almost as if she'd taught me and my sister skills that would get us places in life, but in her own world, she was not the victim...
She was the villain.

Chapter 7

Stumbling back into my bedroom the following morning brought uncertainty and puzzlement.
The wind had increased mildly in the early hours, at sunrise.
My gaze flew to my window. I focused on something flapping in the breeze on the ledge outside. Something white, square. Mysterious.
I walked over, unlocked my window and reached for the letter.
I threw off the envelope without hesitation.
A fat slip of card sat inside. I unfolded it.

Dear Avery Hayloft,
42 Delling Road, East Shallowton. ASAP. Find the money beneath your father's grave. Take it to the police, bribe them. Get them to continue the search for the murderer.

I breathed in.
Shoved the letter into my backpack.
Left the room.

The bus stank of powerful aftershave, ten times better than the stench of weed flowing up my nostrils as I'd waited at the bus stop.
The girl next to me stared intently at my face. I squirmed, embarrassed.
"You're Avery Hayloft, aren't you?" she enquired, jiggling her knee up and down.
I nodded.
"I thought you looked like that girl on the billboard," she gasped. "You were in the newspapers as a child too, weren't you?"
I laughed. "That's me. What's your name?"
The girl instantly yanked out her phone, holding it up to my face. I smiled, out of anxiety more than giving actual consent for her to take a photo of me, and I squinted as the flash went off.
"My name's Summer," she announced, obsessing over the photo.
I raced off the bus as soon as it came to a halt half an hour later.

42 Delling Road wasn't new to me because I'd visited Dad's grave many times before. It was one of the only cemeteries in Shallowton.

I scurried across the town hall, through a children's playground and around the bend of my old street. It was dull and bleak; many druggies were dotted around, and many stabbings had been reported there.

It wasn't an appropriate place for two young girls to live.

There was an aroma of flowers as I neared the cemetery. Not from the actual cemetery, of course, but from all the delicate roses that had been delivered by people who'd lost a loved one. I felt a pang of sadness.

Dad's grave was isolated, only damp grass surrounding it. I gently shifted the roses over and added one of my own. A whole range of artificial flowers were deposited on the ground beneath. An extra one was placed on special occasions, Christmases especially.

I reached behind the grave. Nothing. I removed the note from my rucksack. It didn't elaborate on where it was hidden. Wasn't as if I could dig up the soil.

I stood up and walked a bit further along. I couldn't leave my sister for any longer than an hour... What if she thought I'd run into danger once more?

I kicked something sturdy and white. Bending down, I recognised it at once - the money.

I tore at the envelope, my hair fluttering out behind me as if it were a curtain. I'd always loathed it, admiring Keira's blonde curls, craving to own fair hair myself.

The unpigmented envelope consisted of fifty thousand pounds. My mouth hung open loosely, my eyes widening with shock. Fifty thousand pounds. An unknown individual had donated this cash to allow my dad's murder case to continue. My lips stretched, spreading into a beam. I was over the moon, so obliged.

I slung my locks off my face, gathering my bearings. This made the last couple of days appear less frightening.

Until I heard a sound.

Pivoting on my heel, I scanned the cemetery. Empty.

Subsequently, a hand touched my shoulder, light, casual.
I parted my lips, composing myself. And then screeched.
"Ava, be quiet. You'll rouse the dead." A man's voice. Calm.
I spun around, gritting my teeth.
Eric Chanell.
"What are you doing? You scared the heck out of me," I accused him, flustered. "You recall that just a few days ago I was captured?"
Chanell grimaced. His face was regretful. "I remember." He shrugged. "Sorry." He dismissed my reaction. "You have an appointment at twelve-thirty. Be on time."
I pulled a face. What was he implying?
He rolled his eyes. "The hospital. It's mandatory for you to speak to a professional."
A professional... Who did he think I was? Aside from being a stranger, when did I consent to an appointment? When did I give my permission for him to book anything of the kind?
I crossed my arms, stamping my foot gently. I then realised we were in the middle of a cemetery. I gestured this to him and his eyes widened.
I stuffed the envelope into my rucksack and Eric adjusted his hat, then we trudged off the grass and out of the cemetery. I had an urge to break down and weep. I hadn't said hi to Dad. I hadn't told him I loved him. I always did that when visiting his grave. Perhaps he's lonely in heaven and needs to be reminded that he is thought of. I banished the inner voice quickly.
"Tell me more. Elaborate," I demanded, stopping in front of Eric.
He curved an eyebrow. "No." He shrugged. "But don't bother worrying. I'll be there."
I laughed. "Oh, so you expect me to feel better because you'll be by my side? Eric, I hardly know you. I require the details if you wish to catch my attention."
"You're stubborn." He chuckled.
I frowned, lowering my eyes. "Labelling me as stubborn doesn't really encourage me to trust you," I pointed out.
"I intend to help, madam. Just go to the hospital at the time I gave."

I raised my head halfway, uncertain. I couldn't avoid feeling hesitant. The feeling perched at the depth of my stomach as if it owned my emotions. "I can't. I'll be in A&E."
Eric scowled, puzzled. I decided it best if I elaborated on my own details. "My mum got a phone call. Said to go to A&E for a meeting in one of the spare rooms. The appointment is scheduled for twelve," I explained.
"Right... I don't understand why, but right. So be it. OK, I'll bring the authorities to... A&E? Who's holding the meeting?" he questioned, almost as if I'd organised the thing. Of course, it had been as unexpected as my encounter with Eric himself.
"Angelina... White. Yes, that's the one. Angelina White. Apparently a very pretty woman." The last remark was unnecessary, but I just repeated Mum's words.
Eric paused, suddenly silent. I gulped. His expression changed rapidly. I shook his arm, waking him out of his trance.
"Sorry, Ava. Angelina White was my wife. She... She disappeared, months and months ago," he confessed, keeping his eyes on me.
I blew out a breath. I asked if we were speaking about the same Angelina White.
"Beautiful light brown skin? Fierce brown eyes? That's my Angelina. She went missing while returning from work. Knocked out and kidnapped. That's what the police said. But if she's going to be talking to you... I'll definitely come and sort things out. If she's kept me worried all this time without contacting me, it's over."
I said nothing.
And then noticed the time displayed on the large cathedral clock.
11.45am.

I darted out of Delling Road and around the bend, flying to catch the bus. I arrived there, panting. I banged on the window like a crazy woman. The driver seemed confused, which didn't surprise me; thumping on the window of a vehicle already pulling up is pretty strange. I launched my bus ticket towards him, twisting it round and enabling him to see it clearly.

He nodded. I didn't have time to reach back and grab it, so deposited it.
I didn't even sit.
Keira and Mum were due to leave for the meeting. Keira would probably assume I had been abducted or was risking my life and Mum just wouldn't care.
I winced as the inner ache spiralled through my bones. A child's nightmare might be their mother not protecting them from the dangers they may encounter while growing up. Mine used to supervise me twenty-four-seven. Recently, she'd proven to be untrustworthy. Nothing could be confirmed about whether or not she'd killed Dad this early on, especially as there wasn't a way the police would be able to verify her as a criminal, but nonetheless, she'd acted as if life was normal, even when Keira and I had been missing. For that, I could only visualise her as a dishonest woman, self-obsessed and in her own world.
I reached the house, otherwise known as my destination. Curving into the red-brick driveway, I spotted Keira battling her way through the car door and into the front seat. That seemed unfair. I was the oldest.
I heard her sigh, cursing inappropriately to herself. She stopped in her tracks as she saw me. We looked at each other and, aside from the difference in hair colour, I felt as if she were mirroring me.
And just like that, she raced up to me, flinging her arms around my neck.
"Ava, *what*?! I thought you'd been taken from your bed this morning!" she said. "I was so worried! Mum told me I was being theatrical, but I knew well enough that disgusting events happen, especially to young children."
I cuddled her and she buried her face in my jumper.
"I'm so sorry, Keira," I said apologetically, "but I found money. Money to allow Dad's search to go forward, if the police accept the cash and don't decline it. There's fifty thousand pounds. If they don't snatch it out of my hands, I'll find someone who will."
Keira stared at me, sceptical. She nodded slowly. "Show me the money," she whispered in a hushed tone. "Not because I want to

see a stash of cash, but it's valuable, and... Ava, how did you get the money?"
I stiffened, my legs tensing. It wasn't as if I'd stolen it, but telling anyone how much of a coincidence it was that me, Mum and Keira were attending a meeting in less than five minutes and some unknown individual had just left money at Dad's grave...
Mum walked out of the house. She quickly peeked in my direction and ushered us into the car.
"Three minutes," she complained, chucking her handbag into the passenger seat. "Hurry up."
We all got comfortable. As we set off, I glanced at Keira. I caught the pain in her eyes. Not typical pain. The pain of someone who was fighting to keep it together, who'd experienced a whole range of emotions larger than what she'd shared. I'd been on this earth for nearly thirteen years, and never in my life had I seen a little girl so unsure, so defeated, so fragile.

Chapter 8

The waiting room in A&E was airy and spacious. Soft blue chairs were dotted around, one corner full to the brim with children's toys. A small boy curled up on the floor, a book in his lap, his cheek resting gently against his light brown palm. As Mum, Keira and I perched on a chair, two older teenagers glanced at us with curiosity. One tapped me on the shoulder. It felt mocking, somehow.
I faced him.
He was glaring at me, his eyes shining into mine, piercing my brain. "You're in A&E, you know that, right?" he asked.
I looked down at his leg. It was swollen, the bruise fresh and yellow. "Yes?" I answered. "Obviously I know that."
The other teenager sniggered. "Well, none of you seem injured." He gestured to the three of us.
Keira turned around and the first guy tapped his friend, hissing something in his ear. The second boy got to his feet, guiding the first. "Got to go. We've just been called in." He laughed awkwardly.
They hobbled away together, down the corridor leading to an X-ray room.
"Wow, Keira," I said. "Thanks."
Keira looked surprised and confused at once, but before my little sister could reply to my impressed remark, a woman with shoulder-length black hair and determined brown eyes shouted our names.
"Avery, Keira, Sandra Hayloft?" Her voice sounded a little slurred, but I didn't think twice. She had gorgeous, soft brown skin.
This lady was dressed in a navy blue police uniform. She somehow seemed stiff and fragile, but I guessed she was nervous.
She decorated her face with a homely smile, motioning us into the room beyond.
Keira skipped ahead of both Mum and me, clearly eager to get this over with. I could see her legs trembling slightly and felt

sorry for her. She'd always been anxious whilst meeting new people. Especially police officers.
The policewoman hauled three chairs together and sat on another herself, behind the wooden desk. She situated her hands into a business-like position but didn't look terrifying or big. Instead, she seemed kind, sweet.
"I'm Angelina White," she explained. "I've been on your dad's murder case for nearly six years. They forced me to put it on pause, but I don't care what they say anymore. This is important. They can't keep putting it off because they're too weak to deal with it. They definitely cannot stop me, anyway."
I nodded. Keira sat beside me, her arms moving in every direction possible. I bit my lip.
Mum rested her arm on my own chair. I could feel it gently scraping on my back.
"Sandra, you can sit," Angelina offered.
"Maybe," Mum said. She appeared stressed.
Angelina tugged a red sheet of paper from a plastic wallet. The wallet was orange, so bright it could've blinded me. I should've brought sunglasses.
"Oh, and," Angelina continued, "you may call me Angie."
Keira, Mum and I kept quiet. Angie whistled a little until finally giving in. She lifted a pen, balancing it between her fingers. "So," she said, "what do you know? Anything will be good. Man or woman?"
Keira coughed. She wanted to express her thoughts, but was too frightened.
"I think it's a woman," she stammered.
Mum slapped her fist on my chair. I jumped, startled as the angry gesture hit my upper back.
Mum glided across the room, snatching up the red paper Angie had in her grasp.
"Sandra?" Angie said, bewilderment streaking over her expression. "Talk to me."
"You're going to listen to a child? She's not right!" Mum insisted, her opinion clear.
Keira slid down in her seat, uncomfortable.
I peered at Mum's irritated, infuriated face.

"Well, I think Keira has shared a great thought," Angie said approvingly, trying at the same time to assure Keira and release the anger from Mum.
Mum stared at her youngest daughter. "I don't. She's NINE! How are you about to believe her?"
And with that, Mum lunged her weight at the third chair, sending it flying, smashing through the window and out of sight.
I bounced up.
"This wasn't in the script, Angelina White!" Mum cried out. "How-"
She suddenly became aware of her two children right beside her.
I frowned, feeling my forehead form into a muddled crease.
"Joking, girls. I'm just sure it would be a man. Out in the snow in December, late at night..."
"That's incredibly stereotypical!" Keira yelled, the first time I'd heard her so outraged since years before when I'd stolen her favourite doll and had dipped its head in the toilet.
Mum paused, running out of comebacks as her small, noiseless daughter stood up for her belief.
Angie must have experienced some distressing, threatening actions before in her job as a police officer, but the way her face sat in that moment, you'd have thought she was a woman who sits at home, writing personal letters to friends and family far away, maturing in a way maybe different to one who oversaw crimes and followed murder cases.
It made me feel uncomfortable.
Mum opened her mouth then shut it immediately, possibly regretful. Having raised such a peaceful, silent girl, yet that girl had just spoken so firmly and powerfully - maybe she wouldn't look at her the same way again.
As for me, well, I felt proud of her.
As Angie parted her lips to release another comment, the door flew open and, after hurling himself into the room, a man howled out just one meaningful sentence:
'Darren's murderer has been found!'
Angie stood up, placing her hands behind her back and waited for the man to spill more.

He wore a police uniform too, but didn't look much like a policeman. He had ruffled brown hair, a wart on his forehead and a beard so long I thought it'd touch the tiled floor at any moment.
"Aaron, we need to know more," Angie demanded, narrowing her eyes in his direction.
Aaron groaned, unsure of how to start. "Her name is Pandora Anderson," he revealed. "It came through on that website!"
"Website?" I repeated. "What website?"
Angie quickly became pale. She looked adamant that she would tell me no more, but something in Aaron's head must've yelled at him to tell the truth.
"Eighty people were in Shallowton minutes before and after the stabbing. We didn't know exactly who, of course, so we had to put names of everyone over eighteen in the country on this website page," he elaborated.
Keira rose up, seemingly to argue. "Unreliable, don't you think?" she asked bitterly. "How can you confirm it was this Pandora?"
"So, if there are any suspects you know of, you tick the box of their name. Simple as that," Aaron said. "We receive a notification as individuals choose the culprit's name. We've had none so far, until this morning."
Keira raised her eyebrows. "Unreliable," she repeated. "So unrealistic."
Angie was avoiding the eyes of all, but before I could ask why, Mum thumped my chair again, making me leap half a mile. "She's correct. Impractical could also describe it. It's stupid."
Without taking even another breath, Mum stormed out of the room, slamming the door closed and shaking our chairs dreadfully.
I recalled the scene from the day years earlier when Mum and Dad had had an argument, over something I couldn't remember. It had concluded with Dad stalking out of the house and throwing the door shut behind him, making the house rattle and the chairs Keira and I were sat on wobble uncontrollably.
This had been just before Mum and Dad took a break on their marriage and a few nights later, Dad had died and neither I nor

anyone else could ever have guessed what would've happened to their relationship. Would it have been a happily ever after?
Aaron smiled at my sister, who straightened up her body in alarm, stock-still.
After a few minutes, Mum wasn't back and the room we were in remained quiet, daunting.
Angie clapped her hands together, making me jump once again. "Aaron , see where Sandra has got to," she instructed. "Take Keira with you. I suppose there's something I should tell Ava on her own."
Aaron did as he was told, bribing Keira off the chair with the guarantee of cookies. Keira took his hand and her and Aaron disappeared out the door and down the neat, colourful corridor.
"You've grown so much," Angie said, peering at me with admiration. "I have been on your dad's murder case since that traumatising night. Met you and loved how happy you were, considering your father had just been stabbed."
I laughed unpleasantly. It sounded like a fake laugh, echoey and hollow. My face returned to its original manner. "Me? I guess I always was a merry little girl, even when the worst occurred. It was just who I had always been. I wanted to be a-"
"Therapist?" Angie interrupted me mid-sentence. "Do you still want to be one?"
After Dad had died, I'd been more serious than ever about becoming a therapist. Especially after I saw Keira so broken, so distraught. The idea felt thrilling to me as a person, helping others in their lowest moments of life and guiding them to find that light at the end of the tunnel I'd always been told about.
I nodded, completely sure of my ambition. "I do want to be a therapist, more than anything. As a child I had a desire to become a fairy, but fairies aren't real. I found that out when my dad was killed," I explained, feeling the self-pity flooding in around my feet like water.
Angie slid the red paper over to her left. She adjusted her uniform. "I can't imagine what it was like for you. When I entered your house that next morning, you immediately started blabbing about how amazing your dad was." She reached for a tissue.

"I just knew I had to stay strong. For myself, Mum and Keira. My sister was three at the time. She needed support more than I did. So I decided to be the one to remember Dad and all he did for us." I paused, a tear gradually falling and splatting neatly onto the wood in front of me. "Mum and Dad weren't together at the time. They had some difficulties being around one another with two children."
Of course, Angie knew this. She'd been aware of everything from that night. All the ins and outs. What Dad was doing before, where Keira was, me and Mum too. Why Dad had been in Shallowton. What events had occurred twenty-four hours before.
"Ava, I have been notified that you're unmindful of Lisa's current prison sentence?"
I became scarily engrossed in our upcoming conversation. "I'm oblivious to this information, yes. I encountered Eric Chanell earlier. He didn't seem conscious of it either," I responded.
Hope sprang into my chest, buoyant and enthusiastic. Shortly thereafter, however, my positivity drowned, sinking into the pit of my stomach as another thought ruled it out.
Dan's still out there.
"They're on the lookout for Dan. Said after Lisa had been tracked, he wasn't anywhere to be seen," Angie summarised, as if she'd pulled the contemplation out of my head.
I finally understood how unbelievably cruel the world could be. My dad's bloodthirsty murderer hadn't ever been found, even after five daunting, gruelling years, and now only one of the two individuals who'd kidnapped my sister and held me at gunpoint had been located and punished. The feeling was indescribable. I couldn't accept this as reality. Two criminals were out there, roaming the streets and smiling at others as they paced along. People who didn't know the excruciating pain of their actions. Oh, I'd say they didn't know the least of it.
My body broke out in a cold sweat. I touched my forehead. It was flaming.
"Ava." Angie's angelic voice pulled my consciousness back into the stuffy A&E room. "We'll find him. It's dire, not knowing his

whereabouts. Especially after the trauma you experienced because of that sick man."
I stretched my arm outwards, tugging my sleeve up. The material was tight and woolly, making me struggle to breathe. It didn't mix well with the strong fear in my guts.
"There is just one minor problem," Angie muttered. "What with Dan wandering around, he could emerge at any moment."
Did she think I was oblivious to this? That I hadn't already whirled the possibility around in my head? I couldn't convince myself I'd be prepared, but I knew Dan wouldn't just leave things as they were.
"You are being quiet, so I'm going to resume sharing my thoughts. It's too premature to tell when Dan will step up, but I do have an idea. Firstly, I should tell you my belief, which is that Dan knows your mother. Your family was shown worldwide across the global news, so Dan understood Sandra had two daughters. Whilst Lisa is after Keira, and has been caught and charged, Dan is out to get you. You're remarkable to him. He used his son as an excuse to get close to you and now that's not an option for him, he'll use something else." Angie cleared her throat, looking expectant, eager for my reply.
I paid sudden attention to the finest details of the patchy wood on Angie's desk. Pieces had peeled off, as if they had faded away. It ironically mirrored my own recent emotions. Lost. Uneasy. Scared.
"Yes," I acknowledged. "But please, you're making me nervous."
Angie's dedicated, strong-willed eyes pierced through mine. She set her mouth agape, as if assuming I knew. I did. Her thoughts weren't just predictable and fast-paced. She wanted, presumably, to put my life at stake. Put it at risk.
"No. Are- Are you deranged? Mad?" I shrieked hysterically. "Did- Did you-"
"Ava, calm down. I haven't explained," she said, her eyes scanning my face, tense. "Listen. If Dan attempts to lure you away, which is more than likely what he'll do, you *need* to sprint. Can you run quickly?"
I shook my arms at my sides, anxiety coursing through my whole body. I was particularly pleased with myself because Angie's

request would be daunting, exaggerated; therefore, I must've physically impressed her in some way. However, the bigger side of me, the weak side, begged myself to dismiss any reckless action she'd assign. I couldn't do it. Couldn't undertake her mission.

I breathed deeply, closing my eyes and letting the timidity fade from Angie's view. In my world, it still existed - harsh, squeezing at my stomach and making me want to bend over in agony and wail.

"I can run, yeah," I confirmed. "But not quickly."

Angie swiped her hand. "Doesn't matter. If you see Dan, stand rooted to the spot until he notices you. The dangerous part is, when he does, you *have* to sprint. Faster than ever. Otherwise, he'll catch you, you'll die, and we won't ever find the man. You have to dash. Without stopping," she implored, her hands fiddling with the orange folder.

I shook my head, adamant of my refusal. "I can't. I can't do that. Angie, I'm too young, too weak," I insisted.

Angie caught hold of my sweaty hand, gripping it soothingly. "You'll be completely safe. A member of the police will be spying nearby, a gun and taser at hand."

I twisted my fingers together. "How'll they know when and where I'll see Dan?" I asked reasonably. "Surely it's unpredictable? Unless this policeman can analyse the future."

Angie laughed. I accepted her sudden amusement around my unrealistic query, but this subject didn't seem one to snicker about, not even with a tolerable justification. "The *policewoman* will be me. You'll understand soon, Ava. Jumping back a few steps, you'll sprint here. Bring him here and we'll have a security camera on guard. A photo of him will be logged into the camera and it'll beep when he stands underneath, or anywhere in view," she explained, her voice low and toneless.

I was almost able to fully comprehend her plan of action. Almost, but not quite. "What will happen if he kills me?"

Angie winced, gulping. "Think positively," she said. "If the thoughts distract you from reality, you'll fail, and he *will* murder you. But as long as you dart at full speed, you'll succeed."

I nodded. She spoke sensibly. I'd always been fortunate to be able to focus on the positives instead of the negatives.
Times like these shouldn't be any different.
"Ava, if I'm correct, you kept your mum and sister balanced and sane after your dad's... death." She faltered, stuttering. "You're capable of anything you wish. It is essential we arrest Dan. We aren't achieving finding him through an investigation, so you're our alternative."
I smiled to myself. I was an alternative to catching a criminal. It wasn't ideal, an offender on the loose hungry to seize and kill me, but if the police failed in tracking him and I risked my life and succeeded, it would be awesome.
I looked at Angie, grinning. "I'll do it. Perhaps it'll be like early work experience. Who knows, I might desire to become a police officer instead of a therapist," I suggested with a shrug of my shoulders.
Angie's eyes widened in astonishment. "I... Ava, erm... That's great, but I think the therapist dream is more... realistic."
I raised an eyebrow. "Oh, that's how it is?" I muttered, as though hurt.
"Didn't mean that-"
I stuck out my tongue playfully. "Joking. I got what you meant."
Angie laughed. Her focus on my face forced warmth to flow through my body. She believed in my abilities, more than my mum ever had. It made my heart glow.
I glanced awkwardly around as Angie whistled, shoving papers here and there.
She finished by twining her fingers through one another.
"Now, why I ordered Aaron to take Keira out," Angie said. "The hospital rang me."
I tapped my finger on my arm, waiting.
"They noticed some... scars... on her inner elbow, streaming down her arm."
My heart pounded, *thump thump thump* in my ears. I felt my hand tremble as I reached up and tucked my hair behind my ear. "So... scratches from when she's fallen over? That's Keira in a nutshell, always tripping..." I knew just as well as the rest of my pulsing body that Keira never stumbled over. Not anymore.

Angie looked sorrowful. "Scars... self-harm scars, Ava. We're aware she also tried... killing herself."
My heart rate increased, deafening me from the birds cheeping outside in the tall, beautiful trees, from Angie's small, hollow breaths and my own foot tapping on the wooden floor.
"My sister isn't self-harming," I said sternly. "It's absurd you can even-"
"Ava, when the nurses in the hospital inspected Keira's body, they saw the scars. Keira shrunk smaller as Charlotte gently questioned whether the scars were self-harm. Meaning the answer was yes," Angie interrupted firmly.
My palms were uncomfortably sweaty by now, soaking from the panic and shock mixed together.
Thinking about it, the anguish I'd seen in Keira's bright blue eyes was probably down to her self-harming. She didn't settle well after Dad's death, that I knew, but to the extent she purposely inflicted pain upon herself? With a fierce jolt, I realised Keira couldn't have shaved herself with the razor... but instead, had been torturing herself-
"We're going to ease her into therapy," Angie explained. "We understand it might frighten her, what with her being so young."
I placed my head in my hands, descending into the chair. Angie removed her walkie-talkie from her pocket. I guessed it had been weighing her down, hanging unevenly from her dark blue belt.
"Keira will be scared. She's always been a very fragile girl." I clenched my shoulders, slightly wired.
Angie opened her mouth to reassure me when a knock sounded on the oak door.
She stood up. "Come in."
I held my breath.

Chapter 9

Eric Chanell and a broad, lanky man walked into the room. The man had slick, black hair and dull, grey eyes.
Angie shook Eric's hand lightly.
Didn't he say Angie was his wife? I shook off the thought. Perhaps Eric had been wrong, thinking of a different Angie?
Angie stepped back. "Hello, Eric," she greeted. "Who's this?"
Chanell turned to me, scratching his bald head. "I have a little something to tell Ava." He nodded towards me. "This is Ellis Mayo."
I leaped up, holding my hand out to Ellis. He lazily shook it.
I didn't approve of him.
"What do you need to tell me?" I enquired, gritting my teeth.
Chanell cleared his throat. It sounded like something rough had died inside it and he almost choked. "Aside from holding no proof, we suspect your mum is somehow guilty of your dad's murder," he muttered. "And we don't agree that your mum should have responsibility of one child, let alone two. Keira is so young, hardly yet ten."
I crossed my arms, impatient to hear more. "You couldn't be asking me and my sister to live apart?" I wondered. "That is irrational, if you're asking for my opinion."
"Which we didn't," Ellis piped up.
I pulled a face at him.
"Eric devised this solution, and I think it'll be beneficial for you to move away... for a while. Not far. It will be like a trial to see if your mum can supervise Keira at the very least. After your kidnapping-"
"I *wasn't* kidnapped," I growled.
"OK, after *Keira's* kidnapping, your mum proved to show a lack of protection over you both."
Chanell nodded in agreement.
I arched my eyebrow. "So, you're just expecting me to go... where?"
Eric and Ellis shared an uneasy glance and my attitude vanished. I was tense once again.

“A care home, Ava,” Eric Chanell whispered. “The care home in central Shallowton.”
Despite my earlier reaction, their recommendation wasn’t as bad as I’d expected it to be.
“Jennifer Huxley owns the care home and we’ve emailed her your details. Name, age, date of birth,” said Ellis. He looked at Eric, whose eyes were on Angie.
“It’s Ava’s decision,” Angie reminded them. She turned to me, taking my hand in hers. It felt warm and comforting. “She’s the child. You’ll still have the right to see Keira whenever you please. We’re not restricting you from anything. It’s not you we’re scolding, not even close. Not your mother, either. As Eric said, we have absolutely no proof for the meantime.”
I removed one of my hands from Angie’s, dragging it across my mouth as I contemplated the idea. Eric and Ellis gave each other a nervous look every so often. Angie’s patient, friendly gaze remained on me. I sensed my cheeks were burning.
Keira had always been Mum’s favourite child; that was plain to see. I was a daddy’s girl. He’d admired my aspirations, especially those of becoming a therapist. But Mum? She didn’t seem keen on my dreams. Instead, she praised Keira for every ballet competition she won, for every prize she secured in her nursery’s talent shows. They called it a talent show, but in reality it was a bunch of two-year-olds hopping around on a fake stage. Obviously, she loved me too. Up until recently. After she didn’t show up at the hospital when I was recovering or to help when Keira had been kidnapped, I realised there and then that I was suspicious of her, and had been for a while.
I didn’t ever imagine her betraying Keira, however, and leaving her to almost die if I refused to give answers to Dan and Lisa. Leaving my little sister would be difficult. On the one hand, if this trial worked and Mum proved she could take appropriate care of Keira, I’d be allowed to live with them again. Yet if Mum abused Keira - and I prayed to God she wouldn’t dare - even though Mum would be seen as guilty, Keira would be scarred forever.
I forced my aching heart to take the risk.
Both Eric and Ellis seemed reasonably happy with themselves.
“OK,” Eric said. “We’ll speak to your mum.”

I let out a raspy breath, feeling the discomforting sensation of anxiety eating at my guts, rising to my throat, strangling me. “That won’t go amazingly,” I whispered. “My mum will not listen to two middle-aged men.”
Eric and Ellis shared a glance again. They had something planned. “Come with us, Ava,” Ellis instructed.
I followed them out of the room into the bright, airy space of the waiting area. My feet felt uncomfortably heavy in my trainers, sharp pins and needles piercing through my skin.
Angie trudged not far behind, keeping a firm eye on me. I released an uneasy breath. The upcoming minutes could be life or death.
Mum was cradling Keira on her knee. Keira herself looked discombobulated as we strolled over.
She scrambled off Mum as the two men came to a standstill.
“Hi, Sandra,” Eric said politely.
Mum gasped. “It’s you. Your parents almost killed my little girl.”
“Yeah.” He wiped a bead of sweat off his face. “But I saved them. I called the ambulance for Ava and ensured Keira remained composed.”
Mum looked exasperated. “Still.” She hesitated. “You must have mentioned Ava to Dan and Lisa?”
Eric shook his head. “Sandra, I briefly said a young girl turned up at my apartment, accusing me of a murder. In my discussion, I referred to Ava as ‘a teenage female.’ Nothing more. Dan and Lisa must’ve known it was your daughter.”
“As if.” Mum laughed, rolling her eyes. “Whatever.”
Eric stared blankly at the floor. He didn’t in the slightest want to talk to Mum, especially not about a subject that would possibly cause rage and anger.
Ellis took on the role instead. The smug glare in his eyes told us he wasn’t afraid. Eric had described Ellis as being part of the authorities. I’d expected lots of them to bombard our meeting, revealing life-changing news that’d cause Mum to cry, me to sit wide-eyed and Keira to scream.
Taking in Ellis’s appearance, I realised he was all we needed.
“Sandra.” He coughed. “Shallowton’s care home is in desperate need of volunteers to help them look after their little ones. More

than half of their staff have quit recently, leaving the children lost and upset. There aren't enough people to keep an eye on them twenty-four-seven. Until they can find and hire new staff, they're searching for teenagers to take on the role, as part of... work experience." He paused to scratch his head. "I'd like Ava to be a part of it. She's not yet a teenager, but this... work experience... will boost her chances of getting a phenomenal job in the future."
Mum clenched her jaw. "Would she be working long hours?" she questioned, doubtful.
Ellis peered swiftly at Eric and then slowly turned to Mum again. He stammered as he spoke, suddenly self-conscious. "Mrs Hayloft, she'll be a resident there, for the... meantime."
I glanced to my right where Keira stood, astounded. Her eyes were roaming from Mum to Eric to Ellis.
"What do you take me for?" Mum shrieked. "Absolutely not."
"It's an opportunity for your daughter," Eric said.
Mum laughed. "My *daughter* isn't thirteen until next month. It would hardly be appealing to her."
Eric motioned for me to say something.
"It actually is," I said shyly. "I'll be talking with lots of kids from all sorts of backgrounds when I become a therapist. This will be like a... trial."
I sensed Ellis's large eyes on me as I said the word. They focused on me for a short while, direct and steady, until he switched his gaze to Mum.
Mum was scowling. "Give up lying to me and just admit you think I murdered Darren and might abuse my children next. Well, let me make it clear. There's no reason on this earth that'd justify me killing my husband. Therefore, your suspicions will get you nowhere. As for Ava, I'd never hurt my eldest daughter," she snarled. "But to release some pressure off your shoulders, I'll send her to the care home myself."
My mouth fell open. Eric gaped at Mum. Ellis was speechless. The only person to object was Angie.
"Sandra, what are you doing?" she hissed. "Of course we wouldn't assume... *that*. And you can't throw Ava into a lousy care home."

“It’s not lousy,” Eric interrupted. “It’s the best care home in Shallowton.”
Angie ignored him.
Mum laughed again. “Eric, you and that-” she pointed to Ellis - “*thing* mentioned it to start with. I’m just guiding you towards... whatever you and that irrelevant man have planned. However, I am not a stupid woman. I can tell a lie from the truth.”
“Sandra-” Angie started.
Before she could get another word out, Mum stood up and smacked her solidly across the face.
I heard Mum’s hand collide with Angie’s head. I covered Keira’s eyes as the oozing, thick blood dribbled from Angie’s nose. It smelled strongly of metal.
“That’ll teach you,” Mum sneered, “to not switch up on me.”
Angie crawled slowly across the floor, clutching the chair with the strength she could spare and dragging herself up.
Fortunately for her, the waiting area was deserted, apart from a woman wearing earphones behind the front desk.
“You never said I couldn’t stick up for Ava in your stupid script!” Angie muttered, regaining her balance.
Keira, Eric, Ellis and I all stared at Mum. Mum kept her eyes on me, thumping Angie over the head again, knocking her right back down to where she’d just gotten up.
My throat constricted.
“There’s a script?” Eric enquired stubbornly. “Can I read it?”
Mum growled at him.
“Oh, right. Are you certain you’re not an animal, barking at me like that?” Eric mocked.
Keira snickered.
“There is no script,” Mum huffed, tugging Angie to her feet. “Angie has a big imagination, very creative. She also got drunk last night, she doesn’t...” Mum threw her onto the chair. “... know what she’s talking about.”
Angie whimpered like an endangered puppy, instantly crashing to the ground again. She looked immensely vulnerable, the opposite to a supposed policewoman investigating a world-renowned murder case. She grumbled on the floor.

I glanced towards the doorway. An elderly woman wearing a stylish green bucket hat strolled into the waiting room. She took one look at Angie rolling over on the tiles and strutted out again. Eric snorted, trying to suppress a laugh. Ellis thumped him.
"So." Mum sighed. "Do I have permission to return home with Keira?"
The men shared another brief glance with one another.
Ellis turned to Mum, his hands in his pockets. He looked effortlessly swag. "Yes," he answered. "Any wrongdoing, I'll be straight there to take her off you."
"It's one child. You've confiscated one daughter already, I'm sure I can manage."
Ellis dismissed her. Mum breathed out, exhausted, and let out a small yawn.
I hauled my sister to one side, taking hold of her petite hands. They were warm and smooth. "You're all right living with Mum?" I asked.
Keira shrugged, her eyes wet with tears. "Are you OK living in a care home?"
I stared at her blankly.
She smiled. "Until this... *trial*... is over," she said. "I'll see you soon."
I nodded sadly as she walked off.
Mum caught her hand, waving slyly at the men and Angie. She paused in front of me. "Ava! How cute to be spending time around small children." She yawned again. "I gave my consent to this care home, but in reality..." She winked.
I knew then and there that she wasn't sending me to this care home because she fancied chucking me out of the way, and not even because she felt she ought to after figuring out Eric and Ellis's plan. But because a surprise was coming my way. And what does a surprise mean if the person you're surprising is in front of your eyes?
Well, you can work that out.

Jennifer Huxley, the social worker I'd be staying with, had beautiful, brown skin, wispy brunette hair and warm, striking eyes. Currently, she was filling out about a million forms and slips of paperwork.
"Name, age and date of birth?" Jennifer asked, swishing her hair off her face.
"Avery Hayloft, twelve years old and the third of November."
Jennifer gazed at me thoughtfully. "Do you have any siblings?"
"Yes, a sister. Keira. Shouldn't you have gotten this information beforehand?" I rolled my eyes.
Jennifer put the pen down. "Indeed. Ava, the authorities described you vaguely, but we needed the data from your mother. She refused, so our next best option is to ask you."
I kept quiet.
"So, I personally look after four other children," Jennifer continued. "There's Katy, James, Alfie and Lara."
My eyes widened. "Lara who?" I wondered if I'd recognise this girl as the Lara who'd been my best friend in nursery.
Jennifer walked out from behind the desk. "Lildham, why?" She glanced at me over her glasses.
It *was* her. "I-" I started.
"If you know her, I can't group you up together," Jennifer said firmly.
"No, no, I don't know her, I've just heard of her before," I explained quickly.
Jennifer nodded. "Her parents died in a plane crash, so you would have," she said. "Even though you're the same age as Lara, I'm pretty sure you'd have only been young when her mum and dad died."
She sauntered behind the counter again, speaking into a small microphone that stood on the table. "Can you bring Jennifer Huxley's group down to Reception, please?" she asked.
A man marched up to us seconds later, his head held high in the air, a girl in his arms and two boys following behind. The two boys looked six and nine and the girl looked about three.
Jennifer reached out to hold the girl. "This is Ava," she said in a baby voice.
"Ava?"

I turned around. Lara stood gawping at me, her grey eyes staring into mine.
Jennifer frowned. "Do you know Ava?" she asked suspiciously.
Lara looked at me for a minute before replying. "No... no. Just... seen her on the billboards."
"This is Katy." Jennifer jigged the girl up and down in her arms. She giggled with excitement. Jennifer reached over and patted the youngest boy on the head. "This is James." Finally, she pointed to the eldest boy. "This is Alfie."
I waved, feeling awkward. Usually, I was confident and social, always up to talking to strangers. Today, my stomach churned with nerves.
I swallowed them down.
"Ava, I'm afraid there's no extra room with the kids. Your arrival was unexpected and we're already full up." Jennifer coughed. "You'll take the basement."
I scowled. Surely Eric and Ellis could've offered me a spot in another home, one that could fit in another child? But then I remembered that this was all last-minute.
"I'll take the basement with Ava," Lara said beside me.
Jennifer looked alarmed. "No, no. You have to babysit the children, remember?"
Lara pulled a face of distaste. "Alfie can do that," she argued.
"Alfie is far too young," Jennifer insisted.
Lara stomped her foot on the wood floor, as if she were a toddler in the middle of a tantrum. "It's unfair! The first time a girl of my age arrives, I can't even become roommates with her." With that, she spun around and stormed away, her shoes screeching on the clean floor.
I glanced at Katy. Her green eyes scanned my face in awe. She had a load of brown, curly hair touching her chest from all angles. "Are you adopting me?" she whispered.
Bless her. My heart dropped. She must've been four at the most.
"No, silly," Alfie uttered. "Ava isn't adopting us."
I peered at him. His eyes were a similar emerald colour to Katy's. "Are you two siblings?" I queried, eyeing their identical features.

Alfie nodded. "Sadly. Mum drank lots when she was pregnant with Katy, so Katy was very ill when she was born. Our ugly stepdad threatened to pour acid over our heads, and Mum stood by and listened, taking his side." He spoke so openly, as if he'd repeated his story over and over again.
I opened my mouth to apologise, but my brain hadn't yet comprehended this information. "I'm sorry," I squeaked at last.
James was clutching Jennifer's hand, chewing on his lip as he observed our conversation. I smiled at him. Alfie followed my gaze.
"James's mum and dad disowned him when his sister was born. That's after they began abusing him," Alfie blurted.
James glared at him, defiant.
I shifted from foot to foot.
"Lara's parents died in a plane accident," Alfie carried on.
This time, I looked at him. "I heard. Sad, isn't it?"
He shrugged. "She's always happy."
"Sometimes the happiest people hide the darkest secrets," I said quietly.
I didn't know where that had come from. It wasn't like *my* life was bad, not compared to these kids' who clearly hadn't experienced enjoyable childhoods.
No matter if for me this was a trial - for these children, it was life.
I'd change that.
I would do everything in my power.

Chapter 10

The basement looked very posh and pretty. An expensive double bed lay in the middle, a white canopy draped down from the ceiling and a wooden desk was parked in the corner. One wall consisted of a massive walk-in wardrobe. Fairy lights hung from another wall and the windowsill contained about three fake plants.
Jennifer strutted into the room an hour after I'd settled down.
"Hi, Ava. You OK?" She walked right over to the window.
I hesitated. Was I OK? Would I ever be all right? "Yes," I said bluntly. "I'm fine."
"And... do you like the children?" she ploughed on.
"Hmm." I faltered again. "James is lovely."
Jennifer tucked her hair behind her ear and sighed. "For the nine months of her pregnancy, James's mum assumed her baby would be a girl, so when James - a boy - was born, she gave him up. Turns out, she recently birthed a second child, and he was also a boy, but... they kept him."
I gaped at her. Jennifer must have seen the pure shock covering my face, because she elaborated.
"Alfie doesn't understand the story, so he designs his own, which of course further upsets James. I've told him to stop, but he's been brought up in such an awful environment..." She dwindled into silence.
I nodded enthusiastically, looking at her. Black bags lined the skin underneath her bright eyes and her forehead was creased with wrinkles. I sighed. I hadn't realised how difficult it must be to take care of five children from three different households, different backgrounds.
"If you'd like, I'll take them out for a walk tomorrow?" I offered, forcing a smile.
Jennifer's eyes lit up and I instantly praised myself for asking. It clearly removed a huge weight from Jennifer's shoulders. "Oh, Ava," she said with a gasp, "is that OK?"
I nodded before I could change my mind. "Of course. It'll be a practical way to find out more about each other."

"Alfie will be at school all day, but James and Katy are only in for the morning." Jennifer fished in her pocket, digging out a Mars chocolate bar. She handed it to me and, with a wink, strolled out the room.
I ripped open the wrapper and let the soft chocolate sink onto my tongue, chasing my worries away.
I lay on my double bed as I heard a tiny knock on my bedroom door. I sat up as James ambled in.
He sniffed a few times before stopping in front of me. "Can I talk to you?" he asked in a whisper.
I tapped the bed. "Sure." I paused. "What's going on?"
He perched beside me and I drew him towards me, comforting him with a hug.
"I miss my mum. I wish I was what she wanted. I don't know what I did wrong." He began bawling.
My heart plummeted. He sounded so broken, so exhausted. I pulled him closer, securing him with my arm. He leaned into me, burying his head in my chest. His sobs rose louder and louder.
"Hey, hey," I soothed. "It's OK. There are times in which parents don't see their children in the way they should. It's not your fault, you are just a kid. Don't blame yourself."
James peered at me. Snot hung from his nostrils, but I didn't have the heart to point this out. All I had to do was be there for him.
"Ever since Mum sent me here, I've experienced these strange feelings. As if I'm not really happy anymore," James whispered, his voice low.
"Oh, darling." I looked at his face. If what Angie had implied was true, Keira felt exactly the same way.
Suddenly, I realised that the following day would be Keira's doctor's appointment, the one Angie had eased her into to see if she needed to be referred to a mental health clinic.
"You're much better than any girl," I promised.
My comment was an attempt to make him smile, but his cries grew fiercer. "That's not true. Mum kept my brother; it was me she didn't want. I've never even met him." James sighed and rubbed the tear smudges off my jumper.
"It's fine," I assured him. "But... well, she doesn't know what she's missing out on."

James stopped crying. "Really? I'm nothing special," he said.
"You so are. You're a gift, and if your mother refuses to see that, I strongly promise she's not worth it."
James beamed, cuddling up to me again.
I took a deep breath. "Do you wanna go for a walk?" I asked, unsure of whether he'd agree or decline.
To my great relief, he pushed himself off the bed. "Yeah!" He grinned more widely. "Ooh, let's go to Sallow, please!"
"Sallow?" I'd heard of it before.
James nodded eagerly. "Yes! It's a beautiful place and you'll love it! Oh, please?" He stuttered the last two words.
I smiled warmly. "Sure."
I guided James out of my homely room and across the hallway, towards the front door.
No one was behind the reception desk.
"Get your shoes on," I said, pointing to a pair of small trainers.
James bit his lip. "Shouldn't we tell Jennifer we're going out?" he asked.
I shook my head. "She'll be fine with it," I reassured him.
James smiled as he slid on his shoes and grabbed a navy blue coat. I pushed my own trainers on and walked outside. The air was breezy, nipping at my skin. I wrapped my arms around myself as if they were a warm coat.
James looked up at me as we set off down the road. "You are so kind," he said.
I grinned at him.
That didn't last long. When I glanced up, my guts swivelled, squeezing my chest like a fist.
The three billboards surrounding us contained 7x4 photos of a very pretty woman with multi-coloured hair, and one blue eye and one green. The singular word '*Wanted*' was written beside it, and a small passage of Dad's story too. A photo of Keira sat on my lap with Mum and Dad behind us made an appearance in the background. We were all so young and hopeful. I knew instantly that this was a photo of Pandora Anderson. Aside from the fact that the police were sure the method they were using was reliable, I couldn't imagine how Pandora might be feeling if she really was innocent...

I dropped James's hand and leaned against the brick wall. My fingers felt numb and my head was dizzy.
"Ava?" James said nervously. "Ava, your breathing is weird."
I took a deep breath in. Nausea swamped my body, licking at my insides.
"Ava, stop it. This isn't funny. Please," James wailed. He grabbed my hand and squeezed. "Come on, Ava," he gasped. "You can do this. Breathe!"
I did as he said, keeping my mind focused on the tiny boy stood in front of me. I thought of Katy and Alfie and Keira. Of the other children in the Shallowton care home who were so young, so in need of love.
"You're nearly there, Ava. Your breathing is getting good again," James promised.
I hung onto his every word. As I slowly pushed my way back into the present moment, I gradually realised I had just had a panic attack. I hugged James, thanking him with desperation in my voice.
"Do you have anxiety?" he asked.
"How do you know what anxiety is?" I asked, bolting down the path.
James followed, gasping to keep up. "Mum always used to say I was setting her anxiety off. She told me it's severe nervousness and can cause panic attacks. She also told me the symptoms," he explained, panting as he sped to keep in step with me.
I slowed down slightly. "Where's Sallow? How do we get there?"
James grinned and clutched my hand, darting in front of me and dragging me along behind him.

Sallow was huge.
I don't just mean a large town or city; that'd be an understatement.
Sallow had about three shopping centres, a bright, circular park with vast, emerald grassland for miles and yellow-brick houses. You could get lost in the place.
Sallow was definitely an area for children.

James steered me towards the local toy store. It was a massive, colourful building with a sign that read: *'Come Inside, Come Alive.'*
"Kinda soppy," I said, pointing at the 3D white lettering on the shopfront.
"Soppy?" James twisted his head sideways.
"Lacking spirit," I elaborated. Of course, James was only six.
He took me inside. It was full to the brim of dolls and trains and cars. I'd never seen a place so light before. Several members of staff were walking around, some in magical wizard outfits and some wearing supernatural unicorn costumes. We strolled along the aisles, James staring in awe at everything on display. He picked up a detailed, red toy train.
"I've asked for this for my birthday," he said.
"When's your birthday?" I looked past the squealing children, focusing on the billboard outside.
James replaced the train. "Next Wednesday," he replied.
I nodded distractedly. James seized my hand again and dragged me around the rest of the shop.
I had a couple of quid lurking in my pocket, so I bought James a plastic Ferrari.
We carried it to the counter.
After leaving the toy store, James wanted a walk around the mesmerising park. It was full of broad, towering trees with bright pink petals hanging from the stiff branches. Swings, slides and climbing frames were dotted all around. James ran off to play whilst I sat down to watch him. He had gallons of energy, jumping up onto the roundabout and pushing himself round, then scrabbling up the climbing frame, right to the top.
I'd never understand how parents could abandon or abuse innocent children like him.
His little arms and legs flew everywhere as he clattered down the bars and landed on the ground again.
"Look at how pretty she is."
I turned around. Two teenage girls in black hijabs were together, glaring at me. Meeting my gaze, they strolled over.
"Hello, are you Ava?" the oldest one asked anxiously.
I nodded.

The other held out a piece of paper and a pen. “Can I have an autograph?” She pulled it away. “You *are* that girl, aren’t you?”
The other teen stared at her. “Don’t be so rude, of course she is.” She laughed.
The youngest girl stared at me in awe. “You’re my idol. You lost your dad so young and you’re still fighting through every day,” she said.
The older one hit her. “You’re so mushy. Anyway, can we have your autograph?” She nudged the second girl. The younger one stuck her arms out again, clutching the paper.
I took it from her hands and signed.
“You’re so strong,” the older girl added.
She revealed a name sticker that clung to her grey jumper. She must have been a college student of some kind. Her name was Anya.
The second girl's sticker was already revealed. Isobel.
Anya gave me a hug. “I know we’re, like, years older than you, but you’ve inspired us to be who we are no matter what trauma comes our way.” She looked down.
Isobel spoke next. “Our other sister, Lily, died a few years back. She had cancer,” she confided.
“I’m so sorry,” I said, speaking for the first time.
I glanced back around. James was on the slide, playing joyfully with another boy of his age.
Anya shrugged. “That’s all right. We have to go now because we’re meant to be in school, even though we have no lessons for a while.” She giggled. “But I’m sure you inspire many other children, not just us.”
“Keira, too,” Isobel added.
I smiled as they raced off across the park and into the far distance.
Could there be a worse way to gain fans?
Still, if I inspired young people to not let trauma overwhelm their day-to-day life, I’d remain happy.
I made my way over to James and his new friend. James’s eyes lit up when he saw me. It melted my heart, reminding me of how Isobel had gawped at me just a few minutes earlier.
“Jacob, this is Ava,” he told his fair-haired mate.

Jacob glanced at me. "I've seen her in Spain before," he said.
"I've never been to Spain," I confessed awkwardly.
Jacob nodded. "You're on the billboards. You and a blonde girl, as well as a tall man and a very pretty woman."
"We're on Spanish billboards too?" My mouth fell open.
"Avery Hayloft!"
I spun around.
Anya stood there, staring at me with admiration. "You're on all the billboards, from England to Australia. Most of Europe has had you and your family on them for months with different suspects," she admitted.
"You should create a campaign."
I turned my gaze to where Isobel had reappeared. "A campaign?" I questioned.
Isobel glanced at her older sister. Anya coughed, clearing her throat. "Campaigns can be created to bring attention to a cause. For example, it's been nearly six years since the murder of Darren Hayloft, and no one did a thing until recently. You should put a law in place to ensure that next time, this doesn't happen to someone else in your position," Isobel explained.
"Yeah, there's loads about," Anya chimed in.
"But shouldn't I wait until Pandora is found?" I asked quietly.
Isobel shook her head. "No. What's to say Pandora will ever be found, or if it's even her anyway?" She shrugged.
I stared at her, uncertainty dancing through my stomach.
"Yeah," Anya joined in, "the police have only gone off a single email they received to say it even *was* Pandora. That's so unreliable." She rolled her eyes.
Isobel nodded quickly. "And it's because of her name," she said.
"Because of her name?" I repeated.
"Yes. How many people have you heard with the name Pandora in England?" Isobel raised her eyebrows as if she knew she was right.
"But she's English?" I gulped stubbornly.
"So are we." Anya sounded fed up.
I looked at the dirt under my feet, a blush creeping across my cheeks.

"It's OK, Ava," Isobel reassured me. "We're just explaining that we think maybe someone picked on Pandora because her name is unusual. Yes, she *is* English, but I don't think *anyone* would come down from another country just to murder a random man when they could do that elsewhere."
"Plus, not many people would leave the house with a knife," Anya added smartly.
Isobel turned back to me. "Exactly - who even does that?"
"Some sick idiot." Anya rolled her eyes at her sister.
Isobel looked around. "Where's Keira? And who's that boy?" she asked curiously.
"Erm... I've been temporarily admitted into care-"
Anya's eyes widened dramatically. "Is he your brother?" she interrupted, pointing to James.
"Why were you put into care?" Isobel blurted, a similar expression on her face to Anya's.
I shrugged, ashamed and embarrassed to reveal the truth. "Long story short, the authorities became involved with some trouble my mum may have caused. I'm on a trial run at the care home, to see how she copes with just one child."
Eric had visited me early the previous day. He'd been supportive and sympathetic, understanding that it was complicated and upsetting for me. I'd been blunt, blank. The hatred I felt for Mum spiralled through my body and I had to suck up the unbearable pain.
Isobel gave me a hug. "You can come to visit us any time you like," she offered politely. She gazed again at James. "You can bring him with you."
Anya retrieved the paper I'd signed and tore at the second page. She scribbled something down. "Here's our address, the care home will know where it is," she said. "I'm sure Mum would adore you."
I glanced at both Anya and Isobel. Their hijabs were exactly the same colour and they both had the same-shaped mouth. "Are you two twins?" I asked suddenly.
Anya and Isobel glared at each other and burst out laughing.
"No. Lily was my twin," Isobel explained.
"They were never close though," Anya added.

"Oh." I took the paper. "Thank you," I said, holding it up.
Anya hugged me. "No problem."
"We've really got to get to school now. But remember, tell the police not to put too much pressure on Pandora if they haven't heard her story," Isobel said, checking her watch.
I bowed my head, trudging back over to James.
"Ava, you're famous! I'm not sure how, but everyone recognises you from them billboards!" He grinned.
The last thing I wanted was to use my dad's death to make myself known. That was the sort of thing Lara would do. I guessed that if I was younger, my attitude would have matched hers and I'd have enjoyed being the centre of attention.
Now, I was in over my head.

Chapter 11

Later that afternoon, there was a soft knock at the door. I was just crossing from the hall to the living room when Jennifer glanced up from her paperwork.
"Get that for me, Ava," she said.
I walked over, taking the door off the latch. A lean postman stood outside, a square package in his arms. He handed it to me.
"Thank you."
I carefully shut the door behind him and offered the parcel to Jennifer. She shook her head. "It's a computer for you," she muttered distractedly. "I was told you were home-schooled and your mum said I couldn't get you a phone."
I nodded. Mum clearly thought I was still a little girl, too young for a phone.
I carried the package to the basement room and tore off the brown paper that was attached, annoyingly, with tons of sticky Sellotape.
I panted, finally opening the box, sweat dripping from my hands and forehead. I'd been pulling at the Sellotape so violently and my body hadn't adjusted to the unexpected exercise.
I yanked out the bubble wrap that was keeping the computer secure and tugged out the laptop itself. It was a light blue colour, a very good make too. I removed the charger from a smaller box and plugged the laptop in.
An hour later, I'd set it up and adapted my mind to how to use it. Mindfully, I clicked onto the internet icon, tapping into Google.
I sighed.
It wasn't very considerate of my current eagerness.
As it slowly connected to the internet, I typed in 'news.' It immediately revealed new suspected rumours on my dad's murder. I clicked on the link and the page opened into a petition. It had been created to remove Pandora's name off the suspect list, since she was apparently blameless. That was weird; Anya and Isobel had predicted similar earlier. I typed their names into the tab and the page transformed into a range of YouTube videos. They were old and from many years earlier, but were definitely Anya and Isobel.

I commented on their first video. I breathed deeply and waited.
A rap on the door came not even ten minutes later. I ran and glanced out of the window in the living area. Anya and Isobel saw me and smiled. I sped to the door and flung it open.
"You really wanted to see us again, huh?" Anya laughed.
"Basically, yeah." I smiled.
"Hi, Ava," Isobel said.
I led them through to my room and moved my computer off the bed.
"I thought you were bluffing when you said you were a resident here." Anya flopped herself down on the quilt.
"Yeah, how is it?" Isobel enquired.
I shrugged. "I haven't been here too long. The other children are sweet," I said truthfully.
James chose that moment to sprint into the room. He stopped, backing himself out as he clocked Anya and Isobel.
"No. Come in, James." I pointed to the desk chair.
James slowly shuffled over and sat down obediently.
"We've got to do something," I whispered nervously. "I feel so bad for Pandora."
"People just accuse anyone these days," Anya agreed.
Isobel trudged over to the window and turned around. "I suggest we get everyone in Shallowton to write a statement. Otherwise, it's not fair on Pandora," she rationalised, with a very fair point.
"Yeah, as we said, it was because of her name. People see one person with something unusual and judge them for it," Anya added.
"Anya is correct. It's not right that they brought Pandora into the middle of the matter without having evidence to back it up. I mean, her name was noted down in the records at the hospital on the night of the stabbing," Isobel proclaimed.
Anya elbowed her. "It's more stupid than the arguments Isobel and I used to have."
Isobel kicked her. "*Used* to? You start arguing whenever I breathe."
Jennifer poked her head around the door and plodded in with a tray of spaghetti bolognese, crisp bread on the side. The aroma

filled the room, wafting pleasantly into our nostrils. It smelled delicious. "Some for all of you," she announced.
Isobel leaned forwards and dipped a slice of bread into the creamy tomato source. "This is yummy," she said approvingly.
Jennifer looked at me. "I'll need your help bathing the kids," she said. "You can eat later."
Anya glanced up quickly from where she was helping herself to a plate of spaghetti. "Can we help?" she asked.
Jennifer hesitated. "How old are you both?"
"I'm seventeen, Izzy is fourteen," Anya answered, her round eyes eager.
"I'm guessing you don't have any experience in washing small children?" Jennifer asked Isobel.
Isobel's cheeks turned red. She looked awkwardly stiff. "No... but I'm still old enough," she protested.
"Fine, fair enough. You and Anya take James." Jennifer passed him over to Anya. James clung to her neck. "Ava and I will wash Katy - sound good?"
"Yes," Anya, Isobel and I chorused.
We set off, Anya and Isobel walking James to the bathroom. Jennifer and I fetched Katy. She rooted herself to the spot, refusing to budge and sticking her tongue out.
"Don't do this," Jennifer growled. "Move, Katy."
I knew better than to shout at a misbehaving child. I'd had it with Keira; when she was hurting, she'd become stressed. As a result of this, she would yell if we even went near her. When Mum and I stayed away and gave her space, Keira obeyed.
I explained this to Jennifer. Together, we decided to use my technique. Stepping back caused Katy to scream more and more. Her cheeks were sodden, her beautiful eyes raw.
I wiped my forehead, almost certain that this wouldn't work. However, soon after, the tears subsided and Katy curled up on the carpet, sucking her thumb. I beamed at Jennifer, raising my eyebrows. She patted me gratefully on the back.
Jennifer grabbed Katy, tickling her under the armpit. Katy broke out into hysterical laughter, throwing her weight around.

"How'd you know we had to stand back throughout Katy's tantrum?" Jennifer asked curiously as we trudged to the bathroom.
"When Keira was a toddler, I experienced first-hand that disturbing her fits by yelling didn't make anything better. It made her fight back more. If children realise they're not receiving the same attention, they'll slowly stop."
Jennifer sent me an approving glance. "Is there anything you can't do?"
I laughed. "A lot of things," I said truthfully.
"You're remarkable. You put me to shame." Jennifer giggled. "I've known Katy for two years; she's always been dramatic and forever carries an attitude with her. See, this has been brought on by the trauma Katy's mum and stepdad put her and Alfie through."
"I understand. It must be hard for her, she's so young," I sympathised.
Jennifer nodded solemnly. "Yes. She's experienced abuse ever since she was a one-year-old. That kind of thing sticks with you forever."
I bit my lip anxiously. "Bless her... I guess we can't do anything about it. Hopefully, when she's older, she'll move past that stage and become a happy, independent woman," I said.
Jennifer hesitated, looking at the threadbare carpet. "Perhaps... but did Keira shift out of her tears and breakdowns as she grew up, after Darren died?"
I thought this through, shaking my head slowly. "No, she didn't. Well... it's different. His death was unpredictable."
"Does that make your dad's death superior to Katy's abusive household?" Jennifer frowned, tilting her head.
My eyes widened with horror. I hadn't meant it in the way she suggested. "No, no," I protested sternly. "Of course not. I really feel for Katy, my heart goes out to her..."
We both turned our heads to where Katy stood, copying dance moves from the TV programme she was invested in.
Her little face was lit up with happiness, a complete change to moments before where she'd screamed and yelled in the middle of a tantrum, tears streaming from her eyes. She pirouetted in a

semicircle, stopping briefly as she caught my eye. Her smile broadened and I could sense Jennifer staring at me.
"Fancy adopting Katy after all?" she asked.
I chuckled, keeping my gaze on the child in front of me. She reflected the joy I'd possessed, up until Dad's stabbing.
"I'd gladly beg Mum to adopt all three of them... but Mum and I aren't-"
"I know, Ava. I know," Jennifer empathised. She walked over to Katy, picking her up. Katy sat limply at her hip.
Jennifer gestured towards the bathroom with her free hand. I nodded, trailing after her.
I felt a firm, muscular finger tapping my shoulder. I gasped, spinning around.
No one was there.
I shook myself, and stopped. I caught sight of a small girl in the middle of the room. Squinting, I attempted to see her face. She had sun-streaked blonde curls and astonishingly blue eyes. My first thought was: *She's an angel.*
Another figure appeared, his lanky, slight body swaying before my eyes.
I inhaled a deep breath, realising at once who this little girl and middle-aged man must be.
Six-year-old Ava and her dad...
I knew it was my imagination, but it disturbed me nonetheless.

Anya and Isobel were already in the bathroom. It was a spacious room, with baby blue tiled walls and grey furniture. Scribbles stained the walls, while toddlers' and children's toys scattered the floor and inside the bathtub.
"Yuck, who threw Bradley's nappy on the tiles?" Jennifer gagged, picking up an unpleasant nappy. "Ava, Bradley is Mr. Clarke's child. You met Mr. Clarke earlier - he brought the kids down to me, remember?"
I vaguely recalled the man. He wore baggy blue trousers and a black vest top. He was quite muscular and tall. "I remember him," I said. "Does he look after any other children?"
"Indeed. Max, Sarah and Lucia." Jennifer dug her hands under Katy's armpits and lifted her into the bath.

Katy splashed her feet in the water, a big grin cast across her whole face.
"James, baby, are you ready?" Jennifer walked over to the boy curled up in Anya's lap, sucking his thumb intently.
Isobel guided Anya as she slid James off her knee, ensuring he didn't fall too fast. James screeched, his temper rising sharply.
"James! You're six, not Katy's age," Jennifer scolded harshly. "Quit complaining, please."
James wiped his snotty nose fiercely. I guided him into the bath and he smiled at me appreciatively.
"You're so good with kids," Anya said in awe, shifting closer to me.
"So are you."
Anya frowned, as if contemplating her response. "Yes, perhaps because I grew up with younger twin sisters."
"But still. I grew up with one sister..."
"Precisely." Anya laughed. "But even if you didn't have any siblings, it doesn't mean you can't be good around children."
I agreed.
"Ava, I heard a suspect has been located," Jennifer muttered. She was inserting all her focus into scrubbing Katy. James was cleaning himself, getting more soap in the water than on his own body.
"Yes... but I don't believe this Pandora Anderson has anything to do with Dad's death. For starters, the police received the information from a lousy website. Not particularly reliable," I said.
"Aside from that, Pandora's name was logged into the hospital's computer that evening," Isobel added, brushing down her dress.
"How bizarre." Jennifer inhaled a breath. "Ava, you said about a website..."
I snapped my attention in her direction. "Yes. I don't know much about it, but during the meeting I had with Angie, a policeman - Aaron - burst in and told us he'd been alerted about a suspect... through that exact website."
Jennifer considered this, turning to Isobel. "You think Pandora was in hospital that evening?" she asked.

Isobel shook her head impatiently. "No, I *know* she was. I found the list of names, from the same date in December six years ago. I scrolled through it, scanning for her name. She had a stroke, apparently."
Jennifer's eyes indicated pure shock. "Damn... That makes the situation so much worse. Is there a petition of some sort?"
Anya nodded, motioning back towards the basement room. "Ava found one. I think it needs ten thousand signatures..." She spun around to face Isobel. "Can you not send proof of the hospital's records to the police?"
Isobel glanced at the floor, her cheeks reddening. "I didn't take pictures, Anya. I wasn't even allowed to be sneaking through that stuff. It's private, confidential."
Anya threw up her hands. "Who cares? It's compulsory we remove Pandora from that list."
Jennifer looked swiftly towards James and Katy. Neither of them were listening, both messing with yellow rubber ducks. "Go, Ava. Sign the petition," she said, ushering me towards the door.
I froze. "Me? Why?" I panicked.
Jennifer rolled her eyes, sighing. "You're Darren's daughter. Sign in with your name and your Mum's phone number. I'm sure the creator of the petition was Angie as Isobel also alerted her of her findings, plus only significant individuals have possession of your mum's phone number. They'll know it's you signing and will remove her from the 'wanted' list. Yes, others can sign it, but if it's his own child insisting Pandora isn't the suspect, they will *have* to listen."
I backed out of the bathroom, pausing to look at Anya and Isobel expectantly.
They glanced at each other, beaming.
"Can we do this together?" I enquired anxiously.
"Girl..." Anya started.
I stared at the floor, humiliation flooding through my blood.
"Of course we will," Isobel said, finishing her sister's sentence.
I smiled shyly.
They each hooked a hand through one of my arms and we fell into step with one another, marching down the hall - hopeful, optimistic.

Chapter 12

"Log in, Ava." Anya shook my arm.
I cursed myself for having to think twice. What if Pandora was the murderer? I recalled Isobel's comment about Pandora being at the hospital the same evening as Dad's murder. It couldn't be her, I strongly believed that. And as far as I could tell, Pandora hadn't run away or tried to object, which, if she was guilty, she would've done.
I glared at the screen, seeing Isobel's gaze on my face from the corner of my eye.
"Put your details in. They'll see it's you," she commanded.
I clicked 'sign' and it loaded a page for me to put my name and date of birth. I entered the information. The tab came up demanding a reason as to why I was signing the petition. I glanced up at Isobel. She budged me out of the way and started typing, speaking as she did so.
"Found out hospital records were checked; Pandora was a patient after having a stroke on the night of the murder. She is innocent."
I looked at her. She seemed so concentrated, tapping the keyboard one last time before the petition disappeared.
My eyes widened. "Where'd it go?" I asked.
Isobel shook her head. The laptop refreshed itself and she smiled at me. "It's completed!" she exclaimed. "Her name's disappeared. She's free."
I peered ahead. I was happy that Pandora Anderson was now deemed innocent, but it didn't justify everyone jumping to conclusions without hearing the lady's story first.
It was just another reason this world needed to change.
I desired to achieve just that.
"Ava?"
I looked up.
"You're missing him, huh?" Anya asked sadly.
If I was honest, with Anya and with myself, I didn't miss Dad anymore. The aching had long left my body. I'd cried enough tears and mourned so often when all I could see was my broken future without a father figure in the household. Back then,

despite everything, I'd been a bubbly girl, always seeing the light at the end of the tunnel. Now, if I couldn't do anything to help myself, at least I could do something to help someone else.
Jennifer entered the room. Her phone rang, and she answered.
Ten minutes passed. She was still chatting, deep in conversation. It must've been critical.
Twenty minutes...
"Ava, I need to speak to you." Jennifer ended the call, her fingers shaking.
She led me into the living room, twirling her hands together.
"Is there a new culprit already?" I asked hopefully.
Jennifer shook her head. "They've... They've stopped searching."
My mouth dropped open. "Not again?" I couldn't believe it. It was atrocious.
Jennifer nodded. "That's not what I-"
"Why?" I demanded. "Why cancel it again? What about Angie?"
"She's continuing to investigate, but she's been given a fresh case. Her attention will be on that," Jennifer said softly.
I stared at my lap.
I knew for sure that there were worse criminal cases, but they'd given up so many times already. No wonder my dad's murder was a worldwide investigation, when no one was prepared to keep it going.
"No," a firm voice said.
I spun around.
Angie was leaning against the door, a clipboard in hand and a smile on her face.
"Angie?" Jennifer stood up, putting her hands behind her back.
Angie glanced at her clipboard and picked up a pen. "I think I have a choice over what I want to do." She shrugged.
A tense silence filled the room.
The only noise that could be heard was Katy's squeals coming from my basement room.
Angie scribbled some notes and peered at me. "I choose to remain on the case of Darren Hayloft." She smiled.

That evening, Jennifer told me all the details of her phone call.

Apparently, someone had found out that three-year-old Katy had voted Pandora to be the cold-hearted criminal. . The authorities rang and threatened to take away the little girl, until Lara piped up and admitted she did it.
"I crept into the playroom, grabbed Katy and placed my hand over hers on the laptop mouse," she'd explained in a sneaky voice.
Angie had sat listening intently, jotting everything down.
Jennifer had asked Lara why she had done it.
"Both of my parents died, but there was no investigation. The news broadcast the plane crash and that was it," she'd replied.
"That's because the cause of your parents' death was straightforward. With Ava's dad, there was no evidence anyone was ever there," Angie muttered.
I sat on the arm of the chair, twisting my hands and biting my nails.
Once Jennifer had updated the authorities, they'd arrived and said Lara had acted strangely in the past too. She'd been caught vandalising, stealing... and getting blackout drunk in the middle of the night.
Jennifer explained that Lara showed the behaviours of someone with schizophrenia, but the authorities didn't care and said there was no excuse for Lara's attitude, and that if something else happened she would be sectioned in a mental hospital.
Lara had told them she didn't want to be alive anyway.
Jennifer looked exasperated and I wished I could've been more help.
Later on, Angie led me out and into the basement. I sat rocking on my chair.
"Don't do that," Angie told me. "You'll fall and break your neck."
I swung the stool back onto all four legs. "Why are the police dropping the case... again?" I demanded.
"They cancelled the search after they realised they'd blamed Pandora wrongly. The police added her all over the billboards, even though the poor woman was just as intrigued and determined as half the country." Angie sucked in a breath.
I scowled. "I thought you were the detective and the policewoman in this case?"

"I am. But I have a boss. I don't do this by myself, it's too tricky. Bearing in mind that we go up against brutal offenders, it's dangerous for one person to go out alone, especially when the killing goes viral, like this one." Angie sighed, staring into space. "I'm not leaving this case open, Ava, even if the rest of the world gives up. I once promised a seven-year-old girl that I would continue searching. Now you're almost a teenager and I'll stay true to that promise." She winked at me, her ambitious brown eyes wide with loyalty.
I laughed awkwardly. "Thanks."
Angie stopped smiling. "You always had that grin on your face, no matter how much Darren's death affected you. Of course Keira was strong, but you were something else. I lost *my* mum when I was twenty and I'd never been as brave as you. I fell into depression, and I've heard your mum did too," she said quietly, choosing her words wisely.
I bit my nail. "Yes, and now Keira has too."
Angie patted the bed. I perched next to her on the edge.
It wasn't a lie that my mother and sister were both battling mental illnesses. I hated seeing strangers at such a disadvantage, let alone family.
I looked at Angie. She put her arm around my shoulders protectively.
Anya arrived in the doorway, unsmiling. "Jennifer said to tell you Lara's upstairs hurting herself. She doesn't know how to calm her."
I stared wide-eyed at Anya.
"Talk to her, Ava," Angie urged, poking me.
I sped out of the basement, past the living room and up the stairs.
The room Lara was in had been painted green on one side and pink the other. Two sets of bunk beds were propped against opposite walls.
A pair of scissors lay at Lara's side.
As I entered the bedroom, Lara peeked over the edge of the bunk towards me.
"Ava." She sat up. "Did you want to bring one of the children in here? I can go?"

I shook my head, kicking the threadbare carpet.
"I apologise for what I did. I do things without thinking sometimes," she clarified quickly.
"How are you?" I asked, ignoring her apology. I avoided glancing at the pair of scissors.
Lara smiled. "I'm fine."
"Fine?" I bit my lip. "Fine is what my little sister promised me before we found out how upset she really was, before we found out that she had been hurting herself."
Lara reached for the scissors, slowly, and hid them behind her back.
I knew she didn't really wish to keep everything to herself. Instead of begging her to tell me what was wrong, snapping for her to hand me the scissors, I smiled.
"Hey, Lara? Tell me. What's up?" I whispered, giving her a choice.
Lara looked up into my eyes. In that moment, I remembered us back in nursery years before, playing in the dollhouse. My dad had still been alive and so were Lara's parents. Lara always used to come to mine for dinner and vice versa... until Mum had pulled me and Keira out of school, promising we could return after Dad's murderer was found, but of course, the killer hadn't been convicted, and Keira and I never had the motivation to go back.
I recalled one moment in particular, before I'd left school. My dad had just died and Lara showed up early the following morning to comfort me. She'd hugged me and muttered that it would be OK.
I climbed up the bunk and Lara shifted backwards.
I raised my hand, shaking it, gesturing for her to advance towards me. She did so, cautiously. I put my arm round her and she leaned into me. Her body was shaking and I felt her tears soaking my jumper.
After a few minutes, Lara sat up and reached over to where the pair of scissors was placed on her pillow. I gazed up as she handed it to me.
"You have anything else?" I whispered.
Lara sighed hysterically. "No." She paused. "I miss them, Ava."

"I know. Missing them is OK. It shows you're strong," I murmured.
Lara snorted. "Weak people cry." She pushed my shoulder playfully. "That's why you didn't."
I stared at her. "I did-"
"No. Not when I was with you. You didn't shed one tear. You were more focused on making sure Keira and your mum were OK. Of course you cried, you were a child, but not when I was there. It was like you wanted to show me strength and bravery. Your mother told me you cared for and comforted them both... despite your own sadness."
I scratched my head. "You've spoken to my mum?" I raised an eyebrow.
Lara nodded. "It was just for something... not important," she muttered carelessly.
I shrugged. "I still don't think I suppressed my tears because I wanted to show *you* bravery."
"Yes, Ava, you did. And do you know why? Because of that policewoman downstairs," Lara growled, a hint of anger pushing itself into her tone.
"Sorry?"
Lara hit her head with her hand, irritated. "Come on, Ava. Angie acted more like your mum than Sandra. She always loved you and held you when you were sad. Your mother told me herself. She used to go up to your room and see Angie lying there reading you a story. It was like Sandra took care of Keira and Angie took care of you. She appreciated her for that. They were your mum's words," she said.
As if she'd eavesdropped on our conversation, Angie sauntered into the bedroom. "I need Ava for something," she interrupted desperately, lunging for my hand and dragging me down the ladder.
I was still clutching the scissors in my other palm. They were digging into my skin.
"Of course, Angie. Take your favourite girl, once again!" Lara yelled after us.
I gulped, holding my breath.

"Don't worry, Ava. Lara's aggressive when she doesn't get her own way." Angie's heels clomped against the polished floor.
I nodded slowly. Deep down, I knew Lara's irritation carried more meaning than not getting her own way.
I shook the feeling away.

I didn't hand the scissors over to Angie. She'd asked what Lara had been harming herself with and I'd convinced her that it was a sharp pin that we'd thrown away.
I had a peaceful sleep. Anya and Isobel slept over, one on each side of me, curled up in sleeping bags.
I woke up at 10am, treading carefully off the bed. I accidentally stepped on Anya, gritting my teeth as she jumped half a mile.
"Ava." She yawned. "Good morning."
"Morning." I smiled.
Anya fought her way out of her sleeping bag and glanced at me. "Happy Halloween." She grinned.
We both looked over at Isobel, who lay with her eyelids tightly pressed together. Her nose was scrunched up, as if she were a rabbit.
Anya pointed to her. "She takes ages to wake up. We've got college today, so I'm going to have to shake her awake." She laughed.
I watched as Anya hopped over my bed, bending down and tickling Isobel under the armpit. Isobel growled at her, opening an eye.
"Get up, sleepyhead. We have school." Anya rolled her eyes. "I suppose Ava does too, but online."
Isobel sat up. "Ava's here?" she asked sleepily.
Anya glared at me and raised her eyebrows. "Obviously," she said. "We stayed in her bedroom."
"This week is my half term," I explained.
Anya nodded quickly. "Last week was ours," she said.
Isobel leaped up, pirouetting into my wardrobe.
I giggled half-heartedly, peering at Anya. Her face was warm and lively.
"Your sister is nuts!" I said, still giggling.

Once dressed, Isobel stood staring out of my window, whistling. I bobbed up and tapped her on the shoulder.
She spun around, her hijab flapping as she did so. "Yes?"
I sat down on the bed. "Wasn't me."
Isobel laughed, rolling her eyes. "Oh, shush."
Jennifer poked her head around the door. "Would you like me to drop you and Anya off at college?" she asked Isobel.
Anya strode out of the wardrobe. "Is that really OK?"
Jennifer nodded. "Just come down when you're ready to get some breakfast." She smiled.
Anya stared at me. "You all right?"
"Yes."
Anya shook her head and took my hand, pulling me up. She spun me around in a pirouette. I laughed as I stumbled over her feet.
"Won't get too lonely without us here, will you?" Anya grinned.
I tripped over her leg as she spun me again and fell with a crash into Isobel. Isobel screeched, ear-piercingly.
"Shhh!" Anya and I hushed her at the same time.
"I'm going trick or treating with my sister later," I said. With a lurch of my stomach, I realised Keira was going to the doctor's that day to see whether she needed to be referred to a mental health clinic.
Isobel leaped off the floor. "Can we come?" She gestured to herself and Anya.
I felt my eyes brighten. "Of course."
I was sure Keira would love my new friends. They were crazy and lively, all about positive energy.
Anya and Isobel lunged themselves at me, full pelt.
I hugged them back, softly.
Perhaps if my dad hadn't died, these girls wouldn't know of my existence.
Nevertheless, I felt a rush of pride to have such lovely friends.
I'd forever cherish our bond.

Chapter 13

The day dragged by slowly.
Eric Chanell appeared at my bedroom door at around lunchtime. He smiled at me. "Hello, Ava."
"Hi, Eric," I replied. My heart raced as I spoke.
Eric cleared his throat. "You saw your mum, didn't you?"
Earlier on, Mum had visited and begged for my forgiveness, saying that she missed me and was sorry for abandoning me in the hospital and running off like a coward.
I bowed my head. It wasn't my fault.
"I understand it was not your wrongdoing. You were clueless," Eric reassured me. Honestly, I was more concerned that he'd read my thoughts so accurately.
"Thanks. I appreciate that," I said.
Eric patted my knee. He turned to leave.
"Wait!" I called hurriedly.
Eric halted, his back to me. "Yes?" he enquired promptly.
"You said my description of Angie reminded you of your wife... the one that went missing. In the A&E area, you didn't make any comments. You didn't claim she was your wife, nor did she mention anything about you..."
Eric sniffed. "Sorry, I've got a cold," he lied apologetically. "No, my wife had lighter skin. She... She was shorter too."
I wrapped my arms around myself, shrinking backwards onto the bed. I felt awful.
"Look, Ava. Aside from that, we loved each other. She wouldn't have ever left me without an explanation."
I couldn't find the words to comfort him. Instead, I crawled off the bed, silently easing my feet onto the bare floor.
"I'm sorry. I'll help you find your wife," I promised, touching his shoulder gently.
Eric glanced at me. His eyes were shining, red from crying. I looked away, embarrassed.
"I... Really?"
I nodded. "Of course. It'll be something little to make up for blaming you. I feel bad about that..."

Eric rubbed his eyes. "Yes... that's fine. But please, search for your dad's murderer first. That's your priority."
I bit my lip nervously. If I were to do as he said, Eric might be waiting a while. The chances of me finding the criminal in the near future were low.
Eric left, closing the door lightly behind him. I lay back down on the bed, spreading my arms out over the patterned quilt. I imagined wings growing from underneath me. I always got told I looked like Dad. I wondered if I looked like him now, pretending to be an angel on the bed. That's what Dad was: an angel.

At about 14:30pm, Jennifer poked her head around the door, James and Katy at her heel.
"I've just bought some birthday presents and need to wrap them up," Jennifer explained. "Could you take these two out for a while?"
I nodded. "Sure. 'Course."
She thrust the kids my way and flew out of the room.
"Sallow?" I looked at James.
He nodded eagerly and darted off.
I took Katy's hand and led her into the hall. She slid her shoes on and jumped up, bumping into James who was bending down to tie his trainers up.
"Stinky!" Katy wailed.
I glanced at her. "Stinky?"
"She has a habit of saying it. It's like swearing for her," James said, dragging on his coat.
I raised my eyebrows curiously. "Oh."
I closed the front door carefully behind me. The weather was mild, a light patter of rain falling. James took hold of Katy's hand and together they walked ahead.
"Hey, Ava."
I turned around, my hair sticking against my face. Angie was stood behind me, clearly having the same issue.
She walked up to me. "Here." She handed me a wristband. "If you're ever in danger, or someone else with you is, press this button here." She pointed to a little switch on the band. "It will send an alert to me in my office and will start beeping, loudly.

This means that someone will hear it, even if they're miles away," Angie explained.
I held out my wrist and Angie clasped the band round my arm.
"I've got to go, but have fun with Keira tonight. Remember, chances are, Dan won't be lurking around this area. The wristband is because it gets dark early and you're two small girls." Angie smiled at me.
"Anya and Isobel are coming with me," I said stubbornly.
Angie shook her head. "You know what someone did to your dad, Ava."
I bit my lip.
As Angie wandered away, I peered at James and Katy. They were playing some hand game, giggling as they tickled each other.
"James! Katy!" I called, running up to them.
They abruptly stopped.
"Yes?" James asked.
I smiled, an idea forming in my head. "Race you guys to Sallow," I said.
Katy and James sped off at full speed, squealing with excitement.
I followed behind, taking it slowly on purpose.
Flying past the hairdressers, I collided with a middle-aged man.
"Watch it, child." He looked at me.
I glared back.
He continued staring. I waved my hand in front of his face.
"You're that famous girl?" he asked.
"I'm not famous," I objected.
The man continued gaping at me. I shifted awkwardly. "You should still be careful," he muttered eventually.
"Apologies. Have a nice afternoon." I ambled by him, resuming my pace.
Katy and James were staring at the billboard, their necks craned and mouths in an 'o' shape. I looked up too. The billboard included a photo of a young boy of about Keira's age. He had limp brown hair and fiery green eyes.
Beside it, there was a description:
Boy, Harry Broad, has gone missing. He was last seen outside of the toy store in central Shallowton. His mum and dad are desperately

worried. If you carry any information, please ring the number below.
This was the case that had overtaken my dad's murder. The case the police had picked over ours, the one distracting Angie.
I didn't blame them; this little boy was cute and innocent, while my dad was older and was killed long before.
"Where did he go missing? How?" James asked, his cheeks flushed pink.
I shrugged. "That's what they're trying to find out," I said.
James shrugged too. He took my hand and Katy began jumping at my feet. She reached over to the wristband positioned on my arm.
I yanked it away. "Katy, no. It's in case I'm in trouble."
James thumped my shoulder lightly. "There's a girl coming up to you," he said in a small voice.
My head shot up. A child was strolling towards me. Her blonde curls reached her chest and her rosy cheeks shone in the sunlight. As she slowed down in front of me, I dropped James's hand and locked it with Katy's.
I fell triumphantly to my knees as Keira pushed herself gently into my arms.
We stayed like that for a good minute.
"The doctor's appointment?" I glanced at her hopefully.
She stepped back and stared at me. "I've been referred. It's depression," she whispered, covering her mouth with her hand.
I tapped it carefully away. "That's OK. You'll get the help now," I promised. "You're my little fighter!"
Keira turned her head. "The billboards have already been changed," she said. "I'm glad Angie's remaining loyal to us."
I looked at my sister. Her blue eyes gleamed. Her hands felt powerful on my shoulders. I gave her another hug. "How did you know?" I asked curiously.
Keira pushed her knuckles together, her mouth setting in a thin line. "Angie came to the house yesterday. I was upset because I missed you, so she said she had something that would make me happier." She glanced behind me and spotted James and Katy, shrinking shyly against me.

If I was honest, I'd totally forgotten James and Katy were still there, but was proud that they hadn't run off. "Keira, this is James, and this is Katy." I pointed to the children in turn. "Katy, James, this is my sister, Keira." I wiped my hand across my forehead.

Katy ran over and flung herself at Keira.

I stared protectively at her, but Katy was smiling gently.

I didn't have to worry.

Grinning, I took hold of James's hand.

"Hi, Keira," James said politely.

Keira hugged Katy back, giggling.

"Hi," she muttered nervously.

Together, the three kids and I walked to Sallow. We marched into a small toy store, different to the one I'd visited the previous day with James.

Keira and Katy begged for matching baby dolls, so I bought them one each. Keira's was chalky-coloured, with wispy hair and sparkly blue eyes. Katy's had rough, dark brown curls and wore a navy pair of denim dungarees.

Afterwards, we made our way into a huge, brightly-lit cafe. It was overcrowded with parents, grandparents and small children. The walls were painted a soft lilac and the chairs were draped in deep purple sheets. Katy begged to find a seat. I told her not to go off on her own and she turned her knuckles into a fist and slammed it angrily on the counter.

The man behind it looked startled. "What can I get for you?" he whispered.

I stared at the purple menu behind his head. "Three blackcurrant fruit shoots and a Cherry Coke, please," I decided.

I turned around. The two girls were laughing with one another. Katy's mood had changed drastically. James was trying to join in.

"Names?" the man asked.

I glanced at him curiously. He had a pen in his hand. Three cups stood in front of him.

"The three juices are for James, Katy and Keira," I said, "and the Coke is Ava."

The man stopped writing, his hand in mid-air. "What's Ava short for?"

"Avery," I replied, arching an eyebrow.
The man yanked out his phone and scrolled for a minute. He turned it to face me. The photo of Keira, Mum, Dad and me was on the screen. It was from the billboard from the previous day, with Pandora as the suspect.
The man coughed, a piece of phlegm ringing in his throat. "This looks like you."
I nodded. "That's because it is," I said.
The man's mouth dropped open. "I have a package for you," he said, turning away.
"A package?"
He disappeared through the flappy doors at the back of the counter. His trousers were halfway down his legs. I spun to see if the little ones were looking, but they were entertaining themselves.
I turned on my elbow to glance at the man marching slowly out through the storage room. He had a soft parcel in his left hand. He plonked it down on the desk with a thud.
I peered cautiously at the label on the front, as if it might explode in my face at any moment. The tag read: *'Ava.'*
I opened it. Inside were two Halloween costumes. I unfolded them. One was larger, a close-fitting white dress with silky angel wings and a halo. The other was smaller, a little crimson devil costume. A small, rectangular letter sat on top. I tore it open and read it.
Ava,
Along with the cash, I decided to send you these. They are Halloween costumes for you and Keira. I'm not able to identify myself to you at this particular moment, but soon the whole truth will unfold.
You and your sister are both remarkable.

Chapter 14

I stared at the last word, tears blurring my vision. I glanced at the costumes, tilting my head, astonished. They were probably a few sizes off. Whoever had sent them didn't know us. I vaguely contemplated whether or not I should tell Keira that these outfits were bought by a stranger. I decided against it; Keira would never touch them if I did.

I peered at her. She was still smiling with Katy and James, clutching her side firmly.

"Ava!" she called, meeting my gaze. "We're thirsty!"

I gathered the drinks between my palms and ordered the man to keep the package behind the counter. He nodded vaguely.

James spotted a spacious table near the wide window. We sat down, James and Katy on one side, Keira and me on the other. I placed the drinks down. Katy grabbed Keira's cup.

"This one is yours." I flung it towards her. She caught it with one hand.

Keira frowned at me. "You took ages buying these drinks."

"I know. But I have a surprise for you," I said.

Keira studied me. "Is it a cure for my depression?" she asked hopefully.

My heart dropped and I wished I hadn't said anything. I shook my head. "Keira, I can't cure you." I felt useless.

Keira shrugged. "Just joking." Her voice wavered and she altered the subject. "Pandora's innocent then?"

"Yep. There was a petition to sign," I said simply.

Keira took a sip of her juice. She licked her lips. "Did you sign it?"

"Yes."

"Mum signed it too. She put my name on with hers," Keira gabbled.

I glanced at James and Katy. They were quarrelling, Katy trying to bite James. With a lunge, James knocked her off the bench. She fell with a loud clatter into a heap on the floor.

Bouncing up, she bumped into a gangling, brown-eyed woman. The woman stared at her with a harsh, vigorous glare.

Katy recoiled, hiding her face.

The woman narrowed her eyes, shifting them in my direction. "Watch your kid." She swayed away, hands on hips.
My stomach churned uneasily.
After we'd finished our drinks I ambled up to the man, collecting the gifts from behind the counter. I put them into a little plastic bag and departed from the cafe.
James, Katy and Keira were waiting patiently, standing against a brick wall. They turned their heads as they clocked my footsteps moving closer.
"A man came up to your sister," James said instantly.
I stopped in my tracks. "Oh? What did he say?"
"That it's *your* family who caused all this mayhem. If Darren didn't die, apparently more important news would be broadcast instead of this lark," James whispered, swinging his arms around in circles.
"Yeah, well..." I faltered, unsure of how to word my upcoming sentence. "His dream came true. Keira and I won't ever find our dad's murderer, therefore we cannot ever receive justice. Just as you, Katy and Alfie are not able to break apart the facts and understand why *your* parents neglected or abused you," I croaked. As soon as I'd said the words, I wished I could snatch them back.
Too harsh, Avery.
James gasped at me. His eyes were swollen and red-raw. I gulped, chewing my lip, embarrassment choking me inwardly.
Keira took my hand. Her touch warmed me, abolishing my poisonous turmoil and transforming it into numbness. "We *will* find the culprit. And I know you can help others, just as you've been there for me. Ava, you're the world's best big sister. You've always been there to cheer me up." She squeezed my hand reassuringly.
"Keira's correct. I met you yesterday and you've had such an incredible impact on my life. And Katy's." James smiled.
I spluttered, immensely grateful. I checked my watch. It was nearly 16:00pm. "We'll have to get back soon if you want to get into your trick or treating costumes." I rubbed my hands together determinedly.

James nodded seriously. "Are Anya and Isobel back at the care home?" A grin spread across his face.
"I suppose they will be," I said, nodding slightly. "I'm glad you get along with them."
"They're the only girls that like me for who I am. Apart from you, Ava. You're my favourite," James whispered, not so quietly.
"Charming," Keira muttered.
I begged to differ that my sister hadn't actually fallen in love with James. Maybe it would've been practical if they were both eighteen, but the fact that Keira would be sixteen when James was thirteen didn't sit right with me.
I didn't have to fear it; what James told me next shocked us all.
"I have a girlfriend," he said proudly, beaming.
My eyes widened. "Do you?"
I tried to suppress my excitement. If James and his girlfriend stuck together, I needn't worry of Keira confessing her crush to him.
James nodded. "I asked her out this morning at school."
He skipped along ahead of us.
I picked up Katy. She was slowly drifting to sleep, her eyes flickering and her arms draped limply around my neck.
I stroked her hair, looking around at the others. Keira was scraping her feet along the pavement, her shoes quickly becoming dusty and grey. Katy clung to me, moaning slightly as she dropped off to sleep. James didn't seem to be tired or worn out, but he tripped and fell with a clatter.
I decided it was best to catch a bus home.
"James, are you all right?" I called.
James hopped up, brushing himself down. "Yes. Let's go now!"
I turned to Keira. "Here." I passed Katy over. "Take Katy and follow James to the end of the street. Wait there for me, I need to get some money."
Keira nodded, holding out her arms. Katy didn't stir, but held Keira's hand in hers.
Keira giggled, beginning to walk away.
"Keira!" I yelled. "Don't go any further, OK?"
She nodded again, running off.

I was glad she'd shaken Dan and Lisa's kidnapping off. For the most part, anyway. She seemed confident strolling without me, but whether it was because she had responsibility over Katy and James more than her own anxiety, I didn't know.
Rummaging in my bag for money, I growled. The handbag I'd brought with me had so many pockets, I didn't know which one I kept my wallet in.
"Come on, Ava!" I muttered, glancing towards the kids.
They were laughing, aside from Katy who was asleep.
I dug my hand into the last pocket and grabbed my purse.
"Got it- arghhh!"
My scream became muffled as a cloth was stuck into my mouth. A scrawny hand concealed my eyes with a blindfold, lifting me up by the waist and dragging me sideways.
I kicked and shrieked, but the sound wasn't audible to my own ears, let alone someone else's.
An eternity later, I was thrown to the ground. A firm knee pressed at my throat whilst a hand tackled my wrist. They were unclasping the wristband Angie had given me, the one I'd use if I or the children were in danger.
"Stop!" I gasped. With the cloth shoved in my mouth and this person's knee digging into my throat, I could barely breathe.
At last, my throat was free and the blindfold was yanked from my eyes.
I lay stiffly, adjusting to the light and thinking through what could've happened. I glanced around.
I could see no one for miles.
My trembling hands pushed me up off the hard path. I was behind an abandoned industrial building, rusty and old.
I stared intently at my wrist, twisting it over.
The wristband was gone.
I released a low groan, thumping my head. I had no idea where I was, and without the wristband, I didn't have any way to call for help.
This part of Shallowton must've been neglected, deserted. All I could smell was a nearby fire burning. It wafted into my nostrils, strong and fresh.

My watch had also been stolen, along with my handbag and the money.
One thought coursed through my mind: *the children.*
I'd ordered them to wait at the end of the street, saying that I wouldn't be long. My stomach lurched as a possibility roamed along my bones. The same person who'd just attacked me could be hurting the three little children now.
I clasped my hands together nervously. I couldn't gather my bearings. I felt hopeless. I didn't know where I was or what to do.
Sinking down onto the pavement once again, I cried. My sleeve became soaked with sodden tear stains.
"Ava? Are you all right?"
I snapped my head around. A woman with multi-coloured hair stood over me, smiling kindly.
I wiped my eyes and leaped up. "Who are you?" I whispered.
Her eyes were two different colours. One was an emerald green and the other a sky blue.
"Pandora Anderson?"
She smiled. "Thank you for proving me innocent. If you hadn't signed the petition, I might be in for questioning right now."
I nodded. "I... How did you find me?"
Her face shifted and the smile dropped. "I saw a man exit from this industrial area. No one comes through here, so I became suspicious."
My eyes widened. "A man? What did he look like?"
"His face was concealed." She shrugged. "I didn't pay attention to his build... He did look frightening, though."
I glanced around again. Birds were chirping sweetly, filling the silence with a gorgeous melody.
"I was with my sister and two children from the care home. I told them to wait for me at the end of the street... but now I don't have a clue where I am and they could've been taken..." I began sobbing.
Pandora patted my back. "A car drew up a while ago. Three kids got into the backseat. The woman inside looked kind and friendly, brunette hair in box braids and striking green eyes."
Jennifer.

"Oh gosh, can you show me the way out of here? I need to get home, I'm taking the children trick or treating tonight." I held onto her arm.
She softly stroked the ends of my hair. "Of course. You helped me, it's only fair I help you. This way."

Chapter 15

"Beautiful girl."
I glanced sideways. Isobel was zipping up Keira's velvet devil dress. Keira's outfit as a whole consisted of a little crimson headband with a horn on each side and dainty red high heels. Pandora had driven me home about half an hour earlier. She'd thanked me approximately ten times and hugged me tightly. I still didn't carry any evidence of who might've attacked me, but I grew sure it was Dan.
Anya was curling my hair. It was already wavy but needed redoing. I had my angel costume on, the dress tight around my figure, hugging my waist perfectly.
Isobel planned to dress as a devil, just like Keira, and Anya an angel like myself.
Anya parted my dark hair equally over each of my shoulders. "Man, is it in your genes to be so gorgeous?" She sighed. "Your whole family's beautiful."
I grinned to myself as Anya arranged the halo on my head, mindful not to tangle my hair.
When she'd finished twisting a piece of hair around and over the headband, I jumped up and sped to the mirror.
"No, you need these first," Anya said.
She was holding a pair of white high heels. I took them off her whilst staring her in the eye, until she broke into an anxious giggle.
I might have been twelve whilst Anya was seventeen, but we had the same size feet. I slid the shoes on and wriggled my toes until they were properly over my feet. Anya then covered my eyes with her hands and led me to the mirror.
"Anya, she needs the wings," Isobel gasped, running over.
I could hear Keira's heels as she scurried over too.
Anya eased to the right of me, her hands still over my eyes, and Isobel slipped the wings into place on my back.
She moved backwards. "Wow."
Anya stepped away from me. I peered into the mirror.
"You look just like your dad, Ava," Isobel said, gasping as her hands flew to her chest.

Tears welled in my eyes, hot and salty. I *did* look like him, especially my sharp jawline.
Anya smiled. "Since he's an angel now too," she said gently.
Keira came up beside me. Her hair was temporarily sprayed scarlet, the colour complementing her bright blue eyes. She was flawless.
But right then, so was I.
I checked the clock.
Anya's eyes widened as she followed my gaze. "We've spent an hour and a half getting Keira ready." She smacked her sister and they hurried to put their outfits on.
Keira grabbed my hand and sat on the carpet in front of me. "You had a panic attack, didn't you?" she whispered. "In that shopping centre, that's why you didn't meet us."
Pandora had rung Jennifer to inform her that I was safe and sound. Jennifer had begun sobbing, demanding to know why I'd left the children on their own in a public place. I hadn't had the heart to tell her about Dan and his sudden attack.
As far as the kids knew, I'd felt overpowered with stress and, as a result of that, had suffered a massive panic attack.
"I didn't have a panic attack because of me. I'm twelve and carried responsibility over you, Katy and James. It was a lot of pressure on my shoulders. I broke down and didn't want you kids to see me so vulnerable."
Keira stared at my hands. "Usually you can deal with that," she murmured.
I rolled my eyes. "I'm not Superman, though. I can't look after everyone." I gritted my teeth.
Anya and Isobel came gliding out of the bathroom. Anya was in an identical white, silky dress, though it was a lot looser than mine. Her headband was covered in delicate silver diamonds and she wore white, flat party shoes. A flick of eyeliner skimmed the corners of her eyes.
Isobel was wearing a cherry-coloured top and matching shiny leggings. In her hand was a long, scarlet stick. Red converse trainers were fitted over her feet.
"Let's go. Get your basket, Izzy." Anya snapped her fingers towards a round orange bucket.

I lifted one I'd brought for Keira with a small photo of a devil painted on the front, matching her red dress.
The other kids were already at the door in their costumes. Katy was dressed as an elegant princess, James a plump pumpkin, Alfie a handsome prince and Lara a freaky skeleton.
Jennifer's voice shook and her hands wobbled as she ran through her worries and concerns. "Please keep everyone safe," she begged, her bottom lip trembling.
Anya nodded. "We will. No problem."
Jennifer assumed Angie's wristband was firmly clipped to my wrist. I couldn't tell her that the man who was out to murder me had snuck up and stolen it, while snatching my bag and watch too. No one else knew about the bracelet so I chucked a white cardigan over my dress until we stepped outside.
Nerves licked up my skin, crawling sneakily through my bones and swallowing me up. Anya and Isobel were by my side, but I was still apprehensive. Two teenagers and five children wasn't a fantastic mix. Before Dad died, I hadn't thought twice about the dangers we might encounter. You'd have to be pretty unlucky to be kidnapped or killed or assaulted.
I guess at an older age, you come to terms with the fact that you can't trust anyone other than yourself.
I'd trusted the outside world and they took advantage of it.
Never again.

My mind drifted carelessly off into a different world. I became trapped in a daydream - one so real I thought I might reach up and pinch it.
Dad's cheesy smile as he exclaimed about how he saved money because he wore his Halloween mask all year round. Dad gripping tightly onto mine and Keira's hands, securing us from any hazards whilst trick or treating. Little did he know, he'd be the first one to meet danger. He'd guaranteed he would remove all the chocolate from Keira's basket since she was allergic.
Reminiscing on the past hurt my heart but reminded me to love vigorously, to grasp every minute and celebrate each day as if it was the last.
You never know what could happen.

My dad had woken up optimistic and radiant. He'd tackled his day... but wasn't as fortunate to return home again.
My heart ached. I used to boast about having the best Dad in the world years before, at nursery. I dragged him into my classroom and acted as if I were a little angel, and not the noisiest girl in class. Everyone loved Dad; they squealed when he swung them around and their faces lit up as he swaggered into the room.
Prior to his stabbing, I'd always had faith that my parents wouldn't die until I'd grown old and cranky. My mum was thirty and my dad twenty-nine, very young compared to some. I didn't ever panic I'd lose either one, because I should've had years and years before I'd be forced to even roll the possibility through my head.
Trauma hits hardest when you never expected it to happen. Afterwards, the fat fist slaps you, pushing the realisation into your mind; no more hugs, no more bedtime kisses... no more memories.
Eventually, we pulled up outside the first house in Shallowton. The household inside must have been in the Christmas spirit early because they already had their decorations up.
Isobel screwed up her nose. "I love Christmas, but it's only just November tomorrow. Halloween's not even over yet," she huffed in disgust.
"Shove off, Iz." Anya laughed. "You used to scream until we put the decorations up, even if it was the middle of June."
Isobel folded her arms. "Yeah, all right," she muttered.
The children followed us up to the house. I knocked lightly. Seconds passed and the door opened. A jolly woman stood on the doorstep.
"Trick or treat!" James and Katy squealed.
The woman held out a bowl of candy. Keira, James, Katy and Alfie all took a packet and we strolled up to the next house.
As we walked up the steps, Katy slipped over, crashing to the ground.
"Katy, are you all right?" Lara gasped.
Katy started weeping. Her face scrunched up and her bottom lip trembled.

Anya rubbed her back and held onto her hand protectively.
Keira, James and Alfie hustled in front with Anya and Isobel guarding them on either side.
Lara glanced at me. "You OK, Ava?" She smiled. "You're daydreaming."
She took something out of her pocket. A packet of cigarettes.
I gasped loudly.
"I can see you're in pain." Lara shrugged, trailing her hand through her hair, messing it up. "These really help."
I stood stock-still, staring at her in outrage. Dad had advised me to not smoke. He'd had the odd puff at fourteen, but gave it up immediately after I was born.
He'd never picked a cigarette up again.
I'd been informed that they ruined your lungs, weakened your immune system – however, Lara smoked, and she was clearly healthy.
I reluctantly agreed. "Let's do it."
Anya, Isobel, Keira and the others were already at the next house. Lara and I sat at the foot of a broad tree and Lara lit a cigarette to demonstrate.
"See, it's quite safe," she promised, nearly dropping it as she held it out to me.
I took it cautiously, blowing gently once I'd inhaled.
Lara was right. It made me calmer and happier. I knew in an instant that if Keira saw me doing this, she'd tell Mum and I'd never be able to see her again. I also knew that this was dangerous for an adult and I was only young. But in the moment, it didn't seem as bad as everyone made it out to be.
Suddenly, I realised just how much I was ruining my body. I dropped it to the ground and stubbed it out.
Lara turned to me. "Ava?" she whispered.
I shook my head. "My dad wouldn't want me doing this at all," I insisted.
I don't know why I'd done it or what for. It was never going to numb the pain in my stomach, just decrease my lifespan.
"Maybe if you have another-"
"No," I said firmly.

Lara sighed and flicked the stub of her cigarette. She let it fall to the ground beside mine and stood up.
I marched ahead of her, back towards Anya, Isobel and the kids who were down a few more doors.
Anya smiled as I got nearer. I bet she'd never smoked and she was four and a half years older than me.
I stopped and removed my halo. It was itchy and irritating me, like everything seemed to be at that moment. I chucked it onto the grass.
The man who stood at the door looked suspicious. He went to stick his finger up to tell me to run along from his property, but Isobel beat him to it by explaining who I was.
"She's with us. Avery Hayloft," she said.
The man swallowed his saliva. It made me cringe. "You're that famous one?" he queried sternly.
I gritted my teeth awkwardly. I *wasn't* famous. Famous was when someone changed the world somehow, became significant. People only knew me because of Dad's death.
The man chucked chocolate bars in the kids' buckets and shut the door.
In a panic, I remembered my sister was allergic to chocolate. I snatched her bucket and checked through it. There was just that one bar. I yanked it out.
"May I have it?" James asked eagerly.
I ignored him, flinging the bar onto the grass, and turned to Keira. "Have you eaten any chocolate?"
Keira shrugged. "Don't think so."
Isobel picked her up. "She hasn't."
The rest of the night was full of excitement and amusement. Some drunk man began chasing us up the driveway, pretending to be a spooky ghost.
Once we arrived home, James squatted on the marble floor and fell asleep. Me and the girls trudged into my basement room and plonked ourselves on the bed.
"Wow, that was fun," Anya breathed, placing herself on the silk quilt.
"Yeah, did you have a good time, Keira?" Isobel asked.
I pulled Keira onto my knee and sat back.

Keira held up a packet of sweets she'd been eating for at least half an hour. She stuck her thumb up. "Good," she said, showing half the food in her mouth.
I quickly covered it up.
Lara rolled her eyes. "Leave her, Ava. She's just a kid."
I moved my hand away, humiliation burning my cheeks as if they were on fire.
"Me and Iz are at college all day tomorrow, and on Saturday our Mum and Dad are taking us out. We'll be round on your birthday though," Anya promised.
"If we come out alive." Isobel laughed. "Dad does the worst farts in the car."
Anya stared at her, alarmed. "No, he does not." She smacked Isobel.
Isobel glared at her. "He does."
Keira shuffled on my lap, sending a cramp through my leg.
"Is Keira staying here tonight?" Anya asked, frowning.
I nodded. "Yes, and then she's going home tomorrow morning."
"Well, we'll stay tonight and then get going when Keira does," Anya decided.
By 22:30pm, Anya and Isobel had set their sleeping bags up. Keira and I were topping and tailing on my bed, since it was a double.
"You wouldn't expect it to be comfy on the floor," Anya giggled.
Keira was asleep long before the three of us were. Anya kept screeching, but Keira was too deep in her sleep to notice. She stirred every now and then, however the only noise was her heavy breathing vibrating around the room. She'd clearly worn herself out.
Lara insisted she'd feel too claustrophobic in an area with four other girls.
"It's too small, too crammed," she said, which was a lie because the basement was massive.
Realistically, I knew she was going out to smoke again. It was like a turmoil inside my head; she could kill herself whilst smoking so many cigarettes, but she said it stopped her from causing trouble.

I was split between telling Angie and Jennifer, or just leaving her be.
Anya, Isobel and I spent ages lugging pillows at one another, before eventually changing into our pyjamas. Angie still hadn't bought me any clothes, so I borrowed a burgundy top and shorts from Lara.
Luckily, Lara was the same size as me. The downside was that her clothes smelled nasty.
I threw the covers back and leaped into bed, almost knocking Keira off the other end. Anya and Isobel curled up in their sleeping bags, closing their eyes lightly. Keira groaned, rolling over and hitting me with her foot. "You'll be home soon," she grumbled. "Just wait until Sunday."
She rolled away again, hogging the whole quilt. I stared at her for a minute and then slowly turned on my elbow, tapped the lamp off and eased half of the cover back over my body.

Chapter 16

My thirteenth birthday arrived after a full night of tossing and turning. I'd waited patiently my whole life to become a teenager. I pinched up and down my arms, pausing to examine the birthmark on my elbow. It was only small but shaped like a heart. Yep. I wasn't waking up, meaning this was the present moment. I was a teenager.
An actual teenager...
I threw the bedcovers off my legs and let out a deep breath, rubbing my eyes. I could vaguely hear Katy's soft footsteps padding along the wood. She had to be running, probably away from Jennifer. I swivelled my body to check the time.
8:56am.
It couldn't be almost nine o'clock, could it? I groaned. I'd been desperate to awaken at seven o'clock, as per usual. I lay my head gently into my knees, reminiscing over past memories.
The previous Christmas, Mum had allowed Keira and me to go sledding. It had been a white Christmas, the snow pristine and fluffy. Keira was eight at the time and I'd recently turned twelve.
"Look, Mum!" Keira yelled, pointing a perfect finger towards the hillside. It was covered in thick, crisp snow.
Outside, the air had been bitterly cold. I could see my breath misting in front of my face. I had pulled my fur coat over my shoulders, yet in spite of this, it still felt nippy.
I'd have thought Keira would be worse, but she'd skipped off, her hands in her pockets and her cheeks red from the winter weather. She'd looked unbelievably cute, her blonde, sleek hair clipped back in a ballerina bun, her outfit consisting of navy blue jeans and an elegant, frilly top.
The sledding itself had been awesome; I'd felt fresh, free. Prior to Dad's death, I'd despised snow. I'd hated how it developed into a mushy slush so quickly, how it limited where you could and couldn't travel, especially when a snowstorm struck.
Which wasn't often in Britain.
One Easter in April, the sun had been high in the sky, flamingly hot on my neck. Each one of my intrusive thoughts had disappeared as the scorching spring weather hit Shallowton.

Keira had had a dance class in preparation for a competition. I'd visited the rehearsal, partially to avoid being outside in the sizzling sunshine. Keira would've said otherwise, but she was the most talented in the class. Her teacher agreed too.
"Keira is unbelievably gifted," she'd complimented her, stroking her curls. "Today was the first time I've seen her so happy since..."
Since before Dad died. Keira had commenced dancing after she took her first steps as a toddler and had attended ever since. That Easter was the day she stopped. Quit. Forever.
Her dance teacher's comment had seized Keira's healing heart and smashed it to the ground. Mum and I spoke to her, bribed her with ice cream and even told her that it was what Dad would have wished for.
She hadn't changed her mind. "I know it's what Dad longed for, but he isn't... alive anymore. Ava, Miss Rodger really upset me with her remark. It was completely unnecessary."
I'd contemplated explaining that her teacher hadn't meant any harm, and was simply offering her a generous compliment.
"You and I might have gathered what Miss Rodger's innocent comment represented, but Keira mixed it all up a bit, shook everything in her head and didn't realise her teacher's words were unintentional, or that they weren't meant to weaken her." Mum shrugged.
I'd agreed solemnly, but for days Keira had locked herself in her bedroom, not eating or drinking. I'd eventually kicked myself, groaning about how foolish I'd been to listen to Mum's useless observation.
Two months before, Mum had driven Keira and me to Weymouth Bay Holiday Park. It should've been term-time but Keira and I were home-schooled, so we had the benefit of being able to travel away whenever and wherever we desired.
The short holiday had been astounding; exciting, but interesting to say the least. Both Keira and I picked up some sort of sickness bug, ending up in hospital after ten days of uncontrollable, everlasting vomiting. It had turned out to be a small disease trolling around. Nothing major, but sufficient enough for Keira to be told that she was in danger. Her lungs had been very weak

because she was so young. And for a second reason that the doctors had refused to spill.
Strange.
Funnily enough, Keira had recovered first, three days after she'd been hospitalised. She'd come and perched at the end of my bed, holding my hand and reaching for the bowl every time I needed to throw up.
Shortly after healing from the virus, Mum had ushered the two of us into the car, driving us into the middle of Weymouth where we enjoyed our evening in the middle of an annual festival.
Keira had won a stuffed tiger, orange with black stripes. It was twice the size of her and just as tall as me. She had staggered, carrying it lopsidedly in her arms, tripping over and injuring her foot. This had ended in us trudging into A&E, spending our last few days of the extended holiday at the edge of Keira's bed.
I laughed at the memory, focusing on the clock again. It was nine o'clock by then and I could hear Katy screaming. She sounded hysterical. I gulped. Did I really want children of my own in the future?
There was a knock at the door. I straightened up, brushing my hair with my fingers. I hauled up the mirror from my bedside. My brunette curls stuck up left right and centre. I lifted my hand, stroking them down again. I'd just woken up, though; did it matter if my hair was a bit wild?
Lara walked into the room, pausing as she took in my expression.
"Girl, are you good?" she asked, raising her eyebrows. "Happy birthday!"
I rubbed my eyes. "Thanks, Lara," I said appreciatively. "I'm fine."
Lara nodded, unsure. Her eyebrow was still arched up.
I sighed. "I was just reminiscing," I admitted, embarrassed. I didn't expect my face to give so much away.
"That's OK." She shrugged and, to my surprise, smiled. "Reminiscing is good. It's a healthy way to run through the positives in life."
I looked up at her. The front strands of her hair were dip-dyed blue. A pale blue. It blended in smoothly with her strapless,

sapphire-blue dress. The remainder of her hair was brown, similar to my own. Her eyes shone dark and wide as she parted her soft lips. I glanced at her legs. They were flawlessly slender, and would be eye-catching if she were to walk by in the street.
I sighed. I had to confess, she'd changed drastically since I'd first bonded with her in nursery years before. Saying that, I also had to acknowledge her beauty. She clearly carried the good genes in her family.
I'd only met her mother once, when I was four. She'd had sleek brown hair and curious, unusually striking green eyes. She'd died in an aeroplane accident, along with her dad and others. The reporters had insisted it hadn't been intentional but had never broadcast who the pilot was, nor how the casualty had occurred. The Sun, our daily newspaper, had questionably lacked information and only had two lines written about it. This had included the names of the handful of victims involved in the accident.
"Ava!" Lara lunged herself directly onto my bed. I clawed at the bedsheets to ensure I didn't bounce off and up into the air. "We have a birthday surprise!"
I tapped my finger on my chin thoughtfully, thinking about what the 'surprise' could be. Maybe Eric Chanell would laugh in my face as he told me this whole thing was a joke.
No, Mum gave her consent before sending me here. Deep down inside, my gut held hope. Hope that Mum had designed this whole situation as some cruel prank.
"What's the surprise, Lara?" I enquired, finding myself grinning.
"Oh, you're interested now, are you?" Lara quipped.
I frowned. "Not really," I lied.
"Good. I've temporarily been forbidden from giving you even the smallest details so even if you kneeled down and begged, I'd just reach out my foot and nudge you over," Lara declared, sticking her chin out.
She seemed so pleased with herself for withholding the secret. My body flooded with further anticipation. I was too impatient, too hungry for additional information to accept Lara's response. I needed more.

Lara slid off the bed and strolled to the window. She grimaced, turning to me.
"Stop fluttering your eyelids at me, Avery Hayloft," she ordered. "I'd tell you more if I could... I shouldn't have opened my mouth to even give you a hint. You're too edgy. Is this how you felt when your dad's murderer wasn't caught?"
The smile slipped from my face. Her words pierced through my heart, stabbing my skin painfully, as fierce as a knife. I knew her insensitive words weren't meant harmfully. Nonetheless, an agonising throb danced through my stomach, forcing its way into my throat.
Lara's eyes widened as she noticed the atmosphere in the room changing. "I'm so sorry, Ava," she apologised, shoving her hand to her mouth. "My words are impulsive, unintentional."
I swallowed, a wry smile curving at my lips. "No worries," I muttered. "It's fine."
"Oh, it's not, Ava! I'm so heartless," Lara cried.
Irritation rose in my throat. Now she was guilt tripping me. I nibbled at my nails.
"You said it, not me," I said. "If you're not revealing any extra hints, I'll get ready for my special day."
Lara bit her lip, regretful. I gestured for her to leave. She backed slowly out of the room.
I trudged over to my wardrobe, throwing open the doors. I reached my arm out, pausing as my eye caught a pastel-pink dress lying in a crumpled heap on the floor. I bent down, cringing at the sound of my knees cracking. The material felt soft, velvety. The sleeves were lace, a pale rose colour. My lips angled into a crooked smile. It was beautiful, sophisticated.
I sprinted the short way to the turquoise bathroom attached to my basement room, locking the door firmly and removing my pyjamas.

Ten minutes later, the dress was on. I held my hand over my eyes as I pivoted around. Once I knew I was positioned directly in front of the mirror, I took my trembling hand away. My mouth gaped as I took in my reflection. The dress clung perfectly, especially at my waist. It was knee-length, the material at the

bottom hanging loosely. The lace sleeves hugged my skin, not itchy in the slightest.
I had an idea for a hairstyle. I grabbed a little hairpin from beside the sink, holding it in my mouth as I reached for my hairbrush. I smoothed out my curls, fluffing them down.
Gently, I pulled two strands of hair around the back of my head. I pinned them together and, with fumbling fingers, tugged at two of the front strands so they fell over my forehead.
My brain formed another idea. I raced back into the bedroom, yanking open the drawers. Two shining silver earrings gazed at me. I grinned, picking them up and safely placing them into my ears.
Once I was sure they were secure and wouldn't drop out, I burst out of the door and down the hallway. No one was about. I could vaguely hear Katy's squeals. The faint, distant sound of someone rubbing a static balloon hit my ears. I recoiled in disgust, hating the noise.
"Katy, stop it," a voice hissed.
I resumed walking, stopping as I reached the reception area. Five people stood in single file. Rose gold balloons surrounded them with pink confetti sprinkled inside. Birthday banners draped each wall, rosy pink with silver writing. Katy, James, Alfie, Jennifer and Lara beamed happily, breaking into pure laughter as my mouth opened wider.
"Happy birthday, Ava," Jennifer said warmly.
"Happy birthday!" James, Alfie and Katy squealed with delight.
I grinned, pointing at Lara, my earlier annoyance fading. "You knew!" I chuckled. "This is your surprise, the one you kept concealed."
Lara shook her head. "That's coming later," she explained.
"You're seriously making me wait?" I grumbled. "Until later?"
"Yes," Lara confirmed. "You'll have to hold your horses until then."
"I know the secret!" Alfie bragged, flinching as Katy accidentally popped a balloon. "Don't do that, Katy."
Katy immediately began crying. Her little hands were flung into the air, her feet flying out as she crumpled to the wooden floor.

Jennifer motioned swiftly towards Lara. Lara grasped my hand and dragged me into the living room, her free palm over my eyes.
I tried to fight against her. "Lara, I can't see where I'm going!"
Lara switched hands. "Stop moving. You're not meant to see, that's the whole point," she complained. "I'm not afraid to make you stay still so quit squirming."
I obeyed reluctantly. My feet moved, one in front of the other, similar to how they had that day at the hospital, my steps clumsy and uneven.
Lara yanked my arm as she tugged me to a halt. The sudden force of movement made me jump. Lara then spun me around. She took her hand away from my eyes and I squinted as the light hit my fuzzy gaze.
I was standing on the patio, a long lawn of fresh green grass leading away from my bare feet. Two chunky birch trees stood a few inches apart from one another. A pale pink banner was tied around both trees. '*Happy 13th Birthday*' was written in a bold, silver font on the front. To my left, a rosy-coloured gazebo stood, tall and beautiful, the material on top fluttering gently in the November breeze.
Cakes, party food and drinks were neatly arranged on a long table inside. More confetti balloons hovered on the grass, occasionally bumping into each other. A stack of brightly-wrapped presents were positioned on a chair in the corner. I peered at Lara, my heart beating delightedly. She stared back at me and I flung my arms around her neck, squeezing her tightly.
"Whoa." Lara stumbled backwards. "Calm down, Ava. It's not as if I planned this."
I scowled. "Who planned it?"
Lara rolled her eyes. "Jennifer did, Ava. She's the adult. Who else do you think would've arranged it? Katy?" The sarcasm oozed from her lips as she spoke. She pushed me further away from her.
"Nevertheless, thank you, Lara," I said gratefully.
Her eyes glinted. "I'll get the others." She turned, her wispy, wavy hair soaring out behind her, and disappeared from my sight.

Subsequently, Lara remained unseen for the hour I spent unwrapping my birthday presents. Jennifer shrugged her shoulders, murmuring that Lara simply had some issues of her own to sort out.
I raised my eyebrows. "On my birthday?"
Jennifer hesitated. "Ava..."
I dismissed the conversation with a wave of my hand. "Doesn't matter," I muttered.
I spent time *aww*-ing over each gift, running my fingers over the silk material of my new clothes and smelling the fresh, clean pages of the paperback books. I thanked Jennifer for her thoughtfulness, repeating how grateful I felt, how touched I was that I'd hardly known her for a week and she'd already spoilt me rotten.
"One more present." Jennifer dug into her pocket. I waited patiently, stroking the neat fabric of my pink dress. A moment later, a box dropped into my lap. It was rose gold, square and fragile. I lifted it up, my fingers fishing for the ribbon as my gaze lingered on Jennifer's face.
I only took my eyes off her when the thin strip of ribbon fell to the ground. Inside the box was a small chain. I took it out, my hands shaking, my cheeks burning red. I gasped as I examined the gift. The gold chain featured a small, dainty locket, glistening in the scarce sunlight. It perched in the middle, perfect, precious. I unlatched the locket, blowing out a breath as I caught sight of a memory so vague, so valuable. A photo of Dad stared up at me. It had been taken on my old Polaroid camera years back, one February on Weymouth beach. He wore the largest grin, using his fingers to tame his long, wiry hair as a fierce autumn gust swept it up.
Jennifer knelt at my feet, peering up at me intently. She looked concerned. A salty tear escaped my eye. I felt numb.
"Ava, darling?" Jennifer shook my arm.
I tried to seem emotionless and unbothered as I shifted my gaze in her direction. But a second tear, heavier and more powerful, forced its way down my cheek.
Jennifer silently removed the necklace from my grasp, gesturing me to turn around. She clipped the chain together around my

neck. It felt chilly on my skin. I closed my hand firmly around the locket, inwardly sending him a short message, telling him I missed him, that I wanted him back.
As a little girl, I'd thought that if I squeezed my eyelids together tightly enough, God would hear me and know I needed Dad home desperately. I'd prayed he would send him back to us, to cure Keira's heartache and Mum's misery.
By my ninth birthday, I'd understood that it didn't work like that. I had to get up each day and go to bed each night. I had to force myself to face the reality that Dad wasn't coming home. It wasn't God's fault. He did his best. It wasn't anyone's wrongdoing except the immoral, ugly killer who'd snatched his life and broken his family. Along with my prayer each night, I'd sent the murderer a message, telling them they were strongly guaranteed I'd find them eventually.
Moments when I missed my dad had hit harder lately, a sharp stab in the heart, each more powerful than the last.
"It's beautiful," I said admiringly. "Thank you."
Jennifer bent her head, her cheeks reddening. "It's all right."
The doorbell blared out, shocking me to my core. Recalling my childhood emotions had diverted my consciousness, blurring my mind into a deep daze, and I hadn't been paying much attention to my surroundings.
I scampered after Jennifer as she whizzed through the garden and into the living room. She hurried along the hallway, unlocking the front door and slamming it against the wall.
I recognised the two people who'd stepped out of the black BMW at once.
They were stood right in front of me, but for a few minutes, my brain refused to accept their existence.

Chapter 17

"Angie? Keira?" I gasped, my voice low.
Angie grinned. "Happy birthday, Ava!"
"Happy birthday, big sister," Keira said. She raced up to me, throwing herself into my arms.
My little sister seemed so big, so grown up. Her jeans were ripped at the knees, her t-shirt just covering her stomach. Keira looked remarkably older than the tiny baby she used to be.
"What are you two here for?" I whispered, my voice sounding dumbfounded.
"It's a secret for the meantime," Angie claimed.
I glanced expectantly towards Jennifer. She avoided eye contact, whistling to herself.
"We're stealing you for a few hours," Angie said confidently. "The car is outside."
Jennifer smacked her head in disbelief. "Duh. That's where cars usually are," she quipped sarcastically.
Keira snickered. Angie folded her arms but smiled at Jennifer's remark.
I dithered, wary. Angie wasn't a stranger, nor strange at all; however, I was very cautious about getting into any sort of vehicle after Dan's.
I hesitated. Angie opened the car door and hauled out a blindfold from the backseat. I frowned, my terror transforming into bewilderment.
"Angie..." I began.
"It's OK. If you're really nervous, I'll inform you of what our plan is. The last thing I want is for you to panic after your kidnappi- being held at gunpoint. I'm more than happy to settle your mind..."
I sighed. "I trust you."
Angie raised the blindfold. "You're all right wearing this? You can cover your own eyes instead."
"Blindfolded," I decided, knowing it was unacceptable for me to reject the idea of blindfolds and cars forever.
Angie ambled over to me, binding the blindfold together at the back of my head. She patted it, ensuring it fit. "Can you see?"

I stuck my arms out in front of me. “No,” I uttered.
I tumbled forwards, tripping over my own feet. I thudded onto the dry pavement, scraping my knee in the process.
“Guide her, Keira,” Angie said, helping me up.
Keira seized my arm. I flinched, the moment when Dan had done the same thing pushing its way into my mind’s eye. She eventually steadied it and tightened her small hand around my wrist.
I allowed her to drag me away. Soon enough, I felt the soft padding of the backseat under my bottom, then tiny feet crawling over my lap. I predicted this was Keira, not so carefully scrambling by me to get to the other side. I groaned as her hand hit my thigh.
“Ava, you all right there? You’re looking a bit uncomfortable,” Angie observed.
I lifted my palm up, shaking it from side to side. “Not too OK,” I admitted openly. “But as long as you’re not a slow driver, I’ll be fine.”
I heard Angie blow a breath out. “Debatable,” she said, not so quietly.
I crossed my arms, setting aside her uncertainty and focusing on my own troubles.
Somewhere around the globe, a single individual was responsible for my dad’s murder. They were acquainted with an inhuman assassination, hiding plenty of valuable information from the rest of the world.
One offender. Millions searching. Hundreds of billboards, newspapers and internet articles bringing awareness to Darren Hayloft’s death and what people could do to help. A single criminal was on the loose and no one knew even the tiniest detail about who it might be.
My breath hitched in my throat as a sudden possibility nestled itself into my chest. Considering Dad’s death was almost six years earlier, the chance of me roaming past his murderer was high. The odds of it made me shiver with unease and I instantly blocked it out.
My musing didn’t last; Angie broke the silence minutes later. “I’m incredibly sorry, Ava. Traffic is shambolic,” she said

apologetically. “You must be overflowing with suspense by now.”
“Totally,” I agreed. “Although, I think wearing this blindfold is helping in some aspects. I don’t feel half as nervous as I would if I could see.”
Angie laughed. “The criminals we encounter wouldn’t agree,” she said.
“You blindfold criminals?” I asked.
“On the odd occasion. Not usually. But in Shallowton, who knows. The criminals around here could be arrested in a police car and would still attempt a breakout if they saw a lay-by or a petrol station. Crazy.”
I swallowed. “Perhaps there’s a chance my dad’s killer could potentially be in a prison cell already? If he’s committed other crimes...”
“I doubt it. The culprit doesn’t want to be found at all. He or she definitely wouldn’t perform another criminal act this soon.” I could hear Angie scrambling around on the front seat.
I cleared my throat distinctly. “OK, Angie. How would you make a suggestion like that, unless you were involved somehow?”
Angie spoke through what sounded like clenched teeth. “Ridiculous. I am a policewoman. I’m experienced and I understand why a criminal like Darren’s murderer would not commit another offence whilst he’s still being hunted for the first one,” she snapped. “Besides, I sat round your house for three full days after... his death. Comforted you, supported your mum. If it wasn’t for me, you wouldn’t have been fed. By no means am I saying it’s Sandra’s fault - she lost her husband - but she neglected you, Ava, for at least forty-eight hours. Fussed over Keira but didn’t bat an eyelid your way. I took care of you whilst your mother recovered.”
I blinked, stunned. Not too long before, I’d been notified of Mum somewhat abandoning me at a young age. I’d accepted the inadequate information, dismissing it as a simple mishap, that Mum had been caught up in facing the depressing news of Dad’s death, the drastic change in her reality fresh in her head. If I was being honest, the whole affair punctured through me like a blade. Why should my sister be treated in a different manner to

myself? I knew she was younger, therefore had excessive needs, but I found it tore my heart out, leaving my chest with nothing but enduring pain.

"Anyway, Ava, we've arrived," Angie muttered, unlocking the car door.

I motioned to the blindfold concealing my eyes. "I can't make out which direction I'm going in. What if I bump into a brick wall outside?"

"There's no..." Angie sighed, exasperated. "Keira, guide your sister. I'll get the other half of the surprise ready."

Keira's elegant footsteps vanished as she manoeuvred around the side of the car. The door clicked open.

"You OK, big sis?" Keira whispered, anxiety oozing from her voice.

Gesturing wildly towards the blindfold, I sucked in a breath, willing the raw anger flowing through my body to remain undetectable.

Keira clasped my arm. I treaded tentatively out of the car, leaning my weight against her.

"I'm depending on you, Keira," I warned. "If I bump into a tree, all eyes will be on you."

She said nothing, just resumed tugging at my arm.

Minutes passed. My arm ached from stretching it out so far. Gradually, Keira pulled me to a standstill. I was grateful for this; my eyes tingled under the blindfold.

"Right, Keira," Angie said. "There is fine. Thank you."

My arm was dropped. I replaced it by my side. My fingers cramped up immediately.

"OK, Ava. After three. Remember, this wasn't my idea," Angie promised.

Oh, God. It's going to be dreadful.

"One... two... THREE!"

At this final prompt, I untied the loose knot. The blindfold, thankfully, fell from my eyes, leaving my eyesight dark and fuzzy. I blinked, readjusting my eyes to the blazing sunlight.

"Happy birthday, Ava!" This was a third voice. I registered who it must've been with a single, throbbing pain.

I peered at her, scorn plastered on my face.

Just as I thought. The one woman I'd been strictly advised to stay away from.
Mum.

I sucked in the irritation, gulping down the fury my heart struggled to cloak. Betrayal seeped through my skin, chilling my veins. Anger racked my bones, incomparable to the hatred I'd felt before. Matchless to even the loathing I'd held towards Dad's murderer. This woman had abandoned my sister and me at the time we'd most needed her. She'd dismissed visiting her own daughter in hospital. It was forgivable, but unforgettable.
Unable to suppress my agitation, I spat everything into my mum's face. "What in the world are you doing here? I'm not supposed to see you. If you hurt me-"
Mum laughed. "Ava, you're my daughter. I'm not going to hurt you."
"Let me finish," I said firmly. "I could get into trouble for this."
"You wouldn't get into trouble," Mum reassured me. "I'm the adult, this is my responsibility."
I nodded my head approvingly. "Good. Because I've involuntarily been blindfolded for the last half an hour and it's built up a lot of stress." I turned to Angie. "This better be worth it. Your disloyalty will remain unjustifiable, however. You've gone against the authorities and Eric Chanell. Oh, and you're actually a police officer too. Disgraceful."
Angie looked shell-shocked. Her mouth gaped open, her walkie-talkie stiffly hanging from her palm. An uncomfortable sensation fluttered through my stomach. I wasn't a horrible person. But Angie, as a policewoman, was meant to obey orders, not go against them.
"Ava, I told you I wasn't a part of this. Just... follow your mother. I'm a policewoman, as you said. I'll arrest her if she tries anything." Angie shot Mum a harsh look.
"I guess," I conceded. "I'm still sceptical."
"Understandable." Mum shrugged. "The lies you've been told..." She trailed off.
I trekked behind Mum, ignoring her unbelievable remark. Seriously, who did she think I was? I wasn't foolish, or gullible.

I took advantage of the short walk and gazed around mindfully. Hills stretched out far into the distance. Not normal hills you'd see in day-to-day life whilst on an early morning stroll. Hills equivalent to those in storybooks, films, fantasy novels. The fine, smooth grass shone in the sunlight. It reflected shadows of the trees rooted to the ground, stretched out over the grassland. My eyes felt unusually blessed whilst staring at the attractive setting surrounding me. A lake over to my left sparkled, almost as if it were smiling. The water was unrealistically clean, elegant swans gliding across, some cuddling each other with their huge, angel-like wings.

I grinned, despite my earlier tension. I'd never seen beauty as vivid as this. Almost as if I was in a different lifetime, a different world. The view was contrasting, dazzling to my eyes. Horses roamed around, graceful and intelligent. They were a mixture of charcoal, snow-white and neutral greys. I stared at them in awe.

Keira nudged me. "Ava, don't miss your surprise. It's coming up."

"Is it good?" I enquired, anxious.

"Your surprise is coming up," she repeated, as if I hadn't heard her the first time.

I rolled my eyes, the nerves tightening unbearably. "That's a no?" I guessed. Angie and Mum were walking in front, chatting intently.

Keira didn't reply. Spontaneously, I echoed my question.

"It's not bad," Keira said, rather unconvincingly. "You're just difficult to please. You'll reject the proposal."

Did she just mock me?

"*I'm* difficult to please?" I snorted. "Says you, Keira."

Keira shuffled on, leading me along the stone path and around the glistening lake. I caught sight of my reflection. My hair was flapping unattractively in the breeze. My cheeks were red, almost as shiny as the lake's water.

"This place is beautiful, I'll admit that," I said truthfully.

Keira nodded. "Isn't it? Mum brought me here the other day."

I bit my lip, anxiety continuing to course through my body. Nausea settled itself in my stomach and, for a split second, I considered giving in to the overwhelming consternation.

Until I cursed myself inwardly, reminding my body that I wasn't a wimp, nor was I a coward.
I resumed walking after Keira.
We soon stopped in front of a sky-scraping building. The bricks that formed the structure were pastel pink, an unusual comparison to our old house to the south of Shallowton.
An organised lawn filled the area leading down from the property, with neatly cut hedges and spotless green grass. Still enclosed in the grassland hills, the building seemed oddly misplaced.
Something tender prodded my ribs. I turned, intrigued. A green-eyed, charcoal pony blinked up at me, licking my skin for a second time. I giggled.
"Hello," I said softly, stroking her mane. She was smooth, sleek. Disciplined too. She lingered by my side, still and kind.
"Keira," I called to my sister. "This horse is so cute. Come look."
No response. No noise. My heart thumped, fearful once again. I patted the horse, in case it had noticed my sudden vulnerability. I didn't want her to be scared.
Trudging towards the building, I caught a glimpse of Keira inside. Was she trespassing? Breaking into someone's home? She'd seemed relaxed, which would be completely unlike Keira if she were to commit a crime.
"Keira!" I shouted. "What are you doing?"
She spun around, a smile drawn across her face. "Hi, Ava! Come over here."
I hobbled towards the building, wiping my shoes on the doormat as I stepped inside. My heart plummeted, still cautious that we were breaking into someone's home. My gaze swiftly moved from the grey tiled floor to the cream walls and the high ceiling towering over me. I gasped, noticing the dazzling diamond chandelier hanging low, creating a perfect shadow across the red carpet leading away from my feet.
"Keira, this isn't funny. You're looking suspicious, being in someone's house. I bet you don't have permission... Where's Mum and Angie?"
Keira grinned, but it looked fake. "Weirdo. Do you think we'd break into a stranger's house? Reaching a bit, Ava." She cleared

her throat. “No, Mum and Angie are in the garden. They’ll tell you the news soon.”
“News? Garden? What’s happening, Keira?” I scowled, a mix of confusion and terror spiralling through my bones. Was she ill? This was completely unlike her.
Keira snickered. Again, it sounded forced. “You can keep bugging me about it, but I won’t tell.” She stuck her tongue out at me. “You’re basically wasting your time.”
“Oh, am I?” I teased. “I’ll continue asking. I guarantee you won’t keep your mouth zipped for long.”
Keira bent her head and hesitated. “True. I feel a bit scared in case I do accidentally spill the information...”
I laughed. “Oh, Keira. Don’t be so-”
“Shut up, Ava! I swear, I’ll get whipped if I tell you a thing,” Keira snapped bitterly.
I’d never heard her so angry - not towards me. I nodded slowly. “All right...”
“I’m sorry. I’m just tense, under pressure. Things aren’t good.” Keira lowered her head again.
I nibbled at my nail, speechless.
“I’m sorry,” Keira repeated.
“It’s-” I started.
“Ava! Keira!” Mum called. She poked her head around a door. “Come here, Ava. I’ve got a proposal.”
I swallowed, frowning as Keira skipped ahead of me and vanished through the door. I strained my legs to move me forward. Difficult as it was, I managed. Defeating my anxiety these past days hadn’t been easy. I’d never understand how it took a few minutes to build the trauma but after all that time, the experience still lingered.
I trudged through the door, my legs heavy. I couldn’t deny it, I was very scared. What if Dan was there? Perhaps it was a trap for Keira too? No, she’d been adamant that there was a surprise. My eyes naturally squeezed tightly shut as I stepped through. I opened them, reminding myself once again that I wasn’t a coward. I wouldn’t give up and let the doubt run me over, ruin my life. I refused to-
“Welcome to your new house!”

I looked up warily, Mum's screeching tone snapping me out of my intrusive thoughts. “Huh?” I asked. “What are you talking about? Tell me why I’m here. You know I’m not allowed-”
Mum raised her hand. “You’re living in this house... with me and Keira. That’s why you’re here.”
I stared at her, completely appalled.
Choose wisely, Ava.
But I couldn’t think straight.
The atmosphere grew tense as I considered.

Chapter 18

"No," I mumbled finally. "I'm not even supposed to see you until this trial is over, let alone live with you... No."
Mum glowered. "You're thirteen, Ava. What I say goes. Do you want to abandon Keira, your dearest little sister?"
I gritted my teeth, irritated. Guilt tripping... one of Lara's top talents. "I'm taking it Eric Chanell hasn't a clue about this proposal?" I guessed. "Nor the authorities?"
"Ava, you're my daughter. It doesn't matter wha-"
"Yeah, it does matter. They know what they're doing. You haven't proved yourself innocent yet," I pointed out.
Mum set her hands firmly on Keira's shoulders. Keira flinched, covering her face with her hair. In an instant, I became suspicious. Regardless of whether it was because Keira hadn't been expecting Mum's touch, she'd never usually wince so suddenly.
I kept my eyes on her perfect little face, but she didn't meet my gaze. Mum was glaring at me. I waited for an answer.
Mum just sighed, dropping her hands from Keira's shoulders. Keira instantly relaxed, wiping her hair off her face and catching my eye at long last.
"If that's what you want, Ava," Mum said. "I know this trial is important to you. I also understand the authorities are just doing their job. It doesn't stop me from missing you."
I parted my lips to speak, but Mum resumed her speech. "You think I'm guilty, all because I was absent when you and Keira were kidnapped. I accept that. But I am not to blame. Instead of focusing on me, as I'm clearly not the culprit, let's set our attention to finding the real murderer."
Angie nodded thoughtfully. She stepped forwards, in between Mum and me. "I agree with Sandra," she maintained. "This was our other suggestion. Pandora Anderson was wrongly accused, yes?"
"Yeah," I acknowledged.
"Very wrongly accused," Keira whispered.
Angie looked expectantly at Mum.

Mum rolled her eyes. "That's what they say. It happened to be Lara stirring up trouble, right?" she asked.
"Yes. Lara's been scolded for that, however. It's in the past. But Pandora most likely feels... unsettled. No matter the circumstances, she still got accused of a crime she didn't commit," Angie said sensibly.
Mum scraped a velvet chair across the kitchen tiles and slouched down. She swept her hair off her face, exasperated.
Angie eyed her for a moment. "As I was saying, Sandra and I came up with an id-"
"*You* came up with the idea," Mum corrected her through gritted teeth.
Angie ignored her. "The idea consists of travelling into central Shallowton, where your dad was killed, and picking up the CCTV footage from that evening. We'll have to skip back a long way..." She paused.
I coughed. "How are you expecting to convince them we need the footage? As you said, it was a long while ago. Won't they be suspicious? Unless you're planning on stealing it."
Mum looked impressed.
"Remember, I'm a police officer. I'll say I need it for an investigation. Besides, yes, it was long ago... but that will only make it easier," Angie reassured me.
I frowned, my forehead creasing. "Make it easier? How?" I asked.
"You'll see. After being handed the CCTV footage, we'll host a meeting," Angie carried on, stopping to tighten her ponytail.
Keira's expression was doubtful. Clearly, she wasn't in on this, probably didn't know anything about it prior to Angie's announcement.
"What's a meeting going to do? It's not useful, especially not whilst trying to receive justice for my husband. Unless you elaborate, I'll not be taking part in this." Mum's face was filled with contempt.
I shivered.
"Imagine the position Pandora Anderson was in." Angie shrugged. "Think about her, not yourself. We need to host this meeting because if the murderer isn't Pandora, it has to be someone else."

"But there aren't CCTV cameras everywhere," I pointed out wisely.
"How are we meant to know that the killer will be on caught on camera?" Keira added. "If he or she was, wouldn't it have been explored long ago?"
Angie groaned. "Can you let me finish?"
Keira and I nodded. Mum said nothing.
"Thanks. After we view the footage, seeing their faces, I can go to the police station and find their file. We then call them in, hold the meeting and if they seem innocent, they go. If not, they get further questioning."
I grimaced. "It doesn't seem reliable. As Keira said, wouldn't it have been investigated ages back, straight after the murder? And what brainy criminal kills someone beneath a security camera?"
Angie blew out a breath. "Trust me," she said, "please. It doesn't seem practical, but it'll go much more smoothly than you're interpreting from the minimal details I've given you."
Anxiety gnawed at my stomach. What happened if another innocent individual was blamed? The feeling swamped my insides and I tried to pocket it, convincing myself it shouldn't be worth worrying about. Not yet.
"Anya and Isobel are visiting you later, aren't they?" Angie questioned, her voice rising as she became aware that I hadn't been listening.
I nodded slightly, wondering where this could be going. "Yep, they are. Why?"
"I know it's your birthday, but I think we should start this as soon as possible. Sandra, you take Anya and Isobel into Shallowton, stop the bus outside of Mallow's Cafe. They'd hold the footage, so ask them for it. Beg them, break in if you must," Angie ordered, as if she meant business.
"Fine," Mum agreed. "I'm not you, though. It'll be difficult."
Angie raised an eyebrow. "What do you mean?" she asked.
"I mean that I'm not a policewoman. I'm a middle-aged lady who lost her husband. I need some sort of ID."
Angie reached into her pocket, digging hard for a moment. She produced a small, rectangular wallet and flung it open, revealing her card of identification. "Take this." She threw it at Mum.

Mum, not expecting it, missed the wallet and it glided across the room.
"If needed, show them that. It'll be enough. The photo doesn't match, but tell them... you changed."
Mum bent over, scrambling on the tiled floor to collect the card.
"I'll be with Ava and Keira. We'll start planning the meeting," Angie carried on carelessly. She didn't wait for Mum to confirm it was OK.
I don't even think it was a choice.
"Is that OK with everyone?" Angie scanned our expressions.
"Good, no objections."
The four of us scurried back across the hall and out of the front door. The sun burned down on my forehead, fierce and bright. I squinted to see in the unusual November sunlight.
"Hold on, Ava," Mum called. We were metres away from Angie's car. "I just need a quick word with Angie and Keira."
I reluctantly wandered up the gravel track, admiring the soft hills and beautiful lake.
Back at the car, I nibbled on my nail as I leaned against the cold metal. Two minutes later, the others came over. Keira and Angie were peculiarly quiet. I didn't think anything of it until we all clicked our seatbelts and drove off.
Keira tensed up, hugging herself. Angie stared ahead blankly. She'd allowed Mum to drive, which immediately made me dubious.
I slumped lower on the leather seat, suspicion nibbling at my insides, creating a whirlwind of emotions.
Something was off.
Despite the suspense rising in the car, I couldn't make even one assumption as to what could've turned Keira and Angie so silent. Nonetheless, they'd been fine prior to Mum 'having a word' with them. Which meant that whatever Mum had told them didn't end with happiness.
It ended with an uptight atmosphere.
Little did I know, the truth would unravel in front of my eyes.
Patience, Ava. Patience.

Hours later, Angie, Keira and I found ourselves shifting all the furniture out of the living room, setting up a place for the meeting.
Keira was quietly licking an ice cream, despite the fact that it was autumn. She was perched on one of the grey chairs we'd set up. Music boomed loud and rhythmic from a speaker connected to the television. Me and Angie had wheeled it to the other end of the room so it could be taken out as soon as we'd set up the area.
Every so often, Angie randomly grabbed my arms and boogied. She was, if I had to admit, the most excitable officer ever. Maybe that was because she knew me so well. Without sounding odd, aside from a few sports days when Dad had shown up to watch me, the only memories I'd kept from being younger were when Angie had visited. She'd denied all new cases, just to stick with ours. Sometimes I wondered if anything could have been different if she was mine and Keira's mother.
No, not Keira's.
Just mine.
I turned to my sister. Her arms rested on her knees and her blonde, wavy hair was in braids. Her exquisite, ocean eyes were bright and eager as Angie promised her recovery.
I used to think Keira hogged all the attention to herself, but here I was realising that even a large amount of attention didn't cure such evil, dark feelings.
As I gritted my teeth together, it whacked me right in the face how Mum had gone through depression too when Dad died. That was the reason Angie had cared for me so often whilst my mum looked after my three-year-old sibling. She couldn't be responsible for two children when her husband had just died. It hit like a bomb, like how I'd felt on Wednesday when Mum had chosen to abandon me. No matter how much a part of the plan it was, I couldn't have imagined it being my sister instead of me. Especially years before, when she was a toddler.
And then... Angie would never have chosen to be my mother.
"Ava," Angie groaned. "Help."
I glanced up in a flash. Angie was struggling with the coffee table. I sped over as her walkie-talkie vibrated. Together, we eased it

to the other end of the room near the window. Angie unattached the walkie-talkie and positioned it by her ear.
As she spoke and listened for a few minutes, I straightened up the coffee table. It was so heavy that I nearly tumbled backwards. As I stalked back over to one of the chairs, Angie clicked her fingers to seize my attention.
"Keira?" she mouthed. Her eyes directed me to the kitchen.
I raised my eyebrows. I was about to tell her that yes, Keira was my sister, but then I realised Keira was no longer in the room with Angie and me.
I hurried out into the hall, speeding past the reception desk and into the kitchen. The redness of all the walls and tabletops hit my face like lightning.
On the scarlet tiles, Keira lay face-down on her stomach. Her eyes were rolling back and forth, her body jerking alarmingly.
I screamed hysterically for Angie. She ended her conversation and scurried into the kitchen.
"She's having a seizure," she gasped.

Chapter 19

"999, which service do you require?"
The phone shook in Angie's hand. "Ambulance."
"Who's in need of the ambulance?" the operator asked.
"Erm... I've got a nine-year-old little girl with me, she's... she's having a seizure," Angie stammered.
I clutched Keira's palm. I expected it to be cold, but it was scorching hot.
"Thirty-two Mellow Road." Angie almost dropped the mobile. "I'm a policewoman, but I wasn't ever trained to deal with s-seizures."
She ended the call and glanced nervously at Keira. "Ava, I'd move away. I don't know much, but I know you're not supposed to be close to someone having a seizure."
I placed Keira's hand on the floor and reeled backwards. Her gasps and snorts were increasing in volume, ringing in my ears. I shivered, clasping my arms around my waist. I couldn't bear it.
"Angie, she's not gonna... die, is she?" I stuttered, pressing my palms together to stop them shaking.
Angie shot me a swift look. She stayed quiet. This made me feel even more uneasy.
Ten daunting minutes later, three paramedics flung the front door open and sprinted into the kitchen.
"Does Keira have any medical issues?" One paramedic pulled out a clipboard and a stack of papers.
"No... No, she doesn't." My voice cracked.
The paramedic jotted this down. "Allergies?"
My teeth started chattering and I couldn't speak.
"Darling, calm down. Your sister is going to be OK," the paramedic assured me.
"She's allergic to chocolate," I stuttered.
The paramedic repeated this as she wrote it down. "Thank you. My colleague will check Keira's temperature and then we'll go from there," she said.
I watched intently as the paramedic took out an oxygen mask and adjusted it over Keira's nose and mouth.

The third paramedic stuck a thermometer into Keira's ear. Her movements had reduced and her gasps quietened.
"She's very hot," the paramedic said, examining the thermometer.
I gasped. "What will happen?"
No one answered.
The paramedics fussed over Keira some more whilst Angie phoned Mum. Her, Isobel and Anya were in Shallowton collecting the CCTV footage. Mum had said that as long as Angie kept an eye on Keira, she'd see us later.
"Angie, Ava." The paramedic tapped us on the shoulder. "Since Keira is so young and this hasn't happened before, we're going to take her into hospital for some further tests," she said.
I glanced over at my sister. She was sprawled on the floor, almost motionless. Her breathing had returned to normal but she was groaning as if she were uncomfortable.
"See how I'm not moving Keira, or getting too close? If you try to stop the seizure, the person will fight back as they won't know who you are before they've recovered fully," the paramedic said, standing up. His knees clicked.
"Russel, is Keira breathing OK?" the woman who'd questioned us asked.
Russel, a plump man with eyes as striking as lightening, nodded. "Yes, Sara," he replied, looking at Keira. "Go and get the stretcher from the ambulance."
Sara shoved her pen in her pocket and picked up the clipboard. She disappeared and, a minute later, wheeled a bed into the kitchen. She undid the straps whilst Russel and the second man lifted Keira up.
Russel coughed. "Really, we should wait until she's conscious, but as long as she's not kicking or screaming she'll be all right." He lay Keira on the stretcher, tucking her legs under the blanket.
The third paramedic turned to Angie and me. "Are either of you going in the ambulance with Keira?"
"Yes," we answered.
Sara frowned. "We're really only supposed to let one in with her... but since Ava is a minor, Angie, you can go too."

So that's what we did. Angie, Sara and I walked behind the two men and Keira's stretcher, mindful not to bump into the wheels. The air outside was bitterly cold. I'd almost forgotten it was my birthday. I glanced at Angie, shivering. My hair blew in my face, sticking to my lips and nose.
I couldn't believe my little sister had collapsed so quickly. She'd been fine, neither pale nor showing any signs of feeling ill, but moments later she was having a seizure.
I shuffled closer to Angie. "What could've triggered it?"
Angie stuck her foot out to climb inside the ambulance. She paused. "I don't know."
I sucked in a breath, following Angie's lead. The ambulance inside was warm and toasty. My fingers had numbed from being out in the cold.
Sara whizzed around to the front of the ambulance. Russel and the second man stayed in the back with us.
Keira stirred a few times and her eyelids flickered, but she didn't wake up. I became more and more frightened. My anxiety rose, making my fingers tingle and shooting butterflies through my stomach.
Keira's breath fogged up the oxygen mask.
"See, Keira's alive." Russel smiled. "Her heartbeat is completely normal."
I sighed with relief. At least her immune system was fighting the seizure off.
For now.
Once we arrived at the hospital, the ambulance doors flung open and Sara manoeuvred around to help Russel and the other paramedic three-wheel Keira out. Her stretcher seemed heavy, especially with the low moans escaping Russel. He was almost wheezing.
"Children's ward, we've got a young girl, Keira Hayloft. She's currently unconscious after having a seizure," Sara said into a radio. "Bring her down? Sure, we've got a policewoman and her big sister here with us. Could they come in too?" She bit her lip anxiously. She held the radio to her chest and turned to Angie. "Do you know Keira personally?" she asked.

Angie bowed her head. Never mind her being a police officer - she clearly didn't know what she meant to Keira.
"She's not family... but our mum said it's compulsory for Angie to stay with us. Mum is sorting out something real important," I blurted.
Sara nodded. She repeated my words to the person on the other end. Two minutes later, Sara reattached the radio to her belt and we flew through a set of flappy doors. From the cartoon animals and bright contrasting colours covering the walls, I guessed this was the children's ward.
We marched on. Russel and paramedic three were racing ahead. Angie, Sara and I practically bolted behind them.
I bent over, panting, as Russel eased Keira over onto the hospital bed.
He checked her temperature again. "It's very high." His forehead creased. He and paramedic three spoke amongst themselves.
"Take a seat, girls." Sara ushered us over to two solid chairs, both covered with lilac blankets.
Angie gripped my hand. "You don't have to worry," she reassured me. "Look."
I brushed the tears away from my eyes and followed Angie's pointing finger. I lit up as I registered Keira glaring around the room. She was scowling.
"Confusion," Russel said. "It shows she's coming around."
I nodded, setting free a shaky sob. Keira wasn't dead. Her body *had* fought through the seizure.
I hurried over and stroked her forehead. Russel was correct - Keira was extremely warm and sticky.
"Hey, Keira," I muttered gently. "How do you feel?"
Keira stared up at me, her blue eyes alarmed. "Where am I? What happened?"
I chewed on my lip, meeting Russel's gaze.
He stepped forward. "Keira... you're in the hospital," he said.
Keira's frown deepened. "Huh? The hospital? Is someone hurt?" Her words slurred together.
"No, no... unless *you* are injured? You just had a little seizure."
Keira whimpered, her hands drifting over the crisp blanket she'd been wrapped up in. "What's a seizure?"

I took a deep breath. "A seizure is where you uncontrollably jerk and sometimes hold stiff... like you did." I didn't wish to scare Keira any more than she already was, but I didn't want to lie either.
"It's a brain condition. It could mean lots of things, but we'll need to do some tests before we can find out what caused the seizure." Russel patted Keira's arm.
Her cheeks grew paler by the minute.
I tapped Russel's hand to get his attention. "She doesn't look very well," I whispered quietly.
Russel looked at Keira thoughtfully. Her whole body trembled and her eyes twitched. "Keira," he called. "Can you breathe?"
"Y-Yes," she said.
Russel lifted the oxygen mask off the stand of drawers at Keira's bedside. He shoved it in one of the white drawers.
He then picked up a stack of paperwork. "I'll be right back, I just have to hand in Keira's medical form. I'm sure everything will be fine for the moment while I'm gone but if not, I'm just down the corridor."
I nodded and stepped back to let him through. I heard his soft footsteps padding along the floor and down the hallway. Angie pranced back and forth, chewing her nails. Her vulnerability increased my own anxiety.
Keira's head lolled side to side. Nerves choked me. I was barely able to talk, or to breathe.
"Keira," I said, "are you sure you're OK?"
But Keira wasn't blinking. Her eyes were staring blankly into space. Her head stopped moving and dropped to her chest.
Her body lay completely motionless.

Chapter 20

I could no longer suppress my tears. They bubbled from my eyes, running down my cheeks. I reached for Keira's hand. It was as cold as ice.

"Angie," I whispered, "get the paramedic."

Angie's phone fell to the floor with a clatter as she registered Keira's immobile body. She scampered from the room and I heard her yelling, manic cries that filled the air.

I shook Keira. "KEIRA!"

She didn't move. I waved my hand across her mouth.

She wasn't breathing.

I sank to the floor, crawling across the icy tiles and hunching over in the corner.

Footsteps clattered past me, but I didn't look up. I focused on the cabinet towering above me. If I didn't look at her, perhaps she wouldn't die.

Hysterical screams echoed across the room. My chest tightened, restricting the air I could breathe. Keira's system couldn't fight off the seizure. It was too frail, too languid.

A nurse bustled into the cubicle. "We need the area completely clear." She ushered us carelessly through the curtain and out the door. The fabric being yanked across the rail rang in my ears as we walked down the corridor.

"She'll be all right, won't she?" I hid my wavering hands behind my back.

Angie didn't meet my eyes. "Yes," she said uncertainly.

I sighed. "Don't lie to me, Angie. She won't be OK, will she?"

Angie stopped abruptly and turned to me. "Look, I have no clue if Keira will be OK. It's completely out of my control. I'm a policewoman, not a nurse," she snapped.

My lip trembled. Angie noticed. She pulled me into a hug.

"I'm sorry, darling. I didn't mean to lash out at you. I'm just as worried," she said.

I highly doubted that. Angie hardly knew anything about Keira, yet she had the nerve to comfort me by suggesting she understood how I felt.

My sister was deteriorating in front of my eyes. I'd stared and stared at her, right up until her body surrendered and her energy drained out.
Angie's mobile phone rang as we neared the car. I nibbled on my nail as she lifted it to her ear.
"Yes? You're coming here?" Angie looked around the heaving car park. "Shall I go inside? What about Ava?"
She nodded a few times before ending the call. "Ava, your mum is on her way. Her, Anya and Isobel found the footage. One problem is, they'll let Sandra and me in, but not you, Anya or Isobel. Anya will drive you back to the care home. She passed her driving test last year," Angie said. She pulled a face. "Me and Sandra will need a car too, so I'll ask Anya to borrow Sandra's."
Twenty minutes later, Mum's car drew up. Angie and I were stood under shelter from the sharp drizzle coming down. We were already drenched, water dripping from our hair and clothes.
Mum stepped out of the car first. "Think this is the right footage." She handed it to me. It was a small square-shaped disk. I pocketed it.
"Right, where's my daughter?"
Angie explained her plan to Anya. Anya nodded several times before Mum offered her the car keys and disappeared inside.
Anya led us back to Mum's car.
"You're gonna get into trouble if the police pull you over," Isobel sassed her, walking alongside me.
"As if. Angie's a policewoman, remember?" Anya grinned.
Isobel sucked in a breath. "You don't have insurance for Sandra's car," she insisted.
"Quit it, Iz. It's Ava's birthday and her sister is in hospital. I'm only obeying Angie's orders." Anya unlocked the car.
Anya and I jumped in the front seats and Isobel in the back. Anya stuck the key into the ignition and we set off.
"It's good one of us has a driving license," Anya said, her gaze focused on the road.
Me and Isobel shared a glance. Isobel shrugged. "Well, we're not old enough."

Anya rolled her eyes, tapping her fingers on the steering wheel. "Whatever."
I settled back against the velvety material, crossing my arms. Anya and Isobel resumed arguing.
The only thing I could think about was Keira. My resilient, buoyant little sister.
But was her strength enough to see her through - to push her into recovery?

The kitchen was roasting hot and the stench of sweet chocolate hovered in the air. Jennifer was leaning against the counter, dividing pieces of oozing cake onto party plates. My stomach growled with hunger, but I couldn't give in to it.
That would be selfish.
"Shall we sing *Happy Birthday*, Ava? Or do you want us to just eat the cake?" Jennifer asked, handing the plates out.
I hesitated. I didn't wish to be sung to, or to eat the cake. I just wanted Keira home. I didn't have a clue why or how she'd had the seizure. Physically, aside from her allergy, she was healthy and strong. Perhaps it was a one-off? Maybe she'd go ahead with her life, thriving, with no signs of any further seizures.
I preserved the pleasant thought. For the moment, it blocked out any negative possibilities; therefore, conceivably it might work miracles in the future, too.
"I'll wrap some cake up for later, if that's OK?" I asked.
Jennifer peered at me, replacing her slice of cake on the plate. "Are you all right?"
I nibbled my lip. "Yeah... just not hungry."
I slipped out of the kitchen, convincing Jennifer, Anya and Isobel that I was desperate for the toilet. They believed me. Instead, I leaned against the wall and cried. I tried to conceal my snorts with my hand, but this resulted in snot flying through my fingers.
Disgusting.
I brushed the tears away from my eyes and inhaled a deep breath. I didn't know what was wrong with me recently. What happened to optimistic Ava? Ava who clutched at her dreams, pouncing in with both hands to reach them?

All of the faith and destiny I used to carry had fallen through my fingers, leaving me unstable and lost.
What if I never regained my enthusiasm? My positive outlook on the good and bad? For goodness' sake, I'd guided Keira through times Mum couldn't handle. Dad's death, her never-ending tears and horrible nights in which the nightmares consumed her, biting at her lack of confidence until every remaining piece evaporated.
I swiped back my hair, bracing myself to return into the mayhem of the kitchen. I halted at the door, hearing Anya and Jennifer speaking tentatively.
"She claimed she was joking, but it's an awful subject to joke about," Anya was saying.
I peered inside. Jennifer paced up and down, clasping her hair. Anya was bent over, her face hidden.
"Why would she say that, unless it's true?" Jennifer whispered, throwing her hands in the air.
I strained my ears.
"Ava can't know about this," Anya said in a hushed tone. "Her sister has just had a seizure and is currently in hospital."
Jennifer sighed loudly. "Anya... this is bad. What reason would Sandra have? Maybe she did kill Darren."
My heart slammed against my ribs. My head thumped and my hands began shaking. I couldn't process it, couldn't even summon the possibility.
How could Mum be a murderer?
Furthermore, the killer of my dad?
The intense conversation died down and I could only make out Jennifer whistling. I stuck one foot in front of the door, prepared to interrupt their discussion. As I went to step through, I yanked myself to a standstill.
"I don't believe Sandra killed Darren," Anya said. "I think perhaps-"
I tilted my head around the door. Jennifer's eyes widened and her hand flew up to her mouth in an instant.
"You can't think... Would Sandra *hide* Darren?"
I drew in a breath. My head was a whirlwind of emotions. My skin erupted into goosebumps.

Where would Mum imprison Dad? *Why*?
Unable to apprehend any further information, I sauntered into the kitchen. Anya glanced at me.
"Hi, Ava," she said, smiling.
Jennifer fixed a grin onto her face. She said nothing.
I poured myself a glass of water, slurping it down eagerly. Perhaps it might soothe my mind, collide with the turmoil spinning through my head and shove it away, leaving me at peace.
"You're seriously burying the truth from Ava?"
I spun around. Lara was stood at the door, her hands on her hips. Her lank hair was now dip-dyed scarlet, as red as blood.
"Lara, what are you talking about?" Anya's voice wobbled uneasily.
Lara rolled her eyes. "She was eavesdropping. Ava already knows."
Anya and Jennifer glanced at me, and then at each other.
"She wasn't born yesterday, Anya," Lara carried on.
I felt the colour drain from my face. I felt sick with fear. It stuffed my throat, preventing my lungs from releasing the oxygen I needed to breathe.
"Where's my mum hiding Dad?" I demanded, my hands curling into fists.
Jennifer looked uncomfortable. My throat tightened even more. I felt as if all the life was being squeezed out of my body. Should I be angry, or alarmed?
Silence filled the room. Lara tapped her foot on the floorboards, expectant.
"I... we... don't know. Actually, we have no idea. Sandra could've been lying," Anya stuttered. She readjusted her hijab, keeping a careful eye on my face.
I frowned. Were they being dishonest?
My breath was properly enclosed inside my stomach. Instead of speaking, I turned on my heel.
I dashed from the kitchen, my brain practically begging my legs to move.
Once I was in my room, I sprawled on the bed.
And released the tears that'd been held in my guts for so long.

Chapter 21

Lara appeared at my bedroom door, looping her hair around her index finger. The wide grin spread across her face could only mean mischief. Her eyebrow arched as she tapped each finger against the doorframe.

"I've got a surprise," she claimed.

I shoved down the book I was reading, pushing the blanket off my legs. My feet were cramped and my pyjamas hugged my body, but I was eager to finish my book before sleeping. "What is it, Lara?" I asked.

Lara ushered me towards the door. "Follow me." She hurried down the hallway.

I trailed after her, hauling on my trainers and raising my hand to grab my coat.

"You don't need your coat," Lara said. "I have blankets set out in the forest across the road."

I rolled my eyes, following her into the cold night air. Snowflakes were falling, but not settling; the pathways were still drenched from an earlier downpour. A strong gust of wind slapped my face. I shivered.

The forest sheltered us from the breeze. My foot hit a glass bottle. Lara picked it up and swivelled it around.

Vodka.

I gasped loudly. "What the heck...?"

"That's not all." Lara yanked a packet from the bottom of the bottle, which was firmly attached to the glass.

Cigarettes.

Lara looked amused as she took in my expression.

"Lara... I can't." I took a step back.

She grabbed my arm. "Last time wasn't successful. But today might be different."

She offered me a cigarette. I nodded slowly and she lit it for me, passing it over. I lost my balance and the cigarette nearly fell from my clutch.

"Ava!" Lara hissed. "Careful. Otherwise you'll start a fire and we really will be caught."

My face flushed. With fumbling fingers I held the cigarette to my lips, feeling the hot air swamping my lungs as I inhaled a puff, and coughed vigorously. Lara peered at me and rolled her eyes.
"Not everyone is as talented at smoking as you are," I muttered, holding the cigarette further away.
Lara dismissed my comment, pouring out two glasses of vodka. I sat down, shaking. Nevertheless, something about the cigarette calmed me down. I kept puffing on it until Lara handed me the cup of alcohol.
It was sweet and bitter against my tongue. The taste made me shudder.
"Hey," Lara said. "It's real good to have a healthy friend."
I coughed again, shocked. "Sorry?" I asked.
"Mental health is a con, really. I mean, I know your sister was diagnosed with depression, but personally I wouldn't be able to handle such a large responsibility." Lara licked her lips.
I felt my forehead crease. What was she implying? "How does that have anything to do with me?" I asked.
"Ava, I'm trying to tell you how great I think it is that I'm not required to take such precautions with you."
Lara tilted her head. The sky heaved with golden stars. Each one held a light so bright, twinkling down on us, guiding us towards our destination.
But what if you haven't figured out which direction you need to take?
I stubbed the light from the cigarette and chucked it on the damp grass. A mini crackle sounded and I booted the cigarette, watching it be propelled into the distance.
"Mental illnesses aren't something people voluntarily choose," I protested.
Lara chugged a third round of alcohol. I stared at her, outraged. What was she doing, ruining her life so young?
You're one to talk, Avery Hayloft.
I shrugged the thought away.
"We all die eventually." Lara's head lolled sideways. She was drunk. "If you commit suicide, you're basically asking for attention."

"That's so far from being true," I huffed. "Again, why did you bring me here, just to tell me that?"
Lara gritted her teeth. "Jenny informed me of your panic attacks, but she said it's not severe anxiety. You don't suffer from depression or OCD either. You're healthy."
I winced, folding my arms across my chest.
Lara must've seen through my happy-girl mask. Her eyes widened. She swore. "Gosh, Ava. You do feel suicidal, don't you? I... It's not a bad thing."
"That's not what you just said," I argued, voice raised. "You implied that if you're feeling suicidal, it's basically 'attention seeking.' Wanting to end your life is more than a sad, empty hole in your stomach that rips you apart. It doesn't just last a day and then disappear. No, it's life-changing. Once you have it, it doesn't go. It's always there, even if it partially fades. You're so wrong, Lara. You weren't always like this. You used to be sympathetic and sweet, like a little angel trailing after me." I felt the salty, sentimental tears releasing against my will, unable to hold them in a moment longer.
Lara glowered. "Exactly, Ava. Trailing after *you*. Because you were the princess, not me."
I opened my mouth and closed it again.
"Furthermore, your dad's murder case... or whatever it is now... became known worldwide. All dedicated to your beloved father. My parents' bodies were located, but when will they receive the justice *they* deserve? The commercial around my mum and dad's death wasn't even close to the awareness raised for yours." Lara sniffed. She splashed out another glass of vodka.
I pulled a face. "I... I..." The words I wished to say were jumbled up in my head. I didn't quite know how to state them out loud.
Lara raised her palm, holding it out towards me. She wiped her eyes with the back of her other hand and leaped up, snatching the vodka and cigarettes. "Don't bother, Ava. Clearly you're self-centred. Don't come crying to me when you realise you're just attention seeking."
I brushed my hand across the moistened grass. I was drowning in my own repulsive thoughts. My heart ebbed into millions of broken pieces.

If this was life, I didn't want it.
My body was engulfed by a wave of heavy selfishness. Keira lay in hospital at that moment, probably terrified. Katy, James and Alfie were experiencing a childhood without parents. How could I think about myself when they were far younger? Were they complaining?
I buried my sorrow, sucked in a breath and trailed after Lara.

Once in my bedroom, I sank into the soft, snug sheets, heartbroken.
Although I didn't want to admit it, my mental health *was* slowly deteriorating.
I'd begun feeling overpowered by the never-ending fear consuming me, eating me up. I couldn't describe the desolation, I just knew the gloom remained present, ready to gobble me up.
Lara reappeared, her head bowed. "I'm sorry for saying such harsh, hurtful words... and for encouraging you to drink and smoke, especially if you didn't want to." She paused. "Do you think you have depression?" She trudged in and perched on my desk chair, legs tucked under her.
"No." I shook my head.
Lara dug into her dressing gown pocket. "If you want to call the doctors, or wait until Angie can, this is yours. It's a birthday gift, all right?" She pushed a green-blue mobile phone towards me.
I reached for the phone, turning it over in my palm. "Thank you. Lara, you're not changing too much, are you?" I whispered, the lovely little Lara I knew in nursery springing to my mind's eye.
Lara looked at me sadly. "Sometimes, the best people can adapt in the worst ways possible," she acknowledged, standing up and sauntering out of my room.
I stared vaguely after her, then narrowed my eyes as I checked out the turquoise phone.
It was an iPhone 11, with a large screen. I reached for the charger situated on the crisp sheets and walked over to the plugs near my desk, flicking on the switch.
As the power turned on, the mobile ran into action.
I stared down at the lockscreen photo. Lara and I were pictured, not much older than toddlers, in the little blue playhouse at

school. Lara was holding a teacup, her arm outstretched. I had the largest smile on my face, both of my hands flapping outwards, a fluffy bunny stitched on my dress. I bit my lip. This had been exactly two years before Dad had died. I was five, a cheery, excited kid with two sweet parents and one baby sister. My hair was beautifully blonde back then; it had darkened over the years. My blue eyes were strong and electric, standing out against the bright golden curls draped around my shoulders.
I forced myself to call the doctor.
Even I couldn't fool myself for much longer.
I desired to guide others, but I'd ditched myself in the process.
I craved to become my main priority.
Getting support seemed to be the only rational way to do that right then.

The next morning, Angie phoned Jennifer, informing her that Keira had had another seizure overnight. She'd woken up ghostly white and her breathing had stopped for half an hour.
"She's very ill. We still can't be sure whether or not her body is strong enough to fight it off," Angie said, remorseful.
Jennifer reported all the details back to me. Little did she know I'd overheard the conversation, shivering against the wall in my pyjamas. It was surreal. The situation had gone from awful to unbearable.
Later on, Angie rang again. Jennifer handed the phone over to me.
"Anya watched the camera footage, and the faces seem pretty clear," I told her.
"That's good. I'll leave Keira with your mum soon and come home," Angie said.
I hesitated, recalling Anya and Jennifer's hushed discussion from the previous day. Angie, being a policewoman, had the right to know about our suspicions, about Mum admitting to Anya and Izzy how she might've been involved with Dad's murder.
"OK, please come soon," I begged.
"Of course, Ava. See you soon, my lovely." Angie rang off.
I strolled into the living room and sat down next to Isobel.

Anya was squatting down by the DVD player, inserting the footage.
"Definitely able to see the faces," she declared.
"Doesn't matter." Isobel yawned. "Can't let Angie be too quick to get the files."
Anya rolled her eyes. "That's not what's going to happen, Iz," she insisted. "Sometimes I don't know why Mum didn't stop after having me."
Isobel whacked Anya around the head. "Fun fact, there were two of me. Was there a double of you?" She laughed.
"Well, one of you died. Besides, I would have been too fierce if I was a twin, that's why there's just me, plain Anya Smith." Anya wore a smug look.
Isobel stared at her sister. I knew Anya was joking, but losing your twin had to be equivalent to losing an ear or an eye. Unthinkable.
It quietened Isobel, either way.
"Girls, I was just desperate to watch the footage. I'm too nosy. We're not permitting Angie to go any further with this meeting, duh. I cannot conceal a secret for the life of me," Anya said.
Isobel nudged me, rolling her eyes. I chewed my lip, suppressing my laughter.
"We'll let Angie decide what we'll do," Jennifer said wisely. "She'll be here soon."
On cue, screeching wheels could be heard crunching over the stone gravel, kicking up dust. I rushed to the front door, flinging it open.
Angie pulled me into a hug, cupping my face. "Hi, lovely. I'm sorry your birthday kind of went down in the dumps," she said sympathetically.
Tears poured roughly down my cheeks, scratching at my skin. It didn't bother me if my birthday had been the worst, most disappointing day. Feeling sorry for myself wouldn't cure Keira. She was still my best friend and I missed her.
Keira's birth had been very special. Mum had gone into labour in the early hours of Valentine's Day. Usually, Valentine's Day would be full to the brim of red and pink roses, dinner dates in parks or elegant restaurants and binge-watching cringeworthy

films, but for us the day was dedicated to Keira. Mum and Dad fussed over her, as did the midwife and nurses. Twenty-four hours of kisses and hugs filled Keira's special day. We couldn't complain; Keira's existence had filled our hearts with love and compassion.

Keira would turn ten years old in three months; double-digits, a significant age to many. My sister, however, would fight through another year battling depression.

I brewed Angie a cup of tea, eager to impress her. Isobel poured her, Anya and me a glass of orange juice.

Isobel and I sank down, relaxing on the sofa. Anya squatted on her knees in front of the DVD player, clicking 'play.' The screen displayed the CCTV tape.

Angie yanked her phone out, zooming in and snapping photos of all the faces. Her plan was to drive back to the police station and search through all the files. Once successful, she'd host the meeting. Somehow, she assumed this would be a reliable method to find the culprit.

I thought otherwise.

Isobel nudged me. I drew in a breath, settling my hands in my lap. "Angie..."

Angie glanced at me, phone in hand and pointed at the television. "Yes, lovely?"

"We know who killed him," I murmured.

She arranged her phone near the remote on the timber coffee table and removed her walkie-talkie.

"No, don't record it, don't say anything to anyone," Isobel blurted urgently.

"It was my mum," I said.

Angie picked up her phone and the CCTV footage again, standing up. "I can't do this today," she insisted. "We're here trying to find the murderer in one of the world's biggest cases, right? And you are all telling me the man's wife has been the culprit? This whole time?"

Jennifer's eyes widened. "Angie, it's the truth," she protested.

Anya folded her arms, her expression soft and gentle. Isobel curled her fingers around one another, her legs trembling beneath her.

I gulped, staring Angie in the eye. Would she believe us? Our theory seemed pretty reckless.
Angie's face was masked with scepticism. She turned her head sideways, contemplating. "OK." She sighed. "If you think it was Sandra... do all of you?"
Anya and Isobel peered at each other. Jennifer nodded.
"How do you know?"
"Sandra said so herself. Said she clasped Darren around the throat and shoved the knife into his back. He crumpled to the ground... dead." Anya winced. "She claimed it was a joke... said her intentions were to protect Ava and Keira."
"Ah, when in reality it wouldn't protect them at all? Of course. Because it's had more of an effect on Ava and Keira now it's happened. It's broken Keira to the extent she's been diagnosed with depression, self-harmed and tried to kill herself, at just nine years old," Angie emphasised.
No one understood how *I* was feeling. My irregular panic attacks could easily be forgotten against Keira's need for assistance.
"I can't even speak to Sandra, since Keira is in hospital," Angie complained, wiping a bead of sweat from her forehead.
"So, how?" Anya asked, crumpling her brow.
"I'll sort something out. I'll tell you before I do anything, however," Angie promised. "It's going to be very tough. Sandra aimed to train Ava. She was a therapist in her time... She knew Ava's ambition to become one herself. But we can certainly not permit Sandra near children under any circumstances. Safety precautions."
I'd always assumed Mum despised my dream, believing that becoming a therapist wouldn't work out for me. But surely she believed in me, especially if she were to coach me herself...?
"I'll instruct her. I'm aware Sandra had finer training, what with going into therapy when she was a teenager, but I also maintained a course at a young age," Jennifer asserted confidently.
"Let's leave that for now. Sandra bragged that she was a therapist before Darren died and that's why she was willing to help with teaching Ava." Angie paused. "So, it's James's birthday on Wednesday, right?"

Jennifer nodded, a hint of excitement twinkling in her eyes. "Little boy is turning seven."
"We need to make it special. James is quiet but so sweet," I said. "He likes cars, so perhaps a racing-themed party? Inviting his friends from school, Katy, Alfie and Lara?" I suggested.
Lara appeared at the door.
"I don't want to go to some stupid party with pathetic little kids. I'm surprised you do, Ava," she commented, curling her lip.
Jennifer sighed. "Lara, you love the kids."
"Of course I do. I'm going smoking and drinking on Wednesday, though," Lara admitted. "Today, too."
Jennifer shook her head. "You're going to ruin your life, Lara. I will alert the authorities if you don't stop," she warned.
Lara's eyes narrowed with annoyance. "I'll drink until I can't see and smoke until my lungs are broken. I don't care. Doesn't bother me." She spun and marched out of the living room, her head held high and proud.
Jennifer sighed again. "Don't get caught up with her, Ava. You'll never hear the last of it."
Isobel coughed. "Little late for that," she mumbled.
I froze. She *knew?*
"Shut up, Izzy. Can you smell burning?" Anya sniffed the air.
Isobel shrugged. "Nope, can't smell a thing."
"Perhaps you have Covid?" Anya suggested.
Isobel's brow furrowed. "Huh? What's that?"
Before Anya could reply, a fierce cloud of smoke rushed through the door.
"The heck...?" Isobel peered towards the door.
"Definitely burning," Anya said.
A sharp waft of flaring smoke stormed into the room. It blew up the carpet and sent the television off its stand. The acrid stench loomed over the area. I stared at the door as it was whisked off its hinges.

Chapter 22

The crackle of the nearing fire blared in our ears. Jennifer's hushed voice was barely audible.
"Anya, edge towards the door," she hissed.
"Jennifer, I can't. The fire is entering through that door. Unless you want me to sacrifice my life for you?" Anya quipped, rolling her eyes.
Angie was dialling the fire department. "Phone isn't connecting to the internet," she growled.
"Turn on your data," Jennifer said, shielding her face from the sweltering flames barricading us.
"I have none." Angie chucked her phone onto the coffee table.
Isobel chewed her lip. "Does anyone else have their mobile?"
Anya shook her head. Jennifer frowned. "Mine is at the other end of the room. The flames are blocking the way," she said.
Isobel sucked in a breath and closed her eyes. "Great. Where's Lara?"
"Didn't you hear her? She's gone out to smoke." The flames were surrounding Jennifer's feet.
Fortunately, I was furthest away from the roaring fire.
Not so fortunately, Jennifer was closest.
"So..." Angie hesitated. "Do you think her cigarette caused the fire?"
Jennifer shrugged. "Doesn't matter. If we think too deeply about that, we'll all die."
Isobel hopped from foot to foot. "Ava, come on. You're the smartest. You always know what to do."
I coughed, covering my mouth with my hand. Truth was, I didn't have a clue what to do. Isobel looked expectant, as if I were to yank out a magic wand and transport us somewhere away from there.
"I'm not the smartest," I mumbled. "Funnily enough, I've never been trapped in the middle of a fire before."
I glanced around, anxiety itching at my skin. Flames swarmed the carpet, hammering against the walls. Jennifer tucked her feet under her, backing away.
Her green eyes brimmed with fear.

"Ava, unlock the windows." Anya pointed behind me.
I darted over, digging my feet into the sofa as I leaned over it, tugging at the window latch.
Locked.
"We're trapped." Isobel threw her hands into the air.
"At least if we die, we die together." Anya pumped her fist.
Isobel pulled a face. "Optimism isn't always useful," she said.
Flames were washing over the walls. My coughs became intense, my breathing raspy. Inhaling too much smoke wasn't good... We didn't have much time.
Angie's eyes were fixed on me. She owned the funniest personality, possessed the most flawless skin and gave the best advice. She was determined, sympathetic, witty. Yet, amidst these blazing flames, she came across as scared, vulnerable. Her hair cascaded down her chest, tangled and shiny. Her golden-brown eyes were wide with terror.
Anya and Isobel huddled together, coughing violently. Flames were creeping up the walls, starting in one place and ending in another, teasing us almost. The fumes were strong and deadly. I raised my hand to my mouth, blocking the thick smoke threatening to choke me. Jennifer began gasping, her hand still covering her eyes. She would die before the rest of us. The flames ate at her feet but she kept jumping back, defiant.
"Is there anything that might protect us from this fire?" Anya asked. Isobel gripped her arm, shrieking loudly.
I looked around helplessly.
"Here." Angie threw Anya a slender cloth.
Anya hoisted it up. "This is too thin," she declared.
"Give it back here, then. Or let Jennifer borrow it."
We glanced at her. She was half on the floor, half battling her way up against the fierce flames. Never mind Angie - Jennifer was on the verge of collapsing. I looked around again.
How did this fire start?
Every inch of the carpet was drowned in whopping flames, tearing along the material, ready to pounce at us.
"Ava, can you smash the glass?" Anya gasped.
I stared at her. "What?"

She advanced closer. "The window," she croaked. "Smash the glass. Get us out."
I turned to the window. "What with?"
Anya groaned. "Angie, surely you've got some sort of useful tool? What with being a policewoman and all..." She paused, taking in Angie's blank expression. "Nope? Never mind."
Both Isobel and Jennifer were retching vigorously, clutching at thin air.
I faced Angie. "We've got to do something. Anything, Angie." I looked at the window again.
The flames hadn't yet reached Angie and me, but it was a matter of minutes before they would swamp us too. Jennifer and Isobel, on the other hand, were overwhelmed by the ferocious fumes.
"Do what, Ava?" Angie asked. "There's nothing in here that hasn't caught fire... unless you count the ornaments at the other end of the room."
I turned to her. "Pass me your walkie-talkie," I demanded, waving my hand.
Angie stared at me. "My walkie-talkie won't shatter glass, Ava."
I rolled my eyes. "OK, well, give me the CCTV disk. The case might break the glass," I said.
"That's our only way to host the-"
"Angie, we spoke about this. Mum murdered Dad. We don't need the wretched disk." I snatched it from the coffee table - flames rippled up the sides, but hadn't quite demolished the whole surface - and chucked it at the window.
A mini dent was visible in the glass, but thanks to my wonky aim, the disk had fallen into the flames.
Destroyed.
I glanced at Jennifer. Only one knee was above the flames, her head and shoulders sinking slowly.
"Gosh, Angie, give me your walkie-talkie!" My scream was hoarse.
Angie unhooked the device and placed it in my open palm. I shoved the antenna at the window. It cracked some more. I grinned. Angie doubted me, but I'd proven her wrong.
Until I felt the scorching heat of the flames surrounding my feet.

"Hurry, Ava!" Angie called. "I don't know how you broke a window with the walkie-talkie, but I'm not surprised. Your talents are never-ending." She looked intently at the window.
I drew back and thrust the device at the window again.
Another time.
Again.
"Yes!" I shrieked with excitement.
The glass had a big enough hole for us to crawl through. A big gush of wind entered the room, cold against the roaring flames surrounding us. My skin tingled.
"Push Jennifer through!" I croaked.
Anya shoved her forwards. I forced her to place one foot in front of the other. She scrambled through the window, falling with a thump onto the pavement.
"Isobel, get over here!" I screamed. My lungs were numb, my throat dry.
Isobel avoided the threatening fire, fighting her way over to the window. I poked her in the back, but she turned towards me.
"What about Anya?" she whispered, trembling. "I can't go without-"
"MOVE!" I shoved her. "She'll follow you."
Isobel hobbled through.
Great, at least the weakest of us have found safety.
I gestured to Anya. The flames were at her feet, but somehow she'd managed to remain free of injury. I coughed as she climbed through, shielding my eyes. The heat made them water, and my hand was no longer visible in front of them.
"Angie, GO!" I said, jolting her directly in front of the window. "Get out!"
Angie shook her head. Instead, she prodded me in the back. I staggered forwards.
"What are you doing?" I shouted, my lungs almost giving up on me.
"You go, Ava. You're the child, so go. I'll be behind you."
I gazed around the room. Smoke billowed into the air and flames concealed the walls and carpet. It wasn't an attractive sight.
I looked back at Angie.
"Leave, Ava. Otherwise we'll both die from the fumes."

Sighing, I lifted my foot and clambered through after Jennifer, Anya and Isobel. I thudded onto the ground, Angie landing beside me shortly after.
We all darted away to the other end of the street. Huddling together, we watched the building collapse into nothing but bricks and dust.

I perched on the edge of Keira's bedside. Her face was a sickly pale colour and her eyes unreadable. I stroked her matted hair, glossy in my fingers.
She hadn't woken up, but the nurse had told me she'd had another seizure. I sighed, feeling somewhat soothed by her rhythmic snores.
After we'd fled from the fire, the building burned down. The firefighters had arrived, calling an ambulance to take Jennifer and Isobel into hospital for a checkup.
Their results had come back healthy. Luckily, they hadn't been stuck in the flames long enough to be at major risk.
Eric and Ellis had stayed with Anya and me whilst Angie drove to the police station. Eric had suggested I move to the care home Katy, James and Alfie were in, until they could figure out how the fire started and if my mum really killed Dad.
I'd agreed reluctantly, numbness tingling my body.
I had then slipped out, to visit my sister in hospital.
That's where I was now, after thirty minutes of fighting the nurse on duty.
She strongly believed I shouldn't see Keira until she'd recovered.
I disagreed; she was still my sister.
Keira's blue eyes flickered gracefully.
"Hi, beautiful," I whispered, clutching her hand.
She stared up at me, bewildered. "Am I still in hospital?" She yanked at her hospital gown.
"Don't pull it, Keira. How do you feel?" I asked.
"I have a headache," she muttered, struggling to sit up.
"Should I call a nurse?" I asked.
Keira shook her head.
I sighed. "You ate the chocolate, didn't you?"
She turned away, her cheeks reddening. "Yes."

"You knew about your allergy," I said softly.
"I didn't know it caused seizures." Keira shrugged. "The nurse said you had a phone to call me... but you didn't ring."
I froze. The mobile phone Lara had given me had burnt to ashes inside the building, along with my other possessions. Lara must've told the nurse I'd phone from that, unaware of our current fire situation.
Lara had arrived back at the care home as the ambulance turned up. Jennifer and Isobel were being escorted to the vehicle and Lara demanded all the details. After I'd cried to her, expressing my emotions and weeping that I could no longer ring the doctors - I didn't wish to have anyone else know, therefore wouldn't call from Angie's phone - she told me she'd help herself. I'd frowned at her.
"What do you mean? You're not a doctor."
Lara had tucked a strand of hair behind her ear. "Well, duh," she said sarcastically. "But I can guide you another way."
I'd gulped. Surely I'd received enough advice from Lara Lildham to last a lifetime? The probability of it being another of her unhelpful habits she thought I'd find useful was high. I'd rolled my eyes and smiled. "Go on," I said. "Tell me."
My eyes had widened as her information was digested and I dissolved into nerves.
"So, if you don't have a phone now, we'll move to plan B. Personally, this is my favourite." She had coughed. "My dad owned an aeroplane... since he was a pilot. Only one of Dad's friends and I know where it is. I thought we might go for a little flight?"
I'd struggled to understand her plan at first.
"You're suicidal, clearly. You don't want anyone knowing... but it's obvious," she'd carried on.
And then everything had clicked into place.
"You're saying you'll guide me to... commit suicide? Jeez, Lara. That's assisted suicide... It's *illegal*."
Lara had glared at me. "Don't you think I know that?" she'd snapped. "I'm on the verge of being arrested anyway, so what will this do? I'm always happy to help you."

I had contemplated it. Travelling up into the sky in pitch darkness wasn't appealing. Not to mention the danger we'd get ourselves caught up in. Being honest, I'd felt on the edge recently. My anxieties had slashed my heart into a heap of nothingness. I refused to sleep at night knowing I'd wake up the next day and everything would repeat itself. Feeling exhausted, numb, disconnected. The worst part was, reaching out for help seemed as if I were annoying. Nobody was willing to babysit such a defenceless person, one who could not take care of themselves. I wasn't ready to expose my vulnerability, not until I was able to shake off the frustrating feeling of existing as a burden and not as a human.
Because until I was proved to be otherwise, that's what I'd be.
A burden.
"Fine. You win. So, how will this work?" I'd enquired, folding my arms.
Lara had chuckled. "For me to know and you to find out. Just meet me outside the care home at 10.00pm."
I had glowered at her. "Can't we wait? Until... Friday?" I'd asked.
"Ava..." She'd sighed. "You push my patience. Whatever, fair enough. It has to be Friday, no buts about it."
She'd walked out, swaying her hips.
The discussion was over.
And so now I sat at the end of Keira's bed, stroking her gently and staring into her ocean eyes. "Sorry, Keira. The care home caught fire. It... It burned down. My phone was inside."
Keira gasped. "No... Were *you* in the fire?"
I nodded. "Yes. We all were. Jennifer and Isobel almost died, but Anya, Angie and I were just lucky enough to be furthest away from the flames," I said.
"Damn, Ava. Are they all right too?" Keira struggled to sit up further. Her knees cracked.
"Yes... Jennifer and Isobel needed to be assessed, but they're safe and healthy. As for the rest of us, aside from in the last minute, the flames didn't advance too close." I shuddered, remembering how claustrophobic it had been, being stuck to one side of the room with four others and ferocious flames licking every inch of the area.

Keira's cheeks whitened again, a colour equivalent to a piece of paper. I stayed quiet.
"It's boring here," she said. "Lesson learnt... I'll never eat chocolate again."
I laughed half-heartedly. "You weren't meant to eat it in the first place, Keira."
A plump brunette lady entered the cubicle. She carried a glass of water – ice-cold, for the outside was misty and frozen - and a square packet of paracetamol.
She stuck her nail into the packet and pierced it open, then handed Keira the tablets and water.
"Hi, darling." She looked at me. "Your sister will be taken in for more tests. I'm afraid you'll have to leave for now."
I reached over and hugged Keira. She whispered three words in my ear.
"Don't kill yourself."
I gazed into her bright, hopeful eyes. In an instant, I realised that she knew.
I withdrew from the room, avoiding any eye contact.

Chapter 23

I passed the toilet cubicles, halting sharply as I heard a voice. They seemed to be screaming. I strained my ears, desperate to get an idea of who it could be... or if I even recognised the voice.
"You stupid coward!" they yelled. It was a woman. "You knew I only created you for my sake, yet you buddy up with my daughter!"
There was something I should've been worried about...
"Yes, of course! I stabbed Darren Hayloft." The woman sounded hysterical. "I murdered my husband."
My heart detached, descending into a messy puddle around my feet. The cold-hearted, evil witch was, as Eric suspected from the beginning, *Mum*.
She'd stabbed Dad that night.
He wasn't hidden... He was, indeed, dead.
I sank to the floor, my legs collapsing beneath me. I sat back and wept. I became aware of the footsteps clicking past me every second, but I was too focused on the single sentence I'd just heard:
"I murdered my husband."
We really were searching for a non-existent murderer. Or, even worse, a murderer who was in front of our eyes the whole entire time. I scrunched my hands together, but it didn't suppress the uncontrollable sensation itching my skin. I desired to break through the door and slap the satisfaction from her voice. The cruel, wicked woman on the other side had stabbed my dad - her husband. I slammed my fist against the wall behind me, feeling the anger gripping my throat and choking me. I couldn't breathe, couldn't focus. Neither Dan nor Lisa had killed him, and Eric certainly hadn't either.
"Ava, is that you?"
I vaguely heard the voice above my head and sensed the sweet stench of her perfume, but my vision blurred. I felt dizzy, lightheaded.
It was as if a stone was crushing my lungs, disallowing me from inhaling oxygen. I put my head between my knees, able to focus

more than before. The noise surrounding me faded into distant hums.
"Ava, do you want me to call a nurse?" The voice was louder.
I fisted my clammy hands, shoving them to my head as I looked up. Pandora Anderson was peering at me, concern creasing her forehead.
"No, I'm fine," I insisted shakily.
She patted my shoulder. "You're not fine. You've just had a panic attack."
I stared at her, exasperated. "I did?" I queried.
Pandora nodded slowly. "Yeah, a pretty big one. You were swearing and barking."
I hid my face with my hair.
How embarrassing.
"I'm OK," I protested fiercely. "I just... I've got to go home, please."
Pandora nodded again. "Right, yes. I can arrange that." She paused. "How did you get here?"
"On foot."
"On your own? Jeez, no wonder you're so frustrated." Pandora held out her hand.
I took hold of it, dragging myself up. "That's *not* why I'm frustrated. I'm worried and fed up."
She stayed quiet, holding me up as we went outside. A bitter wind caught my face, blowing my hair wildly. I shrugged it off.
"So, you got trapped in a fire?" Pandora asked.
"Yes," I confirmed. "No one died or was injured so let's not talk about that."
She quietened. The only noise audible was her high heels clomping against the stone pavement as she walked up to a scarlet Mercedes-Benz.
My mouth fell open. "No way. Is this *your* car?"
Pandora's face reddened and she looked away. "I had a rough year, thought I deserved a treat," she admitted.
I was impressed. A couple stopped to stare at the modern, trendy masterpiece. Pandora shot me a sideways glance, grinning. I leaped into the front seat, catching a glimpse of my reflection in

the rear-view mirror. Mascara ran down my cheeks, leaving a black trail. I brushed it off, sighing.
"Ava, love, can you insert the care home address into the satnav?" Pandora pointed towards the device.
I pitched forwards, tapping in the address.
In the process, my nail snapped. I rolled my eyes.
Typical.

James's birthday was a massive success. Isobel blew up all the confetti balloons and displayed them in the living room. She'd planned a huge party, inviting all James's friends. She bought herself, Anya and me matching dresses. They were a shimmery gold, glistening in the strong moonlight.
The party itself was racing-car-themed. It was awesome; full-sized blue and green racing cars, real exhausts firing out behind them. The fireplace and pearl mirror were draped in red banners, words in swirly fonts spelling out *'Happy 7th Birthday, James.'*
Jennifer had hired a red-and-white circus gazebo, paying cash for a colourful, slightly frightening clown and glamorous stuntwomen and men. They performed a few astonishing, imposing acts, flabbergasting us all, bringing us to the edge of our chairs with great tension. James and his friends especially were awestruck, clutching their hands together, their eyes lit up with anticipation.
Anya and Isobel had designed a huge buffet with all sorts of different delicious food and drink. Warm sausage rolls, mouth-watering burgers and rich, creamy desserts: heavenly cheesecakes, divine Victoria sponges and luscious, towering trifles. James's birthday cake consisted of three layers, all including an array of sickly treats and surprises.
Later on, Jennifer blindfolded James and walked him outside. There, on the front lawn, was his favourite singer, Logan Rae. James almost fainted with shock, breaking into tears and sobbing as Logan performed all of James's treasured songs. He stood by Logan Rae and Jennifer snapped a photo of them both, side by side under the gleaming stars.

Regardless of the drizzle falling by the end of the night, James had grinned all day long. Our persistent hard work didn't go unappreciated, for James displayed his gratitude every two minutes.
Forty-eight hours later, I sat cross-legged on my bed. It was the morning of my upcoming suicide.
I called Keira at the hospital at 6:00am. The nurses had ended up prescribing the wrong medication to her. They'd immediately diagnosed her with epilepsy, since Keira's blood tests and ECG returned normal. There were really no other possibilities.
By lunchtime I grew restless, so decided to buy a drink in the cafe ten minutes away. Jennifer caught my arm as I crept to the door.
"I just need a word, Ava," she said, dragging me back into the living room. It was a whole lot airier and more expensive-looking than the previous one.
Jennifer sank into the green velvet chair, but I chose to stand. Angie, who I hadn't clocked beforehand, peered over at me. She sat beside Jennifer, snatching out her mobile and turning it to face me.
"Uh... " I frowned.
"Just watch." Angie pressed play.
Me as a little girl appeared on screen. I wore a dainty tutu, twirling around and toppling to the ground. I vaguely heard Dad reminding me of my movements; I must've been presenting a dance performance. Laughing, I leaped back up.
"My dream is to become a therapist. I don't like people being sad."
Angie pulled the phone away and sat back. I looked up at her, intrigued.
"Why did you show me that?" I paused. "How did you even get the video?"
"Doesn't matter." She dismissed my question. "A company on the internet was searching for young children to take on the role of a mental health ambassador. To enter, a video explaining why you wanted the job was required. I sent this in. Your mum sent it to me ages ago."

I couldn't comprehend this. They'd sent in *that* video? It scarcely even explained *why* I desired to become a therapist. Besides, it was from at least seven years earlier.
I scowled, still uncertain. "When do they pick the winner? Meaning, the mental health ambassador."
"They d-did yesterday," Angie stuttered.
I promptly looked at her.
Angie coughed, stuffing her phone into her pocket again. "They chose you, Ava."
I stared from her to Jennifer. "Me?" Finally, I crumpled onto the sofa behind me.
Jennifer nodded. "Yes."
"If you want to take up the opportunity, I'll email them with your details," Angie went on.
"And if I decline...?" I raised my eyebrows.
Angie shrugged. "Then it'll be passed on to the next person," she said simply.
I tapped my chin, thinking it through. Of course, my biggest dream was to be a therapist, helping people through their toughest moments, adding the spark back into their smiles... showing them that they're not alone.
But at that particular moment, was I ready? I could barely keep myself alive... In fact, what I was going to do in just a few hours would mean another individual reached *their* own aspirations.
"Would I be able to buy a few days to contemplate it?" I asked quietly.
Jennifer frowned. "We thought you'd take up the role without question-"
Angie nudged Jennifer in the ribs. "Yes, Ava. That's fine."
I gave a wry smile and stood up.
Undoubtedly, I didn't stand a chance.
By the following morning, I'd be dead.

Chapter 24

I walked round to the nearest restaurant, my coat heavy around my shoulders. I paused outside of the café Dad brought Keira to on the night of his death. Could I force myself to step foot inside? Was I strong enough?

Sighing, I glanced around, taking in the Christmas decorations. Christmas should be a festive time, a time for blessings and happiness. Dad had taken us for steaming hot chocolate each Christmas Eve. Keira would weep when the marshmallows were soggy and sank into the chocolate.

Once, aside from gobbling up the jar of sickly marshmallows, Keira only took small sips from Dad's hot chocolate. She had been only two and very fussy.

That was before we found out that she was allergic to chocolate.

The waitress came up to me as I sat at the table. "You're Ava Hayloft, aren't you?" she demanded, removing a strand of hair from her mouth as the automatic door opened, blowing in a heavy gust of icy wind.

I rolled my eyes. "Are you going to tell me my feelings are invalid? That my sister is going through a tough time so I shouldn't be so selfish? Or is it that my mum murdered Dad and you want to offer me sympathy?" I snapped.

The waitress looked mildly startled. "Your mother assassinated your dad? Isn't the police officer, Angelina, doing anything about that?"

I shrugged. "Angie's pretty useless," I said, my eyes widening. That had been impulsive.

"Oh?" The waitress seemed more and more uncomfortable.

I wasn't surprised. "My apologies, it's a joke we have. She's not actually useless, just... looking for a good time to arrest her," I explained shakily.

The waitress nodded, stiff and awkward. "It's nice to meet you, Ava. Your story seems more... complex than is displayed on billboards. Aside from your dad dying."

I laughed. "You know."

The waitress sped off as I glanced up and suddenly, I saw six years earlier. Mum had found out about Dad and Angie had

invited herself in, along with a second policeman. This had been before Mum got the chance to inform me of the current state of affairs. Keira had been camping at my aunt and cousin's house but got picked up the following morning. Shallowton Cafe was blocked off with special duct tape, guided by police officers and reporters.
Mum had towed Keira upstairs before Angie interviewed her. I'd stayed downstairs, but could I rewind, see what Mum told Keira?
I squeezed my eyes shut, tight and firm. I followed them into the room, not sure if this had actually happened or if it was my imagination. I stood stock-still in the doorway, listening.
Mum and Keira were in the very corner of the bedroom, hugging one another. Mum pulled away, sliding something into Keira's palm. I squinted.
"Key to Daddy's house," she said quietly. "You know I'd never kill him, right? He needs to be safe, and I need the money. You won't be at too much risk, but your dad will be. When you're ten, I'll book a flight to Japan and you can travel with Daddy. No one will recognise you there."
Keira's blue eyes were fearful. "Ava?"
"Ava... Yes, sure," Mum lied. "She's my girl too. I want to keep my family guarded. Neither you nor Ava are in any danger, but Tim wants to ensure I don't get back with your dad."
I hardly assumed Keira understood; she was only three.
"You still wish to be an actress when you are grown up?" Mum asked, shooting Keira a sideways glance.
Keira bobbed her head earnestly. "Mmm-hmm."
"I'll explain the plan when you're nine. Just remember, this conversation needs to remain confidential, erm... secret." Mum paused, hugging Keira again. "It's too complicated right now."
But Keira already knew.

The waitress snapped me out of my daydream. I bounced half a metre above the chair.
I needed that key and I knew where it was.
"Ava-"

I scrambled up and raced out of the door, pulling on my jacket. I didn't look back.
The conversation between Mum and Keira had been after Dad was 'stabbed,' so why had Mum been so certain that Keira and I would fly to a different country with him?
I didn't know.
I hastily caught a bus and skipped off at the grubby stop in central Shallowton. I followed my previous footsteps to Ruby's Rising Shopping Centre. Unsurprisingly, the area was deserted, so I sauntered into Dad's old mechanic store. I briskly recalled Mum's strict order not to go into the storeroom attached. Unquestionably, that was where the key would be hidden.
Flicking on the silver light switch, I stared at the neatness of the room. Just a desk stood in one corner, its wood top painted a pastel pink. A pencil pot perched on the edge, a concealed drawer underneath.
I reached over and took out the gold key.
I darted out of the shopping centre, faster this time, catching another bus that was speeding by. I pressed the button once we were approaching Delling Road and the bus dragged to a standstill.
I thanked the bus driver and rambled along the pavement to where I knew the metal gates towered over the cemetery. I looked around quickly before dashing over and bashing my fist on the patch of grass above Dad's coffin.
A noise came from underneath.
"Sandra?" A male voice. "Sandra, is that you? Is it night-time already? Can I come out?"
I glared around. How would I be able to get in? I looked to my left. A shovel was planted stiffly in the ground. Pulling it out, I dug at the smooth, damp grass. It wasn't a difficult job; it had rained earlier on, releasing a light wash over the soil.
The coffin was inside, hardened and brown. A small hole caught my eye, bold and round. I yanked out the key and twisted it in the lock.
A figure shivered and made his way up, without a look of alarm or terror.
Dad.

Or was it?
He peered up, angrily. I think he'd been expecting Mum.
I staggered backwards when he noticed me.
"Ava?" he heaved. "My daughter, Ava?"
My mouth fell open, but I couldn't talk.
"Your mum's been hiding me here for years," he whispered, straightening his back.
This man had black hair and green eyes. His face shape was different. His voice made me think it was my father. Now, I thought otherwise.
"You're not my dad," I argued, picking up the shovel and holding it out in front of me.
"I am your dad. Ava, this is all your mum's wrongdoing. I can't explain in the middle of a cemetery, but she's hidden me here for *years*, only letting me out at night as if I were nocturnal," he confided.
I gasped, returning the shovel to my side. "Mum?"
Dad nodded. "She's a freak. A weirdo. I don't get it." He yanked the shovel from my hand and snapped it with his bare hands.
I covered my face. "Dad, stop. We need to talk. Please tell me everything and I'll tell you the rest," I said.
Dad considered my words. He raised an eyebrow.
"Pinky promise?" I tried.
"Pinky promise." Dad beamed. "Oh, my baby girl. My firstborn daughter. Please, can I have a hug?"
Feeling strange, I fell into his arms. He trailed his finger across my cheek, tugging away a stray strand of hair.
"I strongly believed you didn't want to see me," he wept. "Your mum said-"
I smiled half-heartedly. "She's a liar," I interrupted. "Let's go and get a drink."
As I moved my feet to leap up, Dad grabbed my hand. I reeled backwards, almost slumping to the ground.
I saw the terror in his eyes. "It's OK," I reassured him. "Clearly, Mum thought it all through, what with your plastic surgery. No one'll recognise you. I'll say you're a family friend."
Dad hesitated, peering around. If what he'd said was true, he couldn't have seen daylight for years. I followed his gaze. Only

one woman in the distance was visible. She was gently positioning a bouquet of roses on the side of a grave.
Dad looked back at me. "The plastic surgery is one thing I'll thank your mum for." He shrugged, brushing his jeans down. Together we trekked through the bleak cemetery, along the desolate street and down towards central Shallowton.

A slender, blonde-haired woman brought our drinks over to us. She stared at me in awe. "You're Ava, aren't you?" she asked, turning to Dad. "Who are you?"
"He's a family friend. Haven't seen him in a while, so we're catching up," I blurted quickly.
The blonde waitress blinked. "Right... Any further news on your dad's murder case? I haven't seen anything on the news for weeks."
"Well, you see..." I eyed Dad. "No... yes. Actually, the police quit. Except Angie, she's been on our case for years... and..." I blushed, humiliated. "That's it."
The blonde girl looked from me to Dad. She nodded vaguely, then took our orders and walked off. Her hips swayed slightly, reminding me of Lara.
"So." Dad flicked through the menu. "Where's Keira?"
I gulped. "In hospital. She's had several seizures."
"Ah." Dad paused. "How come?"
I shrugged uneasily. "They think it's epilepsy. Really, there's no other rational explanation. Her first one was on my thirteenth birthday. She just... One moment she was fine, the next she'd collapsed on the kitchen floor."
"Epilepsy." Dad chuckled. "Doubt that."
I froze, dumbfounded. "Sorry? What's funny?"
How could he laugh at something so serious? His daughter lay in hospital, critically ill.
"No, no. Keira didn't have a seizure because of 'epilepsy.' No, she had the seizure from the amount of drugs she's consumed."
I stared at him, feeling my forehead crinkling. "*Drugs*? Dad, she's nine!"
"Precisely," Dad said. "Because she is nine, the drugs have worse effects on her body."

I kept my eyes on him as the waitress placed our drinks on the table. "Thanks," I said distractedly.
Dad turned back to me after she left, clasping his hands together.
"*What* drugs?" I demanded.
"I thought *I* was behind." Dad sighed. "Your mum has been giving Keira drugs for months."
My eyes widened. Could that be true?
Well, why would he lie about that?
"I don't get it," I muttered.
Dad sighed again. "Sandra has been manipulating your sister. She ordered Keira to conceal the secret, that I was... *am* alive, and threatened her with the punishment of drugs if she told anyone."
I gasped, my hand flying to my mouth. "Who did Keira tell?" I queried.
"No one. That's how your mother manipulated her. She pushed her to keep the secret, but still went ahead and did what she promised not to do. And since Keira is so young and vulnerable, she believed her." Dad shook his head. "Poor Keira can't stick up for herself. She's too shy, and Sandra took advantage of that."
I slouched in my chair, sipping my strawberry milkshake. Dad pierced the straw through his juice.
"So that's how Keira's seizures began?" I asked, gulping.
Dad nodded slowly. "Yep. I'm surprised her body lasted so long before she had a seizure, or any type of reaction."
I looked at the table. My mum hadn't only hidden Dad, but had mentally destroyed my innocent little sister. With a lurch, I realised that if Keira knew the truth this whole time, her depression couldn't have been triggered by Dad's 'death.' Instead, it must've been Mum's harsh words, her damaging actions. Anger swished through me, crushing my bones with a tight squeeze.
How dare Mum shatter Keira's life like that?
I hesitated. "So, why did Mum hide you?"
Dad slurped his drink, then put it down. "Well, to start with, it was for my own sake. She and this Tim, Lara's dad, were seeing each other but he knew Sandra still carried loving feelings for

me... We were still married. He thought I was a con man, so didn't want her to come running back to me. That's why Sandra hid me... under that horrible grave. So claustrophobic." He shivered. "Well, suddenly one day, Sandra said with a large beam that Tim had died. It was only a short while later that I realised she'd murdered him."
I sucked in a breath. Another thing to add to the list.
"Mum killed Tim, Lara's father, and the other victims? She was the pilot of the aeroplane?"
Dad nodded, gulping. "Yes, that's correct. Afterwards, I begged for my life back, said I didn't need to hide any longer. But your mum..." A tear forced its way down Dad's cheek. He breathed in. "She told me she'd faked my death... said my apparent murder was a major case in which there were searches for the killer..."
I gestured for him to continue, desperately needing him to drop all he knew, allowing us to expose Mum and her illegal actions.
"She said the money was pouring in fast... She chose the cash over me in a split second. We had a row, and I came over to your house one night..."
So that was the voice I'd recognised only too well. Early in the morning of mine and Keira's sleepover, the quarrel had woken me up.
"Did Mum leave you on your own at night? Just to roam around..."
Dad bit his straw. "Mmm-hmm. She claimed that even with plastic surgery, someone might notice me. At night it was less of a risk, but she restricted where I could and couldn't go. Last month, I was too angry and flatly refused to obey your mother."
I suddenly realised I'd picked up my wit and recklessness from Dad. He'd inspired me as a child, and him leaving my life for so long had stabbed at my heart. My chest tightened with the grasping pain that had consumed my lungs for so long.
But now, sat in front of my dad, my head felt clearer - as if because I knew he wasn't dead, I could finally relax.
Kind of.
There was something major I didn't understand. "If the police taped off the scene, whose body did they find and where were

they buried?" I shivered at the prospect of the reporters mistaking someone else's corpse for Dad's.
Dad sat back in his chair, holding his hands over his bulging stomach. "Well, your mother gave a load of police officers and news reporters and journalists money... lots of it. To obtain the truth, but still show up late evening at the cafe. No one else was obligated to view the 'body.'"
"And the grave?"
"Ah." Dad smiled sadly. "The grave was a hoax. Designed by some paid professionals."
I rolled my eyes. By now, nothing shocked me. Mum's measures worsened by the minute.
"That patch of grass above my 'coffin' was also fake," Dad went on, a look of disgust unfurling on his face.
I finished my drink and reached into my pocket.
"How've you been?" Dad asked, resting his head in his palm.
I breathed deeply. Where should I start? The kidnapping? My concussion? How about being a resident in the care home, and then getting trapped in the fire?
Instead, I straightened my posture, slamming money onto the table. "We'll talk some other time. It's almost 4:00pm and I have a meeting later..." I trailed off, unable to pursue my lie.
Dad nodded solemnly. "Of course... I should get back. Are you free tomorrow? For another chat?"
"Yes." I faltered, aware I wouldn't be available tomorrow.
I couldn't possibly be.
I apologised inwardly to Dad. I'd only just figured out the truth, and now I'd be the one departing from *him*.

Chapter 25

9:45pm arrived and I grew agitated of Jennifer's persistent complaining. She continually warned me of Lara's new outbreak of emotions. Said she might influence me into doing something I'd regret.
As if.
"I'm going out," I huffed, barging past Jennifer and sliding my shoes on.
Jennifer rushed out from behind the reception desk. "It's late, Ava. Where could you possibly be going at a time like this?"
I flung open the door. To my horror, Lara stood on the doorstep, tapping her foot.
Jennifer gasped as she clocked her. "*No*, Ava. I forbid you to leave the care home with this... *girl*." She spat the last word.
My eyes pierced into hers. "Why not? Perhaps this'll be the final time seeing me." With that, I turned and stomped after Lara, down the path and along the wide street beyond.
Lara stared at me as we walked, as if I'd impressed her somehow. "Not goody-two-shoes pulling an attitude towards Jennifer." She tossed her hair off her shoulder.
I shrugged, strutting onwards, the night air cool and soothing. The nerves circulating my body decreased to nothing as we rounded the corner. No one was in sight. All the houses were either pitch black or had their curtains closed.
Nevertheless, I slowed my pace as we neared a field.
"Ava, hurry up otherwise someone will see the aeroplane and this won't work," Lara hissed.
I glanced at her. She seemed so confident. In all honesty, I didn't get why I was jumping from an aeroplane. Surely there was a much easier way?
"Lara," I whispered as we trekked across the sodden soil. My trainers sank into the gooey mud and I cringed. "I forgot to leave a note. For Angie, Anya, Isobel and Keira."
Lara looked ahead. "OK," she said. "Guess it'll cause them less pain when you're gone."
I stood rooted to the ground for a moment, close to tears.

We manoeuvred forward after a minute, rubbing our sticky shoes on a patch of grass before boarding the aeroplane.
Lara stepped inside first. As I followed, the aeroplane shook stiffly whilst holding my weight.
"Sit." She pointed to the seat behind hers.
I obeyed, gulping anxiously.
Lara set off, the plane swaying slightly. I felt sick.
"Are you all right?" she called.
I giggled sarcastically. "A twelve-year-old girl is flying an aeroplane high into the air," I said. "No, I'm not all right!"
She pulled a face. "I'm experienced. Dad taught me at a young age."
I raised my eyebrow uncertainly.
Ten minutes passed by. Lara let the plane float gently in the air. She opened the doors.
"Stand on the edge," she said. "Go on."
I did as she said. A strong breeze blew into the aeroplane, smacking my face with a powerful force.
"After three?" she suggested.
I looked down. I could see nothing, except pitch black. It made me feel nauseous.
Shaking my head, I faced her. "Ten."
"OK." She nodded.
My whole body trembled as I placed my foot on the edge. I wanted to scream, plunge Lara out of my way and fly the plane back down to safety.
I couldn't move. My breathing grew shallow.
"Nine!" Lara shouted.
I closed my eyes, bracing myself.
"Te-"
A jarring noise drowned Lara out, followed by a shining light. The helicopter hovering in the air inches away from us thrust a blast of wind in through the door of the aeroplane.
I staggered backwards, losing my balance and falling flat on my back.
Shielding my eyes, I squinted.
"Ava!"
It was Mum. I gritted my teeth.

What was *she* doing?
"Is she OK?" another voice in the background asked.
The speaker peered over Mum's shoulder.
Multi-coloured hair, one blue eye, one green eye.
Pandora Anderson.
Mum stuck her arms out. "Come over here, Ava, we're here to rescue you."
"I'm not in danger," I mumbled, reaching over towards the open door of the helicopter. The gap between where I stood on the aeroplane and the helicopter Mum outstretched her arms from was big, daunting. I closed my eyes tightly, wishing and hoping I wouldn't fall to my death. Cold sweat trickled down my neck, and I lunged forwards.
Which was when Lara appeared out of the shadows behind me.
Mum gasped as she took hold of my wrist, yanking me through the gap with a jolt. "You're with her?" She turned to Pandora. "You didn't tell me that!"
Pandora rolled her eyes.
"You're flying that thing back down to the ground on your own, Lara," Mum said crossly. "I suspect you'll be in trouble."
Lara disappeared and a minute later, she'd steered the aeroplane away and was heading in the direction of the field. I blinked, crumpling back against the seat. I glanced at Pandora, a smile of appreciation masking the fear on my face. "Thank you." I spun to Mum. "We need to talk, now."
Mum looked bewildered. She nodded slowly. "We do."
No one said a word until we were back at the care home.

I wrung my chestnut hair with numb fingers. Unfortunately, but not surprisingly, it had started raining not too long before.
Typical. Just my luck.
Marching angrily through the familiar hall, I peered over my shoulder. Mum was close behind.
Angie explained that there was a private room, right at the end of the hall. She and Jennifer gave me permission to use it, in case I needed to shout or scream.

The walls inside were soundproof. Perfect and very appropriate for the swearing and yelling I'd set free in moments to come. All in Mum's face.
She deserved it.
Tempting as it was, I managed to suppress my emotions until we were inside the room. Just about.
"What the HELL, Mum!" I screamed, slamming the door shut. "Explain everything. You better be completely honest. If you lie, I'll get Angie to send you STRAIGHT to prison without hesitation."
Mum clicked her knuckles carelessly.
"You don't even understand... You look so proud of yourself," I sneered.
"I haven't done anything wrong," Mum muttered.
As if I'd buy her lies. "I strictly told you to NOT lie!" I screeched.
Mum pursed her lips, looking infuriated. "I'm NOT lying," she insisted.
Ugh, does she think I'm that foolish?
I thrust my arms behind my back, glowering. I could barely restrain my contempt. I badly longed to shove all my thoughts and feelings into Mum's smug, evil face.
I pondered, stroking my chin. I allowed myself two options: persuade Mum to confess the truth naturally or deceive her, making her eventually disclose everything, which would prompt her to spend her life in prison.
Forthwith, I chose the latter.
"Right, Mum. I've decided to make this simple. You confide in me, I zip my mouth and keep it shut. Sound good?"
Mum contemplated it, chewing her lip. She was willing to accept, but something held her back. "You already figured everything out," she reminded me. "Why don't *you* tell me what you know? I'll tick it off the checklist."
"Fine," I agreed. "You bullied and manipulated Keira, threatening her with drugs if she didn't obey and fed them to her anyway, killed all those victims in the aeroplane incident, including Lara's parents, and exploited Lara herself." I wrung my hair out again. Droplets of rain splattered onto the bare floorboards.

Mum counted each point off on her fingers. A new type of annoyance swept through my bones. She was so prideful, so smug.
Leaning against the stripped, stark wall, I clenched my jaw, twiddling my thumbs agitatedly.
"Correct," Mum said finally. "Spot on."
Of course, there was also her hiding my dad, crying to the world about his death but knowing his whereabouts all along, hungry for the millions entering her bank account. I couldn't tell her this; if Keira or I were in danger, I might work out how to use my secret and Mum's ignorance to my advantage. If Dad appeared out of the blue, Mum would be thrown - unaware I knew her wicked intentions - and we would win.
"Why'd you hurt so many people?" I demanded. "Me, Keira, Lara... Why?"
Mum grimaced. "I...I..." she stammered. "For protection."
"*What?*" I struggled to believe this. "How can mentally disturbing three kids be for *protection*?" I clenched my fists. "You're lying, AGAIN!"
Mum surrendered, frightened at last. "I'm not, I'm not. Tim, Lara's dad, was all 'in love' at the time Darren and I took a break. Tim and I hooked up. He threatened me, roaring that if I went back to Darren, he'd kill him. So I hid him for an hour or two... That was before he was stabbed. He's not alive now, I promise." Mum shrugged.
I gritted my teeth. The woman thought I was stupid.
Tears spouted from her soft eyes, and I propelled myself off the wall, slumping into the chair opposite her. I felt desperate, helpless. Angie had insisted that Mum would listen to her daughter, but I wasn't sure. Apart from being a kid, I'd lost all confidence, all self-control. My world had shattered, leaving me disorientated, unable to stand on my own feet.
I rested my head in my palms, debating my upcoming actions. "That doesn't explain why you used Keira and Lara," I said.
"They were already both in a vulnerable position. I used that to my advantage... Whatever, you don't need to know everything."
As if she thought her secrets would be private forever.

I already knew her intentions. She'd never stopped hiding Dad. Tim might've threatened him and spoken a load of rubbish, but it was Mum's choice to kill Tim and pursue her dream of becoming rich. That's what it had been about; Mum received two thousand pounds each month, all because it kept her going with two daughters and the small amount of cash she made from work, despite her long hours, wasn't enough. If Dad was found and the public were informed of this, they'd have nothing to pay Mum for since Dad was successful in his job. Therefore, Mum would do what she'd promised Keira at three years old. Deposit her and Dad on an aeroplane, send them to Japan and let them live over there. Meanwhile, she would have won, receiving her money whilst the rest of us suffered. In Japan, no one knew of my dad's murder. Mum had said it'd be when Keira turned ten... which would be in three months.

In the present moment, did I forgive Mum? *Could* I forgive her?

I recalled Dad, cramped up in that grave, waiting patiently for twelve hours a day, just to escape at night when Mum released him. That wasn't rational. It was inhuman.

"You murdered Tim. Lara's mother too. Plus the other eighteen individuals on that flight," I whispered, shaking my head.

"Yes... That was mandatory. Couldn't have him strolling around. Your dad was dead by then, but I felt panicky - what if Tim killed me instead of Darren?" Mum muttered, staring straight ahead.

Seriously... is she all right in the head?

I moaned, scraping my hair off my cheek. "Mum... Fine, fair enough. Why on an aeroplane? Since when could you control one?"

Mum shot me a sideways glance. "Tim taught me." She faltered. "It was quite easy. I knocked the original pilot out, stole the aeroplane, pretended I'd host the flight. Tim met up with Lara's mum again. He'd informed me about their booked holiday. I trooped after them, loitering around the area, stalking them onto the aeroplane. No one else was conscious of the fact that the first pilot was absent. I snuck on, soared into the sky and caused the accident."

She paused. "Tim still loved me... He obeyed my orders, forcing everyone to sit at the back of the plane, therefore it was easy for me to cause the crash and survive."
Her response made sense.
Her attitude didn't.
"Right. Clarify why you killed the rest of them," I ordered, clasping my hands together.
"The police could've linked me to Tim's murder otherwise. I had to think of something bigger. Let's say, I'm not a very good pilot. They'd never have noticed." Mum yawned. She'd ruined so many lives, yet had the audacity to act bored.
I looked her straight in the eye. "That's sick," I spat.
Mum smirked. "Coming from you, Ava Marie."
I gaped at her. "What are you talking about?"
"Keira was almost killed. That's on you. If only you hadn't been so dumb and blamed Eric Chanell," Mum sneered. "See, you read Darren's diary entry, discovered Eric used to abuse your dad and immediately reproached the man."
Her rotten comment wasn't deniable. It'd been my fault. Eric might've kept his mouth shut, not revealing my name, but since Dad's case was out in the public, Lisa and Dan knew *I* was the girl.
"One more question." I coughed, shaking off her ugly reminder. "Who's Ashley?"
Mum's body stiffened, the irritation draining from her face. I'd hit her soft spot, asked a question that'd be difficult for her to avoid.
"Is she another of your accomplices?" I snarled.
"No, Ava. I'll explain. Give me a minute." Mum leaned back on her chair, almost tipping it over. She didn't react, just continued stretching out her arms. Her cheeks turned pale, an ashen, washed-out type of pale.
I rhythmically drummed my foot on the ground beneath me. Waiting seemed like an eternity. I checked my brand-new watch, scrolling through the limited apps on the miniature screen.
"Ava," Mum whispered.
I faced her, raising an eyebrow expectantly.

"Ashley works in A&E. I Skyped her, offering her one thousand pounds if she let me borrow one of the office rooms... for that meeting with Angie." Mum sighed.
I froze, dumbstruck. "Angie didn't plan the meeting? Is she even a policewoman? Investigating my dad's murder?"
"Yes. I've known Angie for years. I lost contact with her after Darren's search stopped... She was banned from speaking to our family due to the drama, but I found her again. Said I had a plan that'd involve her... I didn't expect the stupid woman to slide over to your side. She took a shine to you then, Ava, and apparently that didn't change. But it will. Mark my words."
I shuddered at the edgy tone of her voice. "Angie won't believe you," I said defiantly.
"Ava, it's hard to think of you as my daughter at this moment in time," Mum smirked.
"I feel the same," I snapped.
Mum grinned, displaying her glistening, flawless row of teeth. "I didn't lie. The truth's out, I'm finished, and this conversation remains between the two of us."
"Oh... I lied," I snarled. "I'll divulge this conversation in approximately... twelve hours."
Mum's grin disappeared, along with her intimidating glare. "You backstabbing, deceiving-"
"Deceiving? *Me?*" I shouted, outraged. "You deceived Keira. Instructed her to conceal a foul secret, pushing her to believe a lie, just to please yourself anyway... disgusting."
"You're so oblivious, you sly, toxic girl," Mum hissed, her angry tone returning. This was unfortunate for me.
I sat silently, scratching my thigh. An itch escalated across my body, tormenting me.
Mum stared at me. She watched every move I took, not speaking a single word. I was still suppressing my own fury, attempting to push it down like I did with the voice in my head. It was the only way to punish it. However, it still didn't leave, always haunting me, tightening my chest once in a while.
Mum breathed deeply. "I'm sorry, Ava. I didn't mean this."
I jerked my head up, shocked at her sudden apology. Being honest, it was the last thing I expected after her previously bitter

tone. “Don’t bother apologising now. It’s done,” I muttered, flicking at a loose piece of wallpaper.
“I’m capable of changing... I can pick apart my mistakes and learn from them. I love you and Keira with my whole heart... please.” Mum started weeping, heavy tears falling from her eyes, splatting onto the wooden table positioned in front of her.
My lips quivered slightly. “Mum...”
“Stop. I understand you hate me. I’ve made some disgusting decisions, I’m an adult and should be smarter than that. I beat myself up every day, wishing I’d treated my two daughters like I was family and not a fake friend. Protecting you and Keira wasn’t my main priority... Now I realise it should have been. I want... I want a couple of days to... prove you wrong and myself right.”
I considered this. Would you voluntarily forgive a family member after they’d committed one million crimes in one? Mum was far from aware of my knowledge about Dad still being alive. She’d lied about that, said he’d actually been stabbed that night and that all her wrongdoing had taken place beforehand.
She was a manipulator, a bully to my sister and an exploiter of my pre-school best friend. Not to mention she was a murderer, too. I wouldn’t ever forgive her unexplainable actions, her unhinged mindset... but if I gave her a second chance, perhaps she’d somehow be a solid lead to more answers I could hand over? Possibly about why her intentions were so cruel?
“I’ll give you five days,” I murmured croakily. “Five days. If you’ve not fixed your way of life by then, I reveal all your secrets and you get sent to prison.”
Mum mopped her eyes with her sleeve. I saw a circular stain from where a tear had landed, and hoped I’d made the correct decision.
“Perfect. So perfect. Thank you, Ava.”
The look in Mum’s eyes hadn’t caught up with her change in attitude.
She was fearless, bold. Suspicious, unpredictable.
Far, far from the picture of an admirable, reliable woman.

Chapter 26

Dad and I met up again. Luckily, I knew where to find him. He was cramping up, his legs rigid as he jumped up and out. We walked to the cafe, buying dessert and a milkshake.
It cheered me up. Once I told him one thing, everything else spilled out of my mouth. Soon, he was aware of all the events that'd taken place since his supposed death.
"I can't believe you're my daughter," Dad said, about a million times. "It's been so long."
I grinned up at him, slightly stunned myself.
He explained he'd been the person behind the Halloween costumes and the money. "I longed to do everything possible, send some sort of signal to the police, but of course, they didn't know it was me. I stole the cash from Sandra and I dispatched a bird off with the letter..." He clocked my expression. "Don't ask. Paper blew over twenty-four-seven, and Sandra accidentally left a pen. As for the bird... well, it all became a bit like Harry Potter."
I listened intently. He praised how amazing I'd been, how I'd chosen to put my life at risk to help him. Deep down, I felt awful. Eric and Ellis had sent the wrong sister into care. Poor Keira had had her world shaken up by Mum. Her shyness and fear were attached to a long rope, swinging back and forth constantly. My position was daunting, harrowing, but compared to my little sister's, it was nothing.
"I'll see you again soon," Dad said, drawing me into a hug.
I smiled up at him, my cheeks wet with tears. "Hopefully we won't have to hide our conversations in the future. We just need to gather proof... somehow."
Dad nodded. "Somehow," he repeated.
It wouldn't ever be as simple as that.

Keira had phoned from the hospital earlier that morning. She'd sounded a lot jollier, blabbering excitedly.
The nurse came onto the phone, wanting to speak to me. "Keira's bloods are good. She did have a mini seizure last night..." She stopped.

"What?" I urged, knowing there was something she wasn't telling me.
The nurse sighed heavily. "My colleague prescribed her the wrong medication. We assumed her seizures were occurring because of epilepsy, since she'd had two seizures without any other reason, but it doesn't seem to be that at all."
I bit my lip. Of course, I knew this. But I didn't dare say the truth, as then I'd have to report everything I suspected.
It was too complex.
I ended the call in a daze.
That evening, Lara and I got into an argument. She found out I'd covered up Mum killing her dad and naturally thought that I was involved.
"I totally took you as a genuine person!" she shouted at the top of her lungs. "But you really are the spitting image of your mother. Attitude and everything."
I kept my anger back, holding my tongue. I wasn't like my mum. Not at all. She was foul, evil. I was outgoing and impulsive, but at least I *acted* like a human.
I insisted I wasn't my mum, but she strongly disagreed, fighting my every word.
"You're the most horrible friend. You spread how I'm unstable, wicked, but what about you? Your mum really has rubbed off on you. Honestly, you're pathetic, Ava."
I gave up arguing.
She didn't. "I wish the suicide attempt worked." Her voice carried a daring tone.
I took a breath in. "OK," I said. "Let's try again."
I closed my mouth. I hadn't meant it... or had I? My lips were dry and my throat felt as if it had a million sharp needles stuck inside it. I couldn't breathe, couldn't force my aching legs to keep me upright for much longer. The pain was excruciating, intolerable.
My life consisted of two kind-hearted, beautiful best friends, an admirable, talented younger sister and four exhilarating children stuck in such unpredictable positions, yet persisting to be energetic and hopeful.
Nevertheless, I still found myself feeling more and more lifeless and lonely as the days swept by.

Lara's eyes enlarged. "Ava-"
I held up my hand, interrupting her mid-sentence. "Don't pretend you don't want me gone now," I snapped.
"I don't... Ava, I should tell you something."
"What?" I grabbed onto her arm. "What?!"
I suddenly felt desperate.
Scared.
"Your mum has... Keira."
I gasped. "No... NO! Wait, what do you mean?" I demanded , frantically trying to force an answer from her.
"I can't... Ava, you just said you want to-"
"LARA, tell me where Keira is!" I screamed.
Lara bit her lip, looking me in the eye, guilt swamping her perfectly rounded face. Without thinking, I cornered her, gripping her throat with my hand. She glared at me, her eyes filled with fear and contempt.
"Tell me! Where is my SISTER?" I bellowed, anxiety swarming my stomach as I felt her pulse beneath my clutch. I loosened my grip.
Lara's expression begged me to let her go, to let her answer my question.
I released her.
"Goodness, Ava. You could have killed me!" Lara muttered, clasping her sore throat.
"Yes, and if you don't tell me WHERE my mum has Keira, I'll make your life hell!" I threatened.
Lara attempted to mask her fear. "Your mum is in that house she took you to for your birthday. You know, that one with the hills surrounding it and the lake..."
I nodded, rushing to the door and flinging it open. Lara was running after me. I began panting, my legs trembling as I flew over the pavement, hard and uncomfortable under my bare feet. I gasped for breath, not stopping until I reached the bus stop. I shoved about ten strangers out of my way as I barged onto the bus, not bothering to pay for a ticket. The bus driver didn't seem to care, and just closed the doors and sped off. No one else was on the bus - no one to see my terror, the nerves eating away at my lungs.

No one except...
I couldn't believe it. I turned sideways.
"Eric? What are you doing?" I asked, my guts tightening, my fear spinning out of control.
It seemed the closer I got to my destination, more and more panic clutched at every single muscle in my body.
"Lara rang me immediately. Ava, your mum is out of her head..." Eric paused, stroking his chin.
I instantly realised Lara had alerted him to why my mother had Keira. "She didn't even tell *me* why Mum kidnapped Keira, the little witch," I barked, anger pushing the horror away, my chest cramping, my fists burning with hot rage.
Eric glanced at my clenched hands, avoiding eye contact. I looked at his features, focusing on something other than the roaring fury blocking my throat.
I'd tried so hard to deceive Mum. Yet still she'd put on an act, promising she'd change and make up for her mistakes. I felt numb, hollow. I'd failed, I really had. Mum had killed Tim and the aeroplane victims. My sister was with her now, probably quivering as the very person who'd birthed her screamed and swore and possibly...
"Ava." Eric's voice pierced through me. "I need you to *promise* me you'll be safe."
"Eric, what the hell has Mum got Keira for?" I demanded, ignoring his concern.
Eric looked uncertain, raising his hand to tuck a strand of hair behind his ear and realising he *had* no hair. At any other moment, I'd laugh. But the humour had been squeezed out of me, leaving nothing but an empty, disturbing apprehension curling around my heart.
Eric's face was covered in remorse.
"Can't this bus go any FASTER?" I growled.
"Ava, it's already going too fast," Eric said.
I glowered at him. "Shut up. It needs to go QUICKER!" I yelled the last word and the bus sped up.
Eric held onto the bar in front of his seat, the colour draining from his cheeks. "You're insane!" he shouted over the jarring engine noise.

I slouched down, hoping and praying my little sister would be safe and OK. She should be. What reason would Mum have to hurt her?
Come on, Ava. Your mum may have had a reason to kill Tim, but what about the other victims? She's capable of murdering anyone she desires.
My inner voice was telling the truth, repeating it again and again. It rang in my ears as if reminding me one hundred times...
Keira had been kidnapped.
The woman who'd raised us wasn't a good person.
She'd kill my sister.

Eric followed me off the bus. I covered my ears as his unnecessary chatter rang through them. He eventually gave up, muttering to himself. His footsteps dragged on the pavement. My feet were still bare and cold, often sticking to the ground.
"Ava, you realise that if Sandra has your sister, she could abduct and kill you too?" Eric piped up stubbornly.
I rolled my eyes. "Yes, I figured that. She won't hurt me. I hold information that could throw her in a jail cell to rot." I shoved my hair back.
"Ooh, you're such an angel, aren't you?" Eric mocked.
I stuck my hands in my pockets. They were turning a deep purple.
Freezing to death didn't appeal to me at that particular moment.
"Where's this house?" Eric asked, his brow arching as if he thought I was lost.
I gritted my teeth, holding them tightly together against the chill of the breeze. This man never stopped blabbering.
I kept trailing along, hands on my hips.
Minutes later, I heard Eric snicker behind me. I spun around.
"You look like an idiot," he said matter-of-factly.
"I'm just getting prepared." Irritation pricked at my patience. Eric was getting on my last nerve.
He smiled. "You're a sweet reminder of my daughter," he said softly.
I gaped at him. Eric had *kids?* "Your daughter?" I gasped.

Eric stared sadly at me. "Yes. She was kidnapped, along with my wife."
"I... I'm sorry..." A tear escaped my eye, rolling silently down my cheek. I knew first-hand how devastating it could be to lose a loved one to a cold-hearted criminal.
Eric dismissed my sympathy with a swift swipe of his hand. "*That's* why I pray you'll be safe. Sandra is immoral and deranged. Children certainly do not deserve a parent like that." He hesitated. "Especially not you and Keira."
He turned me gently towards him and put his arms around my shoulders.
I hadn't realised how touch-deprived I'd been these last days, not until I felt his warm arms around me and breathed in his peppermint scent.
I peered over his bony shoulder. The sun was low in the sky, swirly pinks and yellows pirouetting across the horizon. Nonetheless, it was freezing cold.
Eric set me free and I stepped backwards, tripping over my own feet.
"Whoopsies." I laughed as Eric caught my hand. "Thank you."
"No worries," Eric replied. "Now, where is this house?"
I glanced around, collecting my bearings. We still seemed to be quite far away; the house was in the middle of nowhere and the only things surrounding it were the lake and hills.
Problem was, hills were a reoccurring sight. They existed all over, not just around Mum's new place.
"Gosh, this is daunting," I whispered, unable to suppress my terror.
Eric nodded, peering at me. "You've gone pale. Please don't pass out on me." His voice shook considerably.
We trudged across about half a dozen more plain, boring pathways, nothing but trees and hedges nearby. Even the sun gave up on us, leaving the sky grey and bleak.
"Ava, maybe you should call your mum?" Eric suggested unwisely.
I raised my eyebrows, unimpressed. "Oh... my mum? The one that has kidnapped my sister? Perfect, good idea."

He grimaced at my sarcasm. “Well, you continue your journey. It’s making me feel so optimistic that you know where you’re going,” he said.
“Doubting me isn’t helping.” I pressed my lips together.
We prowled further onwards in silence. I often sensed Eric’s gaze on my shivering body, but I said nothing.
I kicked at the damp mud underneath my feet, flicking it up and into the air. Just as I began to feel less confident, I spotted the house across the stretch of captivating field.
The lake lay among the grassland, sparkling blue in the faint light. I glanced at it in awe, the same way I had done on my birthday.
I pointed my finger, extending it further to ensure Eric had seen it too.
“Ava, I’m coming in with you,” he said.
I stared at him as my hair flew gracefully out behind me. To others, I was just a silhouette in the dim light, far away. Too far away to touch, to hold, to visualise.
But here, I felt as if I were the bravest girl in the world. Despite my racing heart beating painfully against my ribs, I was about to fight a murderer, a criminal... my mum.
My mum.
“Perfect idea,” I said. “I need you there.”
Eric looked from me to the house and back again. His smile was shadowed with anxiety... similar to the way I felt inside.

My shaking hand reached for the door handle. I rattled it. Locked.
Eric was looking intently at the windows, all of which had their flowery curtains pulled closed.
“Eric, the door is locked.” I yanked at it one more time, swearing.
“Language, young lady.” He walked over to me, pushing my hand out of the way.
He didn’t seriously think I’d consider my language at a time like that, did he?
“Stupid door won’t budge,” he growled. “MOVE you silly little-”
“Language, old man,” I teased.

He slowly paused, turning towards me. "You are so far over your-"
The door squeaked open. Eric snatched his hand off the handle, retreating.
A towering, burly man stood in the doorway, his dirty-blond hair almost reaching his shoulders. His round, brown eyes glowed in the dim light and I could instantly tell how dominant he was.
The man's eyes widened, flashing with momentary shock as he looked Eric up and down.
And then his glare landed on me. He shot me a sickening grin. "Could it be Avery Hayloft?" he snarled.
In that moment, all my confidence disappeared. I tried to back away, but my legs wouldn't budge, wouldn't follow my lead. My heart pounded, the voice in my head deafening.

Chapter 27

Dan grabbed my wrist, hauling me inside. He gripped a handful of my hair, pulling it tight, all focus on Eric.
"You brought her to me," he said. "Making up for betraying your mother and me, huh?"
Eric's eyes widened and he shook his head quickly. He looked at me. "I wouldn't have brought the girl to you even if you'd paid me." He straightened his posture, sticking out his chin.
Dan bellowed with laughter. "Then why are you here?"
"I was just-" I started.
"Shut up. Did you hear me asking *you*?" Dan tugged my hair harder.
I swore in agony.
"Ava wanted to see her mother," Eric said calmly. "She thought her sister might be here too."
"I can help Avery. You're correct, her mum and sister are right upstairs." Dan released my hair with a final heave and grasped my hand.
It felt warm with sticky sweat. I heaved.
Eric stepped inside, but Dan shoved him backwards.
"I'm capable of showing the girl upstairs," he said firmly.
Eric's eyes widened with alarm. "No, no... Wait, why are *you* in Sandra's house?"
Dan grinned. His nails were piercing through my skin, clawing at my veins.
"You stay put, Eric. I'll take Avery upstairs and I'll be back." He faltered. "I won't hurt her..."
Dan kicked the door shut and pulled at my wrist. I attempted to slap him in the face, but he pushed my hand away.
"Still haven't learned to stay still, have you?" Dan spat, dragging me up the wide set of stairs. Photos of Mum, Dad, Keira and me lined the grey walls, all in gold-rimmed photo frames.
Each photo I trudged by seemed to light up an old memory.
I couldn't stare at them for long; Dan was practically running up the stairs.
I swore.
"You're a little devil," Dan growled as we reached the landing.

Three medium-sized bedrooms were ahead of us. Photos scattered the walls, mostly of me and Keira when we were younger. Baby pictures, toddler pictures, pictures taken recently.
Dan dragged me towards the first bedroom, booting open the door and flinging me inside. I fell with a thump.
I'd landed on a cream carpet, plump and comfy.
"Dan, what the heck are you doing?" a woman's voice screeched.
My blood ran cold as I looked up.
About thirty centimetres away, Keira sat tied up on a wooden chair, a gun pointing at her jaw.
A lady with straggly brown hair towered over her, sneering.
"Conveniently, I'm here with your daughter," Dan said, striding over.
Mum glared in my direction. Her expression registered disturbance, disgust. She marched over, swaying sexily, thrusting the gun into Dan's arms.
She muttered something to him and he disappeared.
"Oh, jeez. Who brought you?" Mum asked, dragging me roughly to my feet.
"I brought myself. Got the bus, found this house..."
Mum frowned. "No, how did you *know* I was here?"
I didn't wish to snitch on Lara. Mum had caused enough trouble for that girl to last a lifetime.
"I... guessed. Guessed you wouldn't have kept your promise, and that you're always going to be an evil witch," I huffed.
"Ahh, yet I got you... again. The lies just keep coming, keep falling off my tongue," Mum seethed, clutching my arm tightly.
I scowled, anger twitching at my palms. "What's your master plan this time? Why were you aiming a gun at Keira?"
It hit me that Mum must have kidnapped Keira from the hospital, the hospital in which the nurses were trying to keep my sister from dying.
From - surprise - the suffering Mum had brought upon her.
Mum laughed. "I take it back, you are foolish." She paused. "DAN!"
Dan appeared in the doorway, his breath lagging.
"Did Eric bring Ava?"

"Yes, I told him I'd go back and fetch him after pulling Avery up here," Dan replied.
"Then go. Collect him. He must've told Ava I was here... She was about to commit suicide. I made sure my intentions were in Lara's hands..."
I gasped. Lara hadn't wanted me dead... Mum had. She'd manipulated Lara, again.
I knew exactly why.
Mum's plan was to shove Keira on an aeroplane with Dad and send them far away to a country where no one knew of their existence, and no one would question why Keira was with a random man - which was what Dad looked like, after his plastic surgery.
Nobody would give them a second glance.
All of this mess, just so she could continue to receive the money.
But me? She couldn't possibly have me around.
So she'd arranged for Lara to guide me, *convince* me, to take my life. She'd backed out at the last minute, not able to conceal Mum's secret for any longer. She'd told me where Keira and Mum were so I could save Keira's life.
I inwardly sent my thanks out to Lara.
One thing didn't make sense...
"Why did you *stop* me, *save* me, from committing suicide the first time? I was about to die... You rescued me."
"OK... That wasn't my intention. But Lara told Keira and Keira informed Pandora. Because of this, Pandora understood everything. Where Lara was taking you in the aeroplane. Stupid girl really thought Keira would remain quiet about such a secret. When she asked me to go with her, I certainly couldn't just say no. But Pandora never informed me you were up there with someone. I didn't think Lara would fly you in an *aeroplane*." Mum scrunched her hands into fists.
"You're cruel. You *promised* me, Mum."
Mum's eyes scanned mine and I genuinely thought she would apologise, pull me into her arms, take Keira and me back home.
"You should've known, Ava, my promises mean nothing," she snarled. "Keira will die and I'll keep you as a slave or something."

“I’ll just tell everyone what I know,” I threatened, raising an eyebrow.
Mum chuckled. “Nah, you won’t. Because if you do, I will kill your dad... I’m serious this time. Whilst the world was searching for a non-existent murderer these past years, they’ll be looking for a real one this time... Mark my words.”
I peered over towards Keira. She was hunched over, her hands trembling, her eyes scared.
She avoided my gaze.
“Why would you consider killing Keira?” I enquired.
Mum shot me a disdainful glare. “Your sweet little sister will not ever be brave enough to fly on an aeroplane with your dad. She’s too vulnerable, too shy. I’ll have to keep your father hidden... and kill Keira. Otherwise, this won’t work. I’m the villain in this story, Avery.”
Dan reappeared, his muscular hand clasping Eric’s neck and Mum’s gun aimed at the side of his head.
She shuffled over. “Get off him, Dan. The gun is meant to murder *Keira*. Quit taking advantage of the weapon,” she grunted, flapping him away.
“I thought we were shooting the other two?” Dan complained.
I shuddered at his words. Suppose we all died? No one would ever realise that Dad was alive and Mum was hungry for cash. The public would continue to search for a murderer.
Mum wouldn’t drop any hints.
She’d win.
Eric crawled over to me. He put his arm around my shoulder.
“Eric, what in the world are you doing? Did you tell Ava I was here?” Mum shrieked.
“I didn’t know you were here,” Eric protested. “After I’d received the phone call from Lara, I...”
Mum pursed her lips, putting her hands on her hips. “Lara told you?”
“No... She didn’t, I promi-” I started.
“Button your mouth,” Mum ordered. “That girl double-crossed me.” She paced towards Keira, the gun held high. Keira winced as the cold metal touched her forehead. “Dan, tie them up.” Mum

nodded at Eric and me. "Setting the care home on fire failed, so this'll be plan B."
I gasped. Mum had burned down the care home, trying to kill us... Plan A *was* to let us burn alive.
Dan obeyed. He removed a roll of string, biting off two strands. He bound Eric first, hitching his hands behind his back.
"Ouch, that hurts... *Dad*." Eric spat the last word and caught Dan's attention.
He opened his mouth, irritation shining in his eyes... then knocked Eric over, sending him flying.
I stood up, striving to reach the door, to escape.
Mum swung round, her gun facing me. "You dare escape..."
Dan grabbed my wrist, twisting me around forcefully. I wrenched myself backwards.
"Stop MOVING!" he yelled.
I felt the rough material of the string digging into my skin, cutting off my circulation. "Please let me go. I'm innocent and so is Eric," I begged desperately.
Mum shook her hair off her face elegantly.
"You're far from innocent," Dan hissed in my ear. I cringed at his stench, his hard voice ringing in my head.
He shoved me over and I landed beside Eric.
Eric had his hands on the floor, trying to manoeuvre them sideways. He stopped right at my waist, pressing his palms back. "I phoned Angie," he whispered in my ear. "She's on her way."
I looked at him doubtfully.
"She's a cop. She'll arrest them," he reassured me.
I focused on Mum. Her gun was again pressed against Keira. She was shouting at Dan, swearing.
Policewoman or not, no one would stop Mum.

Chapter 28

The room we were in must've been a guest bedroom. A bed was folded up in one corner. It was bare, with no covers or pillows. Aside from the two wooden chairs - the one Keira sat on and a spare one - the room held nothing else.

Mum and Dan were curled up on the carpet, chatting between themselves. Keira, who was temporarily untied, perched beside Eric and me.

"I'm really going to die. I can't live the rest of my life... I didn't even make it to my teens," Keira sniffed.

She'd been sobbing for about ten minutes. Mum kept glaring over at us but said nothing.

She didn't have the slightest clue that Angie would be arriving soon.

"Darling, you're not going to die," I promised weakly. Unlike her, mine and Eric's wrists were still bound. I turned my back to her so I could hold her hand.

Eric sent me a sideways glance. He was just as uncertain as me.

Keira shook her head, wiping her eyes. "Mum forced me to keep the secret, Ava. I didn't want to... I haven't seen Daddy for ages."

"Quit the pity party," Dan snarled from the other side of the room.

Keira's lip quivered.

"Yeah... I'm generous enough to offer you another hour alive, to spend sixty minutes with your sister, Keira. Do you want to spend it being so depressed?" Mum smirked, her attention on Keira.

Eric grimaced. "Pretty sure the child can spend it how she wants. You have no say."

Mum licked her lips, her eyes heavy, stern. "Be quiet."

"I'm not being quiet. If you hadn't noticed, I'm an adult too," Eric said.

"Ah, yes. You're an adult... but do you have a weapon?" Mum raised the gun.

"You won't pull the trigger," Eric declared.

Mum's face flushed. She loathed Eric and in that particular moment, she desired to shoot him dead.

Sixty minutes ticked by... Keira's time was up.
Angie didn't approach.
Dan muttered something to Mum as she stood up.
"Keira, over here," she said, clicking her fingers towards the chair.
Keira's eyes flooded with tears.
"No... Mum," I begged, crouching on my knees, my hands stuck behind me.
"Stop yapping," Mum barked. "Keira, *now*."
Keira stirred, but didn't move.
"Oh, goodness. You're nine, you cow," Mum spat.
She nudged Dan's shoulder. He rolled his eyes and rushed forward, seizing Keira and hurrying back over, throwing her onto the chair.
"Mum," I yelled desperately, "please-"
"Shut up. You're irrelevant. I will gag you myself if you don't keep out of it."
Dan tied Keira's arms behind the chair.
I twisted to face Eric. His eyes were closed and he lay on the floor, chewing his lip.
I stood up. "STOP!" I shouted as Mum pressed the gun to Keira's head. "Stop."
Mum chucked the gun on the floor, exasperated. She darted towards me, a cloth in her hand.
"NO, STOP!" I bellowed.
"You've gone too far, Missy." Mum pressed the cloth over my nose and mouth. I turned my head, left, right, left again. Predictably, I'd pass out in the next thirty seconds. The cloth smelled nauseating. My head thumped and Keira's cries became feeble.
My last few breaths were unnerved, distressed. I felt Mum's hand on the cloth.
But before I knew it, my life slowed down. The vile cloth was knocked away from my face. I stumbled, falling into Eric. Noise filled the room, ear-splitting screams and direful moans.

"What the hell are you doing, you low-life? Shove off back to where you came from. It must've been a dark, dreary hole," a voice boomed.

I tossed my hair out of my eyes and gathered my bearings. Keira was still on the chair, whimpering and weeping. Mum lay motionless on the carpet, her hair a splaying mess, draped around her head like a halo.

Angie stood above her. Clearly, she'd wrestled the gun from Mum's clutch. She was waving it about as if it were a child's toy and not a lethal weapon. Dan gawked wide-eyed at the woman, the violence replaced with a flashing awe. Angie's expression was as determined as ever, her brown eyes wide with hot fury. Both Dan's hands were held over his chest, his face glowing. Unmistakably, the man had mega heart-eyes for Angie.

Mum fidgeted on the floor, looking limp. Sitting up, she scanned the room, wrinkling her brow. Undoubtedly her head was sore, for she gripped it tightly, frowning.

Dan made an effort to regain his balance.

He failed.

His stability deteriorated further as he continued to gape at Angie. His legs wavered, unable to maintain his stance.

He collapsed.

"Stupid man." Angie lifted her nose in utter disgust.

Mum groaned, snatching Angie's attention. Angie's high heels clicked as she sauntered over, bending down and pressing the gun against her ribs. Mum's eyes widened with angst mixed with dismay.

"Your disloyalty will bury itself into my chest forever," Mum spluttered, spitting unpleasantly in the process.

Angie levelled the gun at Mum's heart. Mum shifted uncomfortably, sweat dripping from her forehead. Her arms were seemingly pinned to the ground, but from the nerves or heated wrath, I couldn't tell.

"I created you, cow," Mum sneered, thinning her lips. "You'll never be able to kill me, not before I kill *you*."

Created her? Mum *was* out of her mind. Had she convinced herself she was magical... an individual who could design human-like robots?

Angie curled her fingers around the trigger, glaring furiously. In approximately five seconds, Mum would be shot dead, killed. Eric and Keira were huddled up together in the corner, Eric stroking my little sister's immaculate hair. Keira herself was staring blankly into space, mortified, a sharp trace of dread in her eyes.

"Three." Angie's finger was firmly on the trigger.

I didn't dare breathe.

"Two."

I sprinted backwards, my legs wobbling awfully.

"One-"

"GET OFF ME!" Mum booted her leg upwards, colliding with the gun. Angie's fingers slipped and the weapon thudded to the floor.

Mum's raised fist smashed Angie in the stomach, knocking her sideways into the wall. Angie bit her lip, reaching for the gun once more, but she didn't stand a chance. Mum's anger had been building up... Now she'd release her feelings and emotions, no matter who or what she hurt.

Her eyes burned bright, her pearly-white teeth bared. She shot Angie the finger, a simple, unnecessary gesture that meant so much.

Mum was ready for business.

She extended her arm, curling her fingers and flexing them again. With a final click of her fingers, Angie stuttered backwards, smacking her head as fresh blood seeped from her arms and chest.

It wasn't as if a normal woman had just been killed in front of my eyes.

Her unexpected death felt strikingly dramatic... as if a body of pure metal had slammed into the wall, not a human being.

"You killed her!" Eric gasped, his mouth ajar.

Mum glared at Angie's corpse. She didn't look impressed, or smug, which was something. But she didn't seem regretful or remorseful, either.

"I created her, as I said," Mum said.

I braced myself. "You're joking..." I couldn't believe my mother would ever be smart enough to pull off such a feat. Not spectacular, but a talent nonetheless.
Not many people possessed the brains to do that.
"I did. She's a robot, Ava. Get it into your head." Mum kicked Angie's dead body to the right.
"But... there *must* be an Angie. She visited our house the day after Dad's supposed murder," I insisted, tears blurring my vision. Regardless, it certainly justified why Angie was so stiff and slurry when we'd first met in A&E the previous month.
Mum pursed her lips. "Yes, Avery. There is an Angie. But you won't find her. She's somewhere even your intelligence won't think of." She glared at Eric. "His wife... She visited our house the day after Darren's 'death.' Shortly after, she detected my plan and threatened me terribly. I gave her a taste of her own medicine. Kidnapped her daughter, tricked Angie and abducted her too."
Eric's eyes flared with inflamed anger, but he didn't dare fight. Mum possessed a gun, not to mention her heinous companion. On the contrary, if anyone there held the ability to provoke Mum, it was Eric.
"Aaron, Ellis, Jennifer... Didn't any of those people dig up any hints about Angie - the one lying dead on the carpet - and figure it out? That she isn't real... That she's a ROBOT?" I demanded, raising my brows.
Mum clenched her jaw. "Obviously they didn't know. The robot I designed is identical to Angie. Her skin, eyes, hair. I convinced anyone suspecting Angie had gone missing that she was this bot I'd replaced her with."
"I suppose you're impressed with yourself?" I asked, disgust pulling at my lips.
"Darling, I won't be anywhere near impressed until I kill you all." Mum's finger pointed at each of our heads.
I stepped back, blocking her view of Eric and Keira hunched together in the corner. "You'll kill me first?" I arched an eyebrow. "Otherwise, you're not getting to the others."

Mum hesitated, unhooking her gun from the sturdy belt on her jeans. "I think you'll find I'll kill whoever I want first. You're not gonna stop me, you pathetic pig."
I urged my body to operate the self-defence techniques I'd learned in Year 7. *Protect Keira and Eric, stand my guard, ensure they're safe - even if I put myself in intense danger in the process.*
None of this happened.
I was rooted to the spot, my bare feet sinking into the fluffy carpet beneath.
"Exactly." Mum cackled, her teeth bared.
She motioned to the wooden chair, standing bulky and firm in the middle of the room. She spun to face Keira. "Sit."
Keira's eyes widened. The fear plastering her face was unmissable. It sent a cold shiver down my spine. I hugged my arms around myself, my gaze intent on Keira as she crouched beside Eric.
"Fine... I'll mix this up a bit," Mum said. "Keira, if you don't move in five seconds I'll shoot your sister, right in front of your eyes. That'll traumatise you, won't it? I'll then kill you immediately afterwards."
Keira's terrified gaze met mine. She pushed herself up. I could see her legs wobbling, as if she might pass out before Mum could murder her.
My eyes remained on Mum as she aimed the gun at Keira's throat. Keira's eyelids flickered as she closed them, and I could sense the unpreventable adrenaline flowing through my little sister's bones.
My own legs almost buckled underneath me. I had to scream, cry, yell, do *anything* to prevent Keira from dying in front of Eric and me.
I didn't have any energy... I wasn't strong enough.
Mum would pull the trigger.
Keira is going to die.

Chapter 29

Rustling sounds came from outside the room. Dan stirred awake, scowling as he took in our faces.
His eye fell on Angie's corpse, the scarlet pool of crisp blood swirling around her dead body. He shivered.
Mum stormed to the door, gasping.
"AVA!" she screamed, loud enough to wake the dead.
She turned around, her eyes wide and menacing as she stared forcefully at me.
I frowned, confused as to why she could possibly be so angry.
Until I saw him saunter effortlessly into the room.
Mum raised the gun... The barrel was aimed accurately in my direction.
"You backstabbing twit," she said, her voice shrill and clear. "I don't know how, but you found and released your dad, did you not?"
"I... I..." I stammered. "Please don't kill me."
Mum laughed, lowering the weapon. "You're not worthy of living," she snapped nastily. "You mean nothing to anyone, Ava."
It felt as if she'd slapped my weak spot.
I bowed my head.
Deep down, I knew her words carried no meaning... but in my current mental state, I couldn't ignore the possibility of them being true.
"So, Darren. Lovely to see you. I guess you're another fool I'll have to kill." Mum spun the gun on her finger, strutting across the room carelessly.
Dad nodded, shrugging. "Sure. Just don't shoot my... *our* children, Sandra."
Mum's eyes flashed with love, kindness, regret... but the feeling of power must've been stronger, for her face became as hard as a mask moments later.
"You and I raised two beautiful daughters. Are you willing to choose money over family?" Dad asked in a low voice.
Mum contemplated it, chewing her lip. "You didn't raise them, Darren. I did," she spat.

Mum and Dad's bickering grew louder and tenser. I sprinted over to Keira and we huddled together. Dan hadn't regained full consciousness yet and Eric must have fallen into a deep sleep, his snores dainty and faint.

"I didn't reveal my knowledge of Dad's whereabouts to Mum as I figured it'd take her by surprise. I knew we could use this to our advantage in a situation like this... I was right," I explained to Keira between our parents' yells.

Keira clung onto my hand, still tied behind my back, and I yelped.

This sudden cry snapped Dan out of his trance, and he glared at me. "You haven't killed them?" he called to Mum.

"Shut up, can't you see I'm resolving our current situation?" Mum growled.

"Well, are they meant to be hugging?" Dan questioned slyly. .

"No, they're not hug-" Mum turned around. "Oi, get off each other!" she screamed.

I reeled backwards slightly, pulling myself away from Keira and giving her a reassuring look. She smiled, shrinking down in her chair.

Dan grabbed her by the hair, squeezing it tightly in his thick hand.

She quivered.

"Sandra, you're acting like a child. Quit being so selfish and open your eyes! Protect your girls, don't murder them!" Dad bellowed.

Are they still fighting?

"Stay STILL!"

Slap.

Dan had whacked Keira around the head.

I glanced anxiously towards Eric. He was still asleep.

Asleep at a time like this?

I ran over and smacked his thigh. He jumped, opening his eyes.

"Is everything over now?" he wanted to know, sitting up and peering around the room. "I guess that's a no." He chuckled.

I rolled my eyes. "We need your help."

Eric whined. "Why *my* help?"

I swallowed down the moan that itched in my throat. Couldn't he answer his own question?
Not that it needed asking. Dan held Keira, pinning her to the back of the chair. Mum and Dad were quarrelling, throwing their weight around, oblivious to the rest of us.
Eric still seemed clueless. I sighed, opening my mouth to speak...
Bang.
I whirled around. Dad was clutching Mum's head, hitting it vigorously against the wall.
"Daddy, stop!" Keira yelled across the room. "PLEASE!" She was hysterical.
Dad threw Mum onto the carpet. She lay stiff, lifeless.
"Did you just kill her?" Dan gasped.
Dad stared at him. "No. She deserved what she got. I hope she rots."
He walked over to Keira, unbound her and picked up her limp body. Dan didn't react; he was too shocked, too frightened.
My attention was diverted from the silent atmosphere as I remembered the gun. It was a few feet away from Mum who was stretched out on the floor, motionless.
I collapsed onto my knees, reaching out to collect the weapon that, fortunately, hadn't managed to murder anyone.
I hoisted it up, spinning around swiftly and pointing it at Dan.
"You'll let us go?" I asked.
Dan frowned. "Mmm-hmm."
In the meantime, Dad was frantically gesturing something to me. I mimed for him to speak, that I couldn't tell what he was trying to tell me. His emerald-green eyes sparkled with panic and I could only guess that his hurried signals were important.
His index finger and thumb were pinched together and he was twisting them around.
"Turn!" he mouthed.
Suddenly, before I had the chance to react, a hand grasped my waist, colliding painfully with my ribs and rotating me, sending the gun out of my clutch.
Mum tightened her grip. My stomach stung and my bones gasped for air. I was unable to breathe, unable to move. I cried out at the intolerable burn circulating my body. My blood no longer

reached my palms, nestled in my lower body only. I was numb, pushing at Mum's hand and praying she wouldn't squeeze me to death.
I tried to breathe through my nostrils instead of exhaling all the oxygen through my lips. I barely registered Dad begging for mercy, Keira's agonising whimper or Dan ramming them both back harshly.
I was unable to hear, unable to smell, unable to move.
I could feel the tip of Mum's gun stinging my throat, blocking the air I was desperate to inhale.
"I changed my mind," Mum sneered, her menacing voice hot in my ear. "I *will* kill you."
I shuddered, too scared to object.
If you give in and let her kill you, there'll be no hope of saving your sister. Her corpse will lie next to yours. Forever.
The unbearable thought clung to me, as constricting as Mum's hand crushing my throat. It stuck with me as I kicked out my foot, knocking Mum sideways. She tumbled to the floor, along with the gun. I slumped to the ground too, sucking in an excessive amount of air, panting.
Mum straightened her back, licking her lips. Her eyes shone with contempt.
She lunged for me. Groaning, I flew sideways. She missed. Stood up. Pounced for my leg. I lost my balance, thumping down full pelt on my back. I tried to ignore the throb that ate at my muscles and leapt back up. I avoided her punch and dodged her weak attempt at a karate kick.
Mum bent down, heaving up the gun. I permitted her to do so, whistling against the wall whilst waiting.
She aimed it at me. I darted from one corner to the next. Mum spun the gun in all directions. She fired. The perilous bullet lodged itself into the wall, ripping off a chunk of beige wallpaper.
Mum was a few metres away. My body refused to race around any longer. I came to a halt and bent over, heaving.
"Ava, what are you doing? Run!" Dad shouted. Dan was still barricading him and Keira on the other side of the room.
"I can't." My voice was hoarse.

Mum smirked repulsively. She'd gotten her way and she knew it. I stood rooted to the ground, the creamy carpet sticking to the bottoms of my feet. I didn't care about the gun centimetres away from my face. I'd die eventually, after all.
Two long, daunting minutes passed. The room was eerie, silent. I predicted Mum was watching to see if I moved, trying to escape again.
I stayed fixed to the carpet. Mum stomped backwards a few steps, her eyes penetrating through mine.
I heard shuffling from the corner but was too transfixed on Mum, on the gun. She pulled the trigger.
I froze, the bullet flying towards me.
Life felt like slow motion. Until the bullet hit someone...
It wasn't me.
Keira set free a bloodcurdling scream as Eric lost consciousness, crashing down to the floor.
Blood swamped his body, running down every limb. His mouth hung open, showing off his teeth that were also smothered in gore. The bullet was wedged through his heart, poking out from his t-shirt.
Eric was innocent. He'd switched his attitude and become a kind-hearted, caring man.
He'd guided me away from Mum to start with, travelled to this house with me... and sacrificed himself to protect my life.
Remorse flooded through my veins... I wouldn't allow myself to grieve just yet.
I stared at Mum. She gaped down at Eric's dead body, the gun hanging from her hand.
Dad wrestled himself out of Dan's clutch, charging over and whacking her around the head. Her legs lost their strength and she collapsed in a heap on the bloody carpet.
"Is there anything in this darn room to knock her out with?" Dad asked.
I remembered the foul-smelling cloth from earlier. It lay beside Eric's zip-up jumper in the corner of the room. I brought the jacket to my nose. It smelled strongly of sweet peppermint.
I bit my lip, swallowing the tears lurking in my throat.
I didn't allow myself to cry.

“Here.” I scrambled to pick up the white cloth, passing it over to Dad. “Knock-out drug.”
Dad nodded approvingly, pressing the cloth over Mum’s nose and mouth. “That’ll keep her out for longer,” he said.
“Shall we bolt out of here? Whilst she’s unconscious?” I asked, slipping Eric’s jumper over my shoulders.
Dad rubbed his hand across the carpet. I edged closer to the door, certain Keira was at my heel.
“Oh my goodness, the gun,” Dad muttered urgently. “KEIRA!”
I pivoted. Dan, once again, held my sister at gunpoint. Keira sat stock-still, alarmed.
I whizzed forwards. Dad did too.
Neither of us was quick enough.
“DADDY!” Keira’s spine-chilling scream echoed around the room.
My little sister was dead.

Chapter 30

I sank to my knees, my eyes drenched with endless tears, Keira's frail body deposited in front of me. Her corpse, unlike Eric's, was stiff - no blood and no bullet. I refused to accept reality; Keira couldn't possibly be dead. I looked at Dad, my hands trembling where they were pinned to my chest. He was staring at his youngest daughter. His face mirrored my emotions, scared, troubled.

My numb heart ached.

Keira had spent her life being manipulated and bullied by her own mother. She'd felt trapped, uncertain, never sure of what was coming next.

Mum had drained all chances of Keira developing into a confident child. She'd been selfish, only commanding what she wanted. Keira must've hardly coped; her whole world had consisted of Mum's strict orders. Mum didn't care if this cornered Keira, tricked her, lured her into a dark hole she was unable to escape. She was so far up her own backside, she'd cut off her family and focused on the money. Hid Dad, made mine and Keira's lives hell, beguiled Keira, almost killed her with the drugs and kidnapped real Angie and her daughter.

I suspected the list went on.

"Are you going to shoot us too? Or can we go?" Dad enquired, scanning the four bodies around us.

"No. You guys know too much," Dan said simply.

My body broke out in a hot sweat. We would be imprisoned there forever.

"Ew, are these dead bodies gonna stay here?" I wrinkled my nose.

Dan poked Eric. "No. That'd be disgusting," he said.

"Thank you. That is the kindest thing you've done," I blurted.

"It's not for you. Frankly, I don't care if you're stuck in a room with dead bodies with the metal stench of blood filling your

nostrils. I'm doing this for myself," Dan announced triumphantly.
He snickered at my reaction.
I looked at Keira. Her eyes drifted open for a second.
She was alive.
My sister put her finger to her lips and then her neck, pretending to slice her throat. "*Keep quiet. Dan knocked me out with the gun, ensuring the process was realistic enough to throw you off,*" Keira mouthed.
I stared, dumbfounded. Dan didn't shoot her.
So...
"He knocked me out silently. He didn't kill me, but he thinks the punch was enough to knock me out for a while."
Dad had noticed too. I stood up, throwing back my shoulders.
Dan glanced at me.
Jolting, I recalled Angie's past arrangements.
'Bring him here and we'll have a security camera on guard. A photo of him will be logged into the camera and it'll beep when he stands underneath, or anywhere in view.'
"I gotta use the toilet," I lied. "I'm on the verge of-"
"Then get in front and walk," Dan interrupted, using the gun to indicate the door.
Dad tugged me backwards, his forehead creased, his manner serious.
"Don't hesitate. Sprint, as fast as you can. Get Dan to the A&E department, the camera is positioned there," he whispered.
I wanted to curl up in a ball, protest that I shouldn't be the person to carry out such orders... I wasn't strong enough. I would be caught and killed.
As Angie and Dad both said, if I scurried at full speed, I'd succeed and Dan would be arrested... There was no possible way he would know my intentions, hence the camera was stationed outside of A&E and not the police station.
"Come on," Dan grunted. "You can't need it that badly."
Dad kissed me on the cheek. I sauntered in front of Dan, as instructed. We plodded across the landing, past the other rooms. He urged me downstairs, pinching my arm as we turned a corner.

Perfect. I was on the ground floor. The bathroom sat right near the front door.
"Inside." Dan shoved me. "No longer than a minute."
I locked the door, feeling awfully giddy. Taking deep breaths, I braced myself. The upcoming events would be challenging. Nevertheless, Dad and Angie had faith in me. That, at least, made me feel encouraged, determined.
"Thirty seconds left," Dan's menacing voice bellowed.
Realising I hadn't even flushed the toilet to make my fib seem realistic, I pressed down my thumb on the button, cursing. The jarring noise of the flush gurgled loudly, ringing around the bathroom walls.
"Ten seconds."
I tapped my foot on the tiles impatiently.
Hurry up, Dad.
The toilet's vibration dwindled to a low groan. I sighed with relief.
"You've got two seconds. I'll break down the door if you are not out!" Dan shrieked.
I crossed my fingers. Dad had to call out soon...
"OUCH!"
That was him.
Dan grunted. He banged the door.
"I'm gonna see what your dad is screaming about," he called. "Stay there until I come back."
I rolled my eyes. As if I'd listen to that.
Dan's footsteps sounded above my head. I unhooked the lock, pulling the door gently open. I peered out.
No one.
I inhaled a sharp breath, trudging towards the front door. It was on the latch.
Movements could still be heard from upstairs, but I knew as soon as I slammed the door that Dan would come racing after me.
I clawed at the silver chain. It was thick and sturdy. The handle was just as stiff. I tugged at it, sweat dribbling down my forehead.
Moaning quietly, I wrenched open the door. It creaked.

"Darren, shut up! What's that?" Dan's voice yelled.
My breath caught short. Distractedly, I smashed the glass, cutting my finger. I swore, removing my hand and holding it protectively to my chest.
Dan's footsteps boomed down the stairs. His face was purple and he was gasping for air. I turned on my heel and sped down the pathway. The concrete felt uncomfortable under my bare feet. I glanced over my shoulder, still running. Dan pointed the gun.
He wouldn't fire it in public.
I rushed on.
"Avery, I'm not fussy! I'll shoot wherever we are!" Dan bellowed.
I pursed my lips together, clutching my ribs.
I tripped on an uneven slab... Dan approached right behind me, almost too close.
I pleaded with my sore feet to carry me further. This mission was vital, especially now that I'd started.
"I killed your dad, Avery," Dan panted. "Your sister isn't dead, she's just knocked out. If you don't stop running, I'll shoot her too."
I shut my eyes, shaking off his unwanted words.
As Mum had said, I wasn't foolish.
Darting onwards seemed too much. All the oxygen drained from my lungs. My legs throbbed inside my jeans. This part of Shallowton surely had to be somewhat near my destination.
"You don't have your bracelet," Dan snarled behind me. "I stole it, along with your bag."
I ignored him, rounding a corner and almost slipping. A soft drizzle fell from the clouds above. My hair soon became damp. We were two blocks away from the main road.
Without warning, Dan fired the gun. I ducked, just in time. The bullet flew past me.
I looked over my shoulder. Dan zoomed down the path, his fingers grasping the gun. He met my gaze, speeding up.
I gritted my teeth, the rain quickening, my hair hugging my skin.
"Avery, I don't know what you're trying to achieve, but I own a larger brain, extra knowledge and a weapon! You're basically digging yourself further into the hole!" Dan shouted, his footsteps rhythmically thumping against the hard stone.

I considered responding, but my throat had dried up. My breathing felt jagged against my tonsils. I grimaced, swallowing the pain.
The odds of me giving up consumed my insides, and I slowed down.
'You have to sprint. Faster than ever. Otherwise he'll catch you, you'll die and we won't ever find the man. You have to dash. Without stopping.'
Quitting wasn't an option. I quickened my pace, colliding with an elderly man.
"Are you in a hurry, my dear?" he asked.
I nodded, rushing past him and approaching another turning at the end of the street.
Dan concealed the gun with his hand, still running.
I shot around the corner, past a gaggle of teenage boys. They stared at me as if I were crazy.
"Whoa! Where are you sprinting to, beautiful?" one asked, grabbing my arm.
I pushed away his hand, desperate.
Dan was right at my heel.
No matter what, this boy wouldn't let me go.
I shook my arm out of his grasp. Dan halted, right behind me. He waved the gun at the four guys and they raised their hands, then sped out of sight.
"You dumb child." Dan clasped my hair, twisting it up in his fist. He thumped me in the chest, spinning me around and ramming the gun into my ribs. I tried slipping away, but he cocked the gun. "Stay still," he hissed. "Follow my lead and you'll be safe. Move once more, and I'll kill you."
I curled my lip, contemplating my choices.
Perhaps I could shrink backwards, duck under his arm and steal the gun.
"You and Darren are a good team," Dan admitted.
I smiled, satisfied. "We really got you."
Dan scowled, pressing the gun further into my ribs. "Button it. You're as bad as each other."
I arched my eyebrow, then jumped as I felt the metal through Eric's jumper.

Dan yanked at me and I fell into step with him. He walked alongside me, nudging me with the tip of the gun every so often. I registered a road sign. A&E was three minutes away, in the other direction.
Thinking fast, I reeled backwards. Dan's gun slipped from my body and I punched his face, blocking his eyesight for a moment. Ensuring some distance lay between us, I spun around and bolted down the street, fleeing faster and harder than before. Dan's footsteps followed behind.
Angie was right; Dan really was after me.
I ran and ran, my poor feet slamming violently against the solid slabs underfoot.
I could just visualise the rear of A&E. I grinned, begging my limbs to keep flying for a minute more.
Sixty seconds, Ava. Dan'll be captured. He'll receive a bitter taste of his own medicine.
"STOP, AVERY!" Dan's shrill scream rang through the eerie silence.
I peered over my shoulder. His face had turned purple, an ugly, unattractive colour. His eyes flashed with anger, a determination different to my own. He continued to storm behind me, his footsteps deafening. I was dizzy, nauseous. My headache continued to grow, my soggy hair sticking to my cheeks, mouth and nose.
I hurtled around one last corner, encouraging my aching legs to sprint a couple more steps.
RUN. Just for a minute more. You can see the A&E entrance. He hasn't a clue. GO.
"Avery, where the hell are you going?" Dan's voice rose. "A&E won't buy you any security... I'll be waiting outside."
I slowed down, halting right by the entrance. Dirty stares shifted from me to Dan.
"A&E isn't for messing around," one woman said matter-of-factly.
I ignored her, striding backwards shakily.
"I'll stand still," I lied. "Come on, catch me."
Dan advanced forward. I looked up, positive I'd lured Dan directly underneath the camera.

My prediction turned out to be correct.
Beep, beep, beep.
I beamed brightly. An alarm sounded.
I had deceived him.
I won.
Staff scurried from the narrow hallway. One woman smiled gratefully at me.
Which was when Dan cocked the gun.
Launched the lethal bullet.
Towards me.
Screeching, I sprung back, hitting my head on the glass door.
Dan was hauled away by two guards, snarling.
It was the last thing I saw before passing out from concussion.

Chapter 31

"Ava."
I opened my eyes, blinking against the bright light shining from the large window of my hospital room.
I groaned, looking to my left.
Leanne sat beside me, holding my hand. I squeezed it.
"What happened?"
Leanne tilted her head. "You knocked your head... again." She grinned. "Concussion. You've been out for three days."
Three days?
"Concussion? Surely not again?" I moaned, feeling lightheaded. "How?"
Leanne bit her lip. "Don't you remember?"
I shook my head, embarrassed.
Leanne sat up straight. "You brought Dan here. The camera caught his face and the alarm sounded. He fired the gun, right at you. You moved, avoiding the bullet, but whacked your head, terrifyingly hard, on the glass door."
I gasped. "Did the gun hit me? Did it kill me?" My voice sounded desperate.
Leanne patted my hand reassuringly. "No. You're alive, speaking to me now." She paused. "You've... hurt your head quite badly."
I touched my throbbing head. "Oww!" I cried out. "Will it mend?"
Leanne nodded. "Yes, darling. Be grateful the bullet didn't kill you. You're a hero."
I laughed, despite the pain. "Nowhere near a hero. Even Mum told me I wasn't worthy of living."
"Your mother is sick. We found her, she was just waking up..." She hesitated.
Eric. I hadn't had the chance to mourn over his unexpected death yet.
"Mum shot Eric," I whispered, tears welling in my eyes. "She aimed for me... He saved my life."
"I know. We found his... body."
I broke into tears. Not small, meaningless tears... but the tears of someone with a broken heart.
Eric had saved me.

"I wish he didn't die," I sobbed, thumping my fists aggressively.
"My lovely, you couldn't have prevented it. He did it of his own will... to protect you." Leanne bowed her head.
My lungs gave way, departing from the rest of my body. My eyes continued shedding tears, my vision becoming bubbly, blurry. I'd known Eric for less than a month, yet the bravery he'd radiated inspired me greatly. He'd believed in me... even after I'd accused him of Dad's murder.
His memory would stay in my heart forever.
"Dan also knocked Keira out," I said, tears still pouring from my eyes.
"She's not come around yet. Darren said she'd woken up... but Dan gagged Keira and your dad before going after you," Leanne said.
"Are they OK?"
"Darren's been examined... Keira's too fragile right now. After they woke up, an ambulance was called. Keira went stiff and stopped breathing. Another seizure." Leanne wiped my cheek.
I hadn't ever felt so numb before, so lost. Mum had taken everything I knew and shattered it carelessly. She was self-centred, greedy.
My whole world had turned upside down and Mum was the only one to blame. No words, no apologies could ever heal the pain or the torment of the last years. It wouldn't buy that time back and a lousy excuse certainly wouldn't mean anything. Nothing meant anything, not without Eric.
"Angie and her daughter, Chantelle, were also located. Your mum shoved them underground, beneath your old house. She reconstructed the building a while ago, burying them in there. She sent food and water through a pipe." Leanne scrunched up her nose in pure disgust.
I shivered. How could Mum do that? "I want to see Angie," I said.
"She's a bit shaken right now. You will be able to soon, she'd love to meet you again." Leanne removed a clipboard from the drawer beside my bed. "Question time."
I leaned on my arm, my head still thudding immensely.
Deja vu washed across my brain. I glanced around, automatically realising this room was identical to my last one. Both times, I'd

ended up in hospital due to concussion. I laughed to myself as Leanne picked up a pen.
"Tell me everything," she demanded.
So I did.
And, two days later, I had a visitor.

Angie wore a dark blue police uniform. Her baggy trousers wouldn't have looked as stylish on anyone other than her. Her hair was loosely tied in braids, similar to my own.
On Thursday, I'd told Leanne everything I knew, expressed all my feelings... and cried a lot more than I'd like to admit. She'd promised to bring in Angie when she could and also guaranteed that she would update me daily.
All of which she had stuck to.
Angie's luminous brown eyes met mine, dancing over my face and taking in each feature. She smiled. "You've grown up. I remember when you were a little girl, always grinning. You carried the purest heart."
"I'm not so little now. I almost died... I still feel like a coward, as if I didn't try hard enough," I admitted openly.
Angie stared at me, appalled. "Ava, I can't even begin to believe you think that. Aside from finding the courage to lure Dan through the city, you were chased for miles with a gun in his possession. You refused to let that stop you. You're certainly not a coward, to say the least. Ask any thirteen-year-old, they wouldn't have had half the balls to complete such a task." Angie raised an eyebrow.
I looked at the crisp sheets covering my body. My body from my head down to my toes was warm, snuggled up. Nonetheless, my heart still felt cold with the hatred gnawing at my stomach.
"Besides, you rescued Keira. If you hadn't have gotten the bus so quickly, your sister would've died."
I nodded. "Lara's the one to thank for that. She went against Mum's request, telling me the truth so that I *could* save Keira."
"And you did. Ava, in a snap of your fingers you could've turned around and disbelieved her honesty. But you listened and didn't falter. Keira's not in the best position, but she's safe. That's on you," Angie said.

I drew in a deep breath. "I may have saved Keira, but Eric saved *me*."
Angie perched on the end of the bed. "He did. That was his choice, putting himself at risk to protect you."
"I didn't want him to do that," I murmured. "Now he's dead and I can't thank him."
Angie's eyes welled with tears. In an instant, it hit me that Eric had been her husband. She hadn't seen him for years. Neither had her daughter.
"Oh... I'm so sorry," I said, lowering my head.
"Hey, I can't go back and change it. Don't let it worry you." Angie patted my hand.
I twisted around. My legs were inflexible; lying in bed for five days didn't favour me. "How old is Chantelle?" I asked.
"She's eighteen. Would you like to meet her?" Angie offered, stroking my hand gently.
The last month's trauma nuzzled at my head. Dan's tenacious touch on my arm, his thunderous footsteps trailing behind me, his gun weighing me down dreadfully.
Mum's betrayal, her money obsession.
Eric's murder.
Angie must've sensed the uncertainty in my delayed response. "Chantelle is lovely... Er, of course I'd say that because she's my daughter, but truly, she'll love you."
I plucked up the bravery that had always been written under my name, pushing aside the torture pecking at my thoughts. "I'd love to meet her. But... I wish to see my sister first," I said.
Angie nodded earnestly. "I understand. Any recent news on her?"
"She hasn't awoken yet. Mum caused a lot of damage to her lungs... with the drugs. She was really out to kill her. No one can be certain whether she'll make it."
"Ava, Keira is, alongside you, one of the strongest little girls ever," Angie said. "Your sister will fight through this."
My current optimism dissolved into an ocean of fear. Raw, merciless terror clawed at my heart... the heart that wouldn't accept anything other than wrenching pain from now on. Eric was dead, Mum jailed and Keira unconscious.

Almost six years earlier, I'd grieved over Dad's overpowering death... It had consumed me, torn my heart to shreds and left me anxious and lost.
Now that I had Dad back, Keira's illness gnawed at my chest, Mum's selfishness dug at my heart like a knife and Eric's death made my blood transform into incoherent, dominant poison.
"Hey, you're crying." Angie nudged me. "C'mon, Ava. Keira will be fine, I promise."
I twisted my fingers. "No way on earth can you promise me that," I muttered. "Besides, you'll jinx it."
Angie's phone rang. "Hi, darling." Angie stood up, heading towards the door.
She closed it lightly behind her.
I slid onto my wrist my bracelet that Dad had found and returned to me.
Angie reappeared. "Chantelle called me, she needs me at the police station." She paused. "She's in for questioning. I'll see you soon, my lovely."
Her arms wrapped around my body. That was all it took for the careless poison to slide away and for my foggy brain to clear.
Her eyes held such love, such gratitude.
She'd provided me with the proof that not all women carried the same evil mindset as Mum.
Determination curled at my fingers, and I pinged the bell at my bedside.

"My idea will work," I promised, clutching Keira's hand. I shifted restlessly in the chair positioned by her bedside.
Keira's oxygen mask filled with traces of her sweet breath. It reassured me that she was alive.
Just.
Dad sat on her other side, staring at her closed eyelids. "I've tested your method, Ava. Your contribution was lovely, but I guarantee it won't-"
Keira's eyes snapped open. She moaned, looking around, attempting to peel off the oxygen mask.
"Baby, keep it there for a moment. I'll call a nurse." Dad clanged the metal bell.

Two minutes later, a blonde-haired nurse shuffled into Keira's cubicle. She fussed with her mask and some equipment attached to it.
Keira cried out, her knees springing up.
"Hey, calm down," the nurse urged. "You're doing fine, darling." She gently pushed Keira's legs back under the covers. "Her heartbeat is good. Blood pressure normal. ECG returned natural, no signs of any problems." The nurse removed Keira's oxygen mask, disposing the remaining equipment into a basket.
I squeezed my sister's hand, peering into her ocean eyes. Her head lolled and eventually her gaze met mine. We shared a moment admiring each other.
"Are you feeling OK, baby?" Dad asked, stroking Keira's forehead.
"Daddy." She broke into tears. "I missed you."
"I missed you too, Keira. We're all together again now. You're OK, sweetheart, you are," Dad soothed.
His eyes brimmed with liquid too. Soon, we were all a heap of soggy eyes and salty lips.
Rap, rap, rap.
"Come in!" Dad shouted, catching my eye and shrugging.
Who could it be?
Angie strutted into the room, her bouncy hair tied back in a high ponytail. Her police uniform looked as immaculate as before.
"Hi!" Dad's voice was high-pitched.
I smirked. Dad and Angie were staring at one another so intently that even a gunshot wouldn't snap them into reality.
Keira raised an eyebrow. She giggled.
I gazed at them in awe.
Dad and Angie were in love.

Chapter 32

Chantelle's almond skin made my stomach curl with jealousy. Her hair hung loose around her head and as she bent down to hug me, it brushed against my cheek, glossy and sleek.
Her deep brown eyes resembled Angie's. Only one feature of Chantelle's mirrored Eric's: the similar shaped nose.
"I'm sorry," Chantelle and I chorused.
I folded my arms. "Why are *you* sorry?"
Chantelle's face reddened. "You're in quite an interesting situation right now. Erm, I worded that wrong... I-"
"You worded it perfectly," I said approvingly. "I'd say 'amusing' fits better, though."
Chantelle laughed. "Fair enough. Amusing it is." She held up her palm.
I frowned.
She squinted. "Aren't you familiar with high-fives?"
Humiliation burned at my cheeks, hot flames that rose swiftly up my skin. I reckoned Dan's recent actions had scarred me to my core, resulting in me flinching suspiciously every time someone reached out a hand.
"Right - you've just escaped a murderer, you're bound to be wary," Chantelle said solemnly.
"Definitely," I confessed. "How are you doing?"
"Yeah... not too bad. I miss Dad, but he gave his life to save you. I'll forever thank him for that."
"You're not mad at me?" I whispered.
Chantelle snapped her head up. "Never. Ava, you kept my dad sane. You forgave him and held onto your instincts, offering him a chance. That's a different kind of strength."
I chewed my lip, relaxation spreading around me like a quilt. Chantelle's reassurance virtually convinced my miserable heart to repair. The recent sorrow dispersed, like tiny pieces of sawdust lingering in solidarity.
Perhaps not yet, or in the months approaching, but as life returned to normal I expected I'd regain the faith and optimism I'd previously connected with so well.

Chantelle cleared her throat. "I too experienced trauma as a child. Abused by Lisa and Dan, just like you were. Dad disconnected himself from their lives, only receiving a phone call each month to catch up... It was Lisa and Dan's deal. The police rejected our complaints, our never-ending reports. Panic attacks were a recurring concern, until I was diagnosed with anxiety at nine years old."
"Why did they abuse you? Did they hold you at gunpoint too? Oh my goodness, are you OK?" The questions poured out of me. I was horrified that this sweet girl had been through such mortifying trauma.
Chantelle's eyes filled with tears. I reached out to her. Inward pain scratched at my throat. "They didn't, no," she admitted. "They... didn't approve of Angie... for being a woman of colour. Since I'm mixed, they decided to hurt both my parents by bullying... me." She dabbed at her tear-streaked face, shaking.
No words could describe the loathing fury rolling through my blood, seeping into my bones, forcing my fists to curl and my heart to beat faster by the minute.
"Dan and Lisa have been convicted of abuse towards children and murder, but it's frightening that their punishment only came about due to having such a lethal weapon in their possession. Otherwise, they'd still be out there. More to the point... you'd be dead."
I shuddered, hugging my knees. Recalling how close I'd come to being killed scared me to the core.
Knock, knock, knock.
Leanne poked her head around the door. She carried a steaming mug of hot chocolate, topped with pink and white marshmallows.
Suppressing the anger swamping my body, I plastered a smile on my face. Leanne ambled in, swaying her hips graciously as if she were gliding to music.
Chantelle leaped up, untangling our hands from one another's. "I'll leave you with Leanne," she said.
I lowered my voice as she leaned over. "Thank you for sharing your story. It makes me feel stronger, in control."

Chantelle hesitated, nodding. "You're a warrior, Ava. Little girls all over desire to be as strong as you. Anyone else would strive to obtain such attention, so don't take it for granted."
I watched her flee from the room, absorbing her meaningful words in my vulnerability.
Leanne waved vaguely, reaching for a placemat at my bedside. She set the mug down. Reclining in the chair, she crossed her legs neatly. "I'm afraid I must take some blood tests," she claimed.
I wavered, thinking it through. Hate wasn't a strong enough word for what I felt about needles - the feel of them puncturing my skin, drawing thick, scarlet blood, leaving a pinprick the size of an ant, yet an ache as large as a kick in the thigh.
"It's more ideal than you walking out of here with major life-threatening issues that'll affect you in the long term," Leanne rationalised, placing her hand on my messy quilt.
Last time, I'd whimpered and refused on the spot. Leanne had been lenient since I'd just been manipulated into a stranger's car with a gun to my head. This time was the same, but I'd put my life at risk already. Leanne couldn't possibly tolerate the same behaviour when, compared to being feet away from Dan's soaring bullet, a gentle blood test wouldn't cause any harm.
Reluctantly, I swung my feet off the snug bed and stood up. My head had gotten lots better since I'd gained consciousness, but my balance wasn't so remarkable.
"Steady." Leanne caught my arm and eased me into a chair.
I groaned. "I'm so over this."
"Why?"
"I'm dizzy, lethargic and exhausted." I whacked my foot against the cupboard. My muscles tightened, twinging horrendously.
"Ava-" Leanne croaked.
I interrupted her. "It's difficult." Tears surged in my red-raw eyes. "I can't go through this again."
"Since when were you a quitter?" Leanne asked quietly.
I glanced at her. She couldn't be bluffing; her pupils gleamed with sincerity. I blurted out the truth.
"I lost myself, Leanne. Didn't acknowledge my emotions until recently... My entire world collapsed. I tried and tried to keep it

together, but the universe wasn't co-operating. It deserted me and soon after, I neglected myself. I didn't care. But I want to care now... it's just every time I attempt to pick up my missing pieces, they fall through my fingers again." I gulped through tears. "Gosh, look at me."

Leanne kneeled in front of me, her expression concerned, devoted... warm. "Sweetheart, thank you for speaking up. By allowing yourself to express your emotions, accept reality, you'll find the stress departing... You'll be free. I'm going to put your name forward for a mental health assessment. Referral may take a while, but there's a mental wellbeing clinic for children from eleven to fifteen."

I hunched over, concealed my sodden face with my hands and wept. With each sob, I snorted. Loud snorts that echoed around the thin walls. I was beyond embarrassed, but sitting slumped in that chair, the self-pity beat the humiliation. Leanne held me in her arms. I clung to her, soaking her top with tears. Once I stopped crying, I began choking. Leanne tilted back my head, pleading with me to calm down.

"Thank goodness," she said as my tears were brought to a halt. "You scared me."

"Sorry," I muttered. "We can do the blood test now."

Leanne shook her head seriously. "I need to know you're OK first. That was a genuine panic attack, a pretty big one."

I shrank down. "I'm all right. It's happened before," I said flatly.

"It's happened before?" Leanne repeated.

I blinked. "Yeah, it's normal." I shrugged.

Leanne looked aghast. She lowered me against the chair and sat back on her heels, frowning. "No," she said. "It's not normal."

"It is," I insisted, eager to move on.

I lay back against the chair, frustration building inside me.

"Right... Perhaps I should send you straight to a therapist here." Leanne brushed down her jeans, standing up. "Would you rather lie or sit?"

My hoarse voice squeaked, "Sit."

I extended my arm and felt the sharp needle pierce my skin. I broke into shivers.

"Results should return tomorrow. If they're normal, you can go home. Keira's already on the mend." Leanne got up and placed her hand on the door handle.
I coughed, wincing at the pain. "Leanne?"
She turned back, shooting me a puzzled glance.
"How's Keira doing? Mentally and physically?"
Leanne bit her lip. She dragged herself across the room and hauled a chair over, perching beside me. "Your sister is ill. The withdrawal of drugs will have effects on her wellbeing. Dr. Levonette will prescribe her medication and within a month, it should calm the seizures down." She looked at me. "Mentally... she's struggling. PTSD is a difficult disorder to overcome. Her depression on top of it drives her to the edge."
"In that case... I'd like family therapy," I said.
Leanne slipped the blood test into a tray. She stopped and stared at me. "Family therapy?"
I decided to reinforce my statement. "Over the past years, Dad, Keira and myself have encountered an extraordinary amount of heartache. It's only fair to heal as a family."
"I'd encourage separate therapy... but I will pass on and discuss your request. We'll also ensure it's what Darren and Keira will be up for too." Leanne reached for my arm.
With a sudden burst of energy, I heaved myself up and Leanne guided me towards the bed. I lay back, propped against the headboard.
"Hot chocolate's yours." She pointed at it with her index finger. "It may be lukewarm."
I grinned, sitting up and lifting the mug. Raising it to my lips, I caught a whiff of the rich, sickly chocolate. My mouth watered, eager to taste the delicious contents.
Leanne edged to the door, smiling as I took a sip.
"That's surprisingly amazing," I said, my lips smothered in liquid.
"Surprisingly?" She raised an eyebrow. "Glad I could satisfy the Miss."
She opened the door, almost crashing into Anya and Isobel.
"Hi - do you wish to see Ava?" Leanne asked, half backing them out the room.

I peered past her. Isobel caught my eye.
"Yes. We brought her presents," Anya replied.
Leanne looked at me expectantly. She knew I'd be apprehensive under my current circumstances.
I nodded convincingly. "Thank you, Leanne."
She moved aside, holding her arm out to shake Anya and Isobel's hands welcomingly.
"Ring the bell if you need me," Leanne said, creeping out into the corridor.
I smiled gratefully at her, watching her disappear and hearing her heels clash against the floor as she walked down the hallway.
I set my tepid mug of hot chocolate on the placemat to my left.
"Hi," Anya and Isobel chorused.
In turn, they gave me tight hugs. Isobel sat back and wiped her forehead. Her face was etched with worry.
Guilt swamped my body.
"Are you OK?" Anya queried anxiously.
"I guess," I said. "It's a shock."
Isobel sighed. "We were so worried. Lara described your disappearance as unforeseen. She mentioned Keira's departure too. Tracking Eric down was easy, but he rushed past us, adamant he had to catch the next bus."
"We phoned Angie, but again, she didn't answer. Me and Iz watched the news that evening. That's how we knew you were unconscious and Eric was dead."
Eric's death reappeared in my mind's eye. His stiff body lying limp and lifeless on the carpet. Blood seeping out of his heart, oozing around him.
Whirlwinds of emotion coursed through my bones, chilling me to my depths. If Eric hadn't followed me onto the bus and into the house, I'd be dead. Mum would've shot me. Dead.
I shivered at the prospect.
"Ava, you're prone to danger zones," Anya quipped, assuming my silence to be an invitation to continue.
Isobel elbowed her. "It's not funny. You're lucky she's alive," she hissed.
I laughed. "Izzy, it's all right. I am perfectly fine."

"Still, you nearly *did* die." Isobel shrugged, her cheeks reddening.
I reached over and patted her arm. "Thanks for worrying about me."
She looked at me. "It's what friends are for," she said solemnly.
"Anya and I are your best friends. Forever. Aren't we, An?"
Anya pretended to vomit. "Mushy or what?" She laughed. "Yes, we're iconic best friends."
Anya chucked a bag onto my lap.
I opened it.
Her and Isobel spoiled me with chocolate, perfumes and face masks. My mouth watered whilst poring over the bars of chocolate, viewing their tasty contents.
A blanket of protection fluttered across my chest, conscious that Anya and Isobel were loyal, fond.
Best friend material.
Isobel and Anya launched themselves towards me. I staggered back, slumping onto the neat pillows beneath me. We hugged, a cluster of arms and legs.
I untangled myself. "Thank you so much-"
Before I could finish, the door was thrown open and three women bundled in, two of them strenuously holding the third back.
"I can see my daughter whenever I please!" she screamed, kicking against the women.
My breath caught in my throat. I quickly shoved Anya and Isobel behind me, cloaking them from Mum's view.
"You need to stay back, ma'am," one policewoman said, blocking my vision.
Anya and Isobel each held an arm, shielding me. Mum's squeals rose, blasting in my ears, deafening me.
"Are you suggesting I never see my daughter again? Assuming I'll whip out a gun and shoot her?" Mum yelled, punching the woman on her left.
"No, I'm advising you to complete your prison sentence first. You've been convicted of murder and kidnapping, which you know already," the woman groaned.

Mum unleashed an ear-splitting shriek. "Shut up!" She turned to me. "Ava, you don't wish for our little disagreement to break our bond, right?"
"Little disagreement?" Anya spat. "You almost KILLED her!"
Mum paled. "I don't know what she's talking about."
I gawped at her. "You're kidding?" I stood up and strutted over.
"Ma'am-" one policewoman started.
I raised my palm and she faltered.
"Mum, forgiving you for almost murdering me could've been possible. But you traumatised Keira... Gosh, you *shot* Eric..." Tears brimmed harshly in my eyes, cutting through my words. I cursed myself for exposing my vulnerability.
Mum scowled. "Eric basically asked to be shot. He stood there!" she declared.
"Eric saved Ava's life," Anya objected.
"Lara topped herself because of *your* cruel threats," Isobel snapped.
I gasped, clapping my hands over my mouth.
Silence fell across the room.
"Ava didn't know about that, you freak!" Mum shrieked.
She lunged for Isobel, but the police held her back.
"Ava," the policewoman said, "what do you want us to do?"
Mum pouted at me innocently.
"Why did Lara kill herself? How did Mum have anything to do with it?" I asked, rubbing my trembling hands together.
"After Lara told you where Sandra and Keira were, she knew Sandra would come for her too, due to Sandra's threat..." The officer poked Mum. "Tell her what the threat was, Sandra."
Mum tightened her lips. "I said that if she revealed any significant information, I'd kill her the same way I murdered her parents."
I turned to the policewoman. "When did Lara top herself?" I demanded.
"The same night Eric was shot," she replied.
"We found her body in the forest, just minutes away from the care home," the second woman explained.

I swayed backwards. Lara, my childhood best friend, was dead. Mum had manipulated and exploited her, killed her parents and on top of that, forced her to convince *me* to commit suicide. She'd lived an unfair life.
Thanks to Mum.
"No." I spun around to face her. "I don't ever want to see your wicked face again."
Mum clenched her jaw and, with that, the two policewomen dragged her out of the room.
I stumbled towards the bed, clutching my sore head.
"Are you OK, Ava?" Anya sat next to me.
Isobel bowed her head. "We didn't want to worry you."
I looked at both of them. Despite the aching pain and the gnawing anger absorbing me, my brain lit up with an idea. "Isobel, you mentioned a campaign on the first day I met you, right?"
Isobel jerked her head towards me. "Right... why? Your dad's no longer missing, or 'dead.'"
I nodded seriously. "Yeah. But in case it happens again."
"I don't think the same thing would happen twice, not to your dad," Anya said.
I felt slightly irritated. "The police cut off my dad's murder search. For years, they were too lazy and too smug to do anything about it. If it happens to someone else, we'd want the police to *not* give up, right?"
Anya and Isobel shared a swift glance. "That's correct," Anya said.
"So you'd create a campaign, insisting that if someone else's parent was murdered, it'd be compulsory for the police to search ASAP?" Isobel guessed, holding her hands to her chest.
I clicked my fingers, grinning. "Precisely. I would hate someone else to experience similar heart-wrenching discomfort." I lowered my voice. "Would you help me?"
"We'd be crazy not to!" Anya laughed.
Isobel jolted suddenly. "Ava, your dream is to become a therapist, isn't it?" she asked excitedly.
"Ye-es," I confirmed. "Why?"

"You can transform Ruby's Rising Shopping Centre!" she squealed. "Make it a partial therapy centre, and the other half-" "-A children's care home. Providing them with food and drinks, almost as if they were residents. For people like Keira, struggling at home with their parents," Anya picked up from her sister. Isobel nodded frantically.
My heart pounded in my throat. Anya and Isobel were suggesting I convert Ruby's Rising Shopping Centre into a therapy unit. On top of that, a place where a young child could escape to from their toxic household if necessary.
Through providing hope to others, I'd finally find myself.
My own hope.
My own destination.

Chapter 33

December slipped by quickly. I shared Anya and Isobel's idea, emphasising the significance of what I hoped to achieve. When Keira and I returned home, I'd spoken to Angie and Dad. They'd checked it with the owners of the trust... and it was a yes.
Physically, I recovered rapidly. Mentally, I struggled most days.
Dan and Mum were locked up in prison, charged with abduction and murder.
Leanne forwarded my request and Dad, Keira and I attended family therapy once a week. It guided me and Dad. Addressing Keira's mental health was a more difficult task. She'd been scarred for life. Fortunately, however, my little sister hadn't self-harmed or attempted suicide for months.
A person's mental health is just as important as their physical health. It's fragile, breakable. I hadn't realised this beforehand, but the lonely chill of Mum's actions had made me rethink.
Keira and I roamed around gloomily, approaching each day downcast, expecting more exhausting events to occur. Weeks earlier, my blood tests had returned normal, but a nerve in my head was permanently damaged.
I didn't care.
Both Eric and Lara's funerals arrived and passed by. Numbness tingled through my bones throughout. My mind continued drifting to Eric's dead body, the blood trickling from his chest, oozing in a puddle on the soft carpet around him.
He'd put his life on the line to protect me.
This, my brain couldn't understand.
Why had he saved me? He could've let me die and saved himself.
He didn't, and that made him a real hero.
I would be forever grateful.

I wrote off this entry the day before Keira's tenth birthday.
Ruby's Rising Shopping Centre had transformed into two luxurious, towering buildings: one beige, and the other a contrasting yellow, for the children. Pastel flowers scattered the grass, pretty and flattering.

Over three hundred individuals had signed up for my therapy clinic, run by Angie and Jennifer until I was old enough. My favourite part of Shallowton was no longer deserted or depressing. It snapped people's attention in seconds, turned their heads and made them stare in awe at my artwork, at the fine prints and inspirational quotes traced onto the firm bricks. Most important were the photos of little girls and boys who'd taken their lives due to the harsh reality of the world. They'd become too good for the universe and so had gathered their wings and flown up and away, deciding to paint the sky in swirly oranges and pinks each night, reminding us they're just above us - too far to touch, but close enough to hold in the heart.
'Darren Hayloft's campaign' was established. Trialled and passed by the government, my law became global. It ensured that if a family lost a parent, it'd be mandatory for the police to launch a search immediately.
I'd been notified of three reports so far.

"Whoa, Ava!" Isobel shrieked.
Anya crushed my hand in hers. "You're going to be famous!"
Inviting them both the minute after the construction had finished was perfect. They made me feel even prouder of myself. I'd pushed through and attained my dreams. I knew my destiny and my best friends knew it too.
My best friends, forever.
Katy, James and Alfie pestered Jennifer to allow them to move into my children's care home.
"I'm sure you'll love that," Jennifer told me, scratching her head. "So will the kids."
I beamed.
My life had changed in a lightning bolt.
No matter what Mum had done, I prayed she was proud of me.
Even if I couldn't be proud of her.

Chapter 34

"Ava! The party is about to start!" Keira screeched with glee, bursting into my bedroom.
I turned to face her. She wore a mid-length turquoise dress. Sequins were scattered around the skirt that loosely draped from her waist. A matching sapphire headband adorned her hair, which was pinned up with a baby blue flower hair clip. Her eyes shone like the ocean.
I felt relaxed for the first time in ages. Keira seemed at ease, so why shouldn't I? She'd grown over the past month, developing into a mature, confident young woman.
"I'll be there in a second, Keira." I smiled.
Keira grinned, baring her pearly-white teeth. "I'll be waiting." She giggled, throwing a pillow at me.
I turned back to emptying the rucksack I'd carried whilst confronting Eric months earlier. I hadn't brushed off his death for more than a minute at a time; it was far too recent to unpack. My hand skimmed a folded-up piece of paper. I took it out carefully, scanning over its golden words.

If Mr. Chanell somehow proceeds to hurt me and goes too far, Sandra, this is where he lives. Give it to the police. I'll be fine. However, it's just in case. Of course, unless that occurs, you won't read this.

The letter I'd found, leading me to wrongly blame Eric for Dad's murder.
Shame swamped my mind, chomping me up carelessly.
I decided to replace the letter in Dad's office. I retreated onto the landing, peering around. Photos of Keira and I decorated the walls, pictures of us with large grins filling our faces. Me tickling Keira, her sulking at my side, us hugging tightly.
I blushed.
Scampering across the landing, I heard small voices echoing from Dad's office. I glanced around the door.
Dad was hunched over a binder sat in front of him on his desk. I squinted, begging my eyes to zoom closer. The folder was the

one I'd searched through in October... when I thought Dad was dead.
So much had changed.
My cheeks burned with embarrassment and my palms became sweaty whilst clasping the paper.
I couldn't admit I'd stolen it.
I pushed the door open further, walking inside. I placed my hands behind my back, dropping the paper and falling onto my knees.
Dad looked over, raising an eyebrow as he spotted me. "Ava, what the heck are you doing?"
I picked up the paper again. "You dropped this." I shrugged.
Dad shot me a sideways glance, his expression suspicious. He'd figured out the truth.
Angie stood above Dad, patting his shoulder.
"Oooh, Dad!" I quipped. "Are you and Angie in love?"
Dad dismissed my comment with a flick of his hand, but his cheeks turned a beetroot colour.
Angie winked. "Perhaps, Ava." She rubbed Dad's back through his t-shirt.
I sauntered over, flinging my arms round him. "I'm so glad we found you," I whispered.
"Me too, princess." Dad hugged me back. Angie joined in, holding us tight.
A small rap sounded on the door. I turned my head.
Keira.
"Hey, Keira. Let's have a group hug." I held out my hand.
She faltered for a moment but, not able to resist temptation, flew over towards us and into my arms.
I kissed her forehead appreciatively.
She looked up at me. Her eyes held tenacity...
My sister was a warrior.
And so was I.

Important!

Mental health is a serious issue that affects many people's day-to-day life. If you happen to relate to any of the feelings Ava or Keira expressed throughout this book, don't hesitate to reach out for help.
You're valid. Don't suffer in silence.

Helplines & websites:
If you need help urgently, but it's not an emergency, call 111, option 2
UK mental health text support – text SHOUT to 85258
NHS Every Mind Matters
YoungMinds
Kooth

Wishing you all the best.

Acknowledgements

Thank you to Mum, Dad, Nannie and Grandad for making my dream come true.
I love you!

I'd like to thank my friend Annabel for naming my book and helping me gather ideas for my front cover.

Thank you to my friends and all of my family and teachers for believing I can achieve my dreams. A massive thanks to my TikTok friends too, for encouraging me forwards. I'm forever grateful, and shall continue to show my gratitude in the future.

Most importantly, my deepest thanks to everyone who chose to read my book!

About me

I'm Lauren, a 17-year-old schoolgirl from England. I've always loved to write, right from the young age of eight, and creative writing has always been a personal favourite. I began this book in August 2020 with no plot or plan. Many months later, I'm extremely proud of how well this book has been put together. I hope to continue writing in the future, and perhaps become a bestselling author one day!

Instagram – laurenpullanxx – follow for future book content!

Printed in Great Britain
by Amazon

63192964R00139